PRAISE FOR <u>THE X-FILES</u>

"*The X-Files* is a true masterpiece. There's no more challenging series on television and, as a bonus, it's also brainy fun."

—Howard Rosenberg,
Los Angeles Times

"The most provocative series on TV."

—Dana Kennedy,
Entertainment Weekly

"*The X-Files* is a rip-roaring hour of TV: suspenseful, scary, fun, imaginative, entertaining, and weird, wonderfully weird."

—Jeff Jarvis,
TV Guide

"An original gem, mined with passion and polished with care."

—Andrew Denton,
Rolling Stone

Read all the official books based on the Fox television series

Published by HarperPrism

THE X-FILES™

RUINS

Kevin J. Anderson
Based on the characters created by
Chris Carter

HarperPrism
An Imprint of HarperPaperbacks

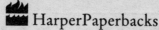

HarperPaperbacks
A Division of HarperCollins*Publishers*
10 East 53rd Street, New York, N.Y. 10022-5299

The X-Files is a trademark of the Twentieth Century Fox Film Corporation.

This is a work of fiction. The characters, incidents, and dialogues are products of the author's imagination and are not to be construed as real. Any resemblance to actual events or persons, living or dead, is entirely coincidental.

ISBN 0-06-105736-3

A hardcover edition of this book was published by HarperPrism in 1996.

First mass-market printing: February 1997

HarperPrism is an imprint of HarperPaperbacks.

HarperCollins®, 💠®, HarperPaperbacks™, and HarperPrism® are trademarks of HarperCollins*Publishers* Inc.

Cover illustration by Cliff Nielson

Printed in the United States of America

Visit HarperPaperbacks on the World Wide Web at
http://www.harpercollins.com/paperbacks

To Christopher Schelling

my editor on several books, who always kept his cool
and his sense of humor even when dealing with an
author!

ACKNOWLEDGMENTS

This book couldn't have been written without the assistance, dedication, and flexibility of the *X-Files* people at Fox Television—Chris Carter, Mary Astadourian, Frank Spotnitz, Jennifer Sebree, Debbie Lutzky, and Cindy Irwin, as well as the editorial champions at HarperPrism— John Silbersack and Caitlin Deinard Blasdell.

Lil Mitchell transcribed my dictation in record time. Kristine Kathryn Rusch and Dean Wesley Smith offered their home during the worst storm in decades so I could accomplish some tight-deadline writing (electricity or no electricity!). Paula Vitaris shared her valuable Spanish expertise, though I probably still managed to make mistakes. Debbie Gramlich and Chris Fusco provided much-needed background material. And finally, my wife, Rebecca Moesta, gave her love and support during writing dead- lines of her own.

1

Even after days of hard excavation, they had barely scratched the surface of the ancient city. But Cassandra Rubicon had already seen enough to know that the ruins held unimaginable secrets about the birth of the Maya empire.

At the far western edge of the Yucatán, where the limestone plateau butted up against volcanic highlands and steamy jungles, the lost city had been hidden by nature for more than a thousand years. The native helpers had called the place Xitaclan, their voices tinged with awe and fear.

Cassandra rolled the word over in her mouth, reveling in the images it evoked of ancient sacrifices, pomp and splendor, blood priests wearing ornaments of jade and green quetzal feathers. *Xitaclan.*

In the late afternoon, she alone worked inside the Pyramid of Kukulkan, shining her flashlight ahead as she crept deeper, exploring. This place was absolutely alive with secrets. In the chalky bitterness of the air, she could taste the mysteries waiting for her to discover them.

Shining her flashlight ahead, Cassandra ran a dusty hand through perspiration-dampened cinnamon hair—

the color of cinnamon bark, freshly peeled from the trees, her father always insisted, not the faded reddish-tan powder found on grocery-store spice racks. The color of her eyes hung midway between green and brown, like rich copper-bearing ore.

Outside, her partners in the University of California expedition kept themselves busy with the external excavations, mapping the overall layout of the city, with its ceremonial plaza, temples, and monolithic limestone obelisks—stelae—carved with fearsome images of mythical feathered serpents. They had found a vine-overgrown "ball court" arena, where the ancient Maya had played their bloody sport in which the losers—or winners, depending on some historical interpretations—were sacrificed to the gods.

An archaeological treasure trove, Xitaclan provided far too many ruins even for a large, well-financed crew to explore in anything less than a year. But Cassandra and her four young companions would do their best, for as long as their meager university funding held out.

Numerous moss-covered stelae towered at strategic astronomical points throughout the jungle, while others had toppled; all of them, though, contained rich and exciting glyphs. Christopher Porte, their team's epigrapher, delighted in attempting to translate them, transcribing them into the battered record book he kept in his pack at all times.

The showpiece of Xitaclan, though, was the magnificent stair-stepped Pyramid of Kukulkan that loomed over the center of the city. Though overgrown with weeds and underbrush, it was still beautifully preserved. Its architecture rivaled the great ziggurats at Chichén Itzá, Tikal, and Teotihuacán—but this one stood untouched. The locals' paralyzing superstitions had protected it from prying eyes. Until now.

Topping the pyramid's highest platform stood the many-pillared "Temple of the Feathered Serpent," with its amazing carvings and ornate friezes depicting calendars, myths, history. Cassandra had named the temple herself after noting the dense motifs that showed the wise god Kukulkan and his feathered reptilian companions or guardians—a common symbol of power in the Maya mythos. The intricate bas-reliefs added a new richness to the Quetzalcoatl/Kukulkan legends of the early Central American peoples.

Her team had also found an unfathomably deep cistern behind the pyramid, a natural limestone sinkhole filled with oily black water in whose murky depths Cassandra suspected hid many artifacts, relics . . . and quite probably the bones of sacrificial victims. Such limestone wells, or cenotes, were common in Maya cities of the Yucatán—but this one at Xitaclan had never been ransacked by treasure seekers or explored by archaeologists.

Her team planned to break out the diving equipment within a week, and she herself would descend into the depths—but for now they still had too much initial cataloguing to complete. More breathtaking discoveries, more work—but too little time, and too little money.

For now, she concentrated on exploring inside the pyramid.

If her team didn't do an overwhelming job here on their first visit, someone else in the competitive archaeological community would no doubt return with a larger expedition, better funding, and superior equipment. It could completely overshadow Cassandra's work.

The crews of native workers recruited by her team's local guide—Fernando Victorio Aguilar, a self-styled adventurer and "expediter"—had worked for days already, hacking and chopping at the underbrush, removing mahogany and ceiba trees, slashing ferns with their machetes, uprooting creepers to remove the shroud of time and nature from around Xitaclan.

As soon as they saw the carvings of feathered serpents, though, the native workers had retreated in terror. They whispered to each other fearfully and refused to come closer to the site or to help with cleaning the ruins, even when she offered to increase their meager payment. Finally they fled. And then Aguilar ran off, abandoning her team in the deep jungle.

In her work, Cassandra had always respected native traditions and beliefs—it came with the territory—but her excitement at these discoveries had grown so intense that she found such superstitions frustrating, and her impatience flared up.

The archaeologists continued working on their own. They had supplies for a few weeks and a transmitter to call for help, should they need it. For now, she and the four others enjoyed their solitude.

Today, Kelly Rowan, the team's second archaeologist (and, as of recently, the man with whom she shared her tent) was spending the last hours of daylight on the outside steps of the pyramid, studying the Maya hieroglyphics. Christopher Porte bent beside him with his battered sketchpad, excitedly trying to translate the chiseled glyphs as Kelly used brushes and fine tools to remove debris from the designs.

Cait Barron, the team's historian and photographer, took advantage of the late afternoon light to work on one of her watercolors. Quiet and highly professional, Cait did her official work with the cameras and logbooks in a no-nonsense way. She took rolls of archival photos rapidly and efficiently—but once finished, she preferred using her paints to recreate the spirit of the place.

It was a long-standing tradition of Yucatán explorers to capture the detail their eyes saw, to depict something more than simple, two-dimensional photographic plates could. So far Cait had filled three portfolios with beautiful paintings that evoked the history of the Maya: diptychs pairing images of the ruins as they now appeared and as she imagined the city must have looked during its golden age.

While the team's quiet but frenzied work went on outside, the simmering jungle sounds increased with the fading light. Daytime creatures sought shelter against the darkness, while nocturnal predators awakened and began to search for their meals. Biting flies that swarmed in the day's heat flew off to sleep, while mosquitoes, bloodthirsty in the cooler air of evening, swept out in clouds.

Deep inside the Pyramid of Kukulkan, though, the damp shadows knew no passage of time. Cassandra continued her explorations.

After she and Kelly had worked together to pry open the long-sealed outer door, careful not to damage the masonry or the stone carvings, Cassandra had spent most of her time combing through the rubble inside, cautiously penetrating deeper, picking her way from one intersection to the next. She had spent days working through the chambers and vaults, mapping the incomprehensible passages within the immense stone structure, trying to solve the maze.

She had spent the afternoon inside again, taking only brief breaks to check on Kelly and Christopher, who worked at deciphering the heiroglyphic staircase, and John Forbin, the grad-student architect and engineer who was studying the other half-fallen structures. John's wanderings took him farther into the jungle as he marked the locations of ruins on the wrinkled topographical map he kept with him at all times. Being an engineer, John had no imagination for naming discoveries. John relied on simple numerical designations— Temple XI or Stela 17.

Cassandra glanced at her compass-watch and pushed deeper inside the labyrinth, aiming her high-powered flashlight ahead of her like a weapon. The cold shaft of light raked across rough-hewn limestone blocks and the crude support beams. Stark shadows leaped at her with exaggerated angles every time she shifted the flashlight. She moved cautiously, smelling the moldy air. Something dark skittered into a wide crack in the wall.

Cassandra carried a small microcassette recorder in her hand, as well as a sheet of graph paper on which she kept track of her movements. So far, most tunnels she'd explored had turned into blind alleys that might have been designed to confuse trespassers ... or they could have been sealed treasure chambers. Even more exciting—from an archaeologist's point of view—the dead-ends could be sealed-off burial crypts or storage vaults for collected volumes of ancient writings.

If her team could find an intact Maya codex, one of the gloriously illustrated books written on mulberry-bark paper, it would increase knowledge of the Central American empire a hundredfold. Only four Maya codices were known to exist. Most of the others had been destroyed by Spanish missionaries overzealous in their attempts to squash all beliefs but their own. Xitaclan, though, had been abandoned long before the Conquistadors had arrived in the New World.

Cassandra worked now with dust in her hair and powder smeared under her eyes, across her cheeks. Her arms and legs were bone-tired, stiff and sore from too many nights on an uncomfortable bedroll, her skin inflamed from hundreds of insect bites. It had been too long since she'd had either a cold drink or a warm shower.

But the wonders she had already found were worth all those sacrifices. *Archaeology isn't for wimps,* she thought.

Her father always called her beautiful, claiming that she was wasted in the cobwebs of ancient civilizations, but she only laughed at him. Her father was quite a character. It was his own fame as an archaeologist that had driven her into the field in the first place. The great Vladimir Rubicon had gained renown as one of the foremost authorities on Native American cliff dwellings, particularly the once-thriving Anasazi civilization, though he had begun his career studying the Maya.

Cassandra wanted to make her own mark in the field, not just continue her father's work. Her original passion had been geology, analyzing the composition of the terrain beneath the jungles of Central America—but as she continued her studies, she found she knew as much about the ancient Maya as did Kelly, the team's self-proclaimed archaeological expert.

Together, they had made an impressive pair, able to talk the Board of Regents at UC–San Diego into funding their modest expedition to Mexico. The team would be all students, willing to work for the possible credentials and the right to publish striking new research, without being paid more than a starvation-level stipend. It was the bane of academics everywhere.

Luckily, like a surprise gift, they had been blessed with matching funding from the Mexican state of Quintana Roo, in which the ruins of Xitaclan had been found. With the Mexican money Cassandra had been able to obtain the diving equipment, hire the native workers, and pay Fernando Victorio Aguilar . . . for all the help he'd been. She snorted at the thought.

So far, their expedition had been a success, and it seemed they would all share a page in the history books.

Cassandra worked her way deeper into the temple, dictating a description of her path as she went. She ran her fingers over the stone blocks, and her voice rose and fell—fiery with excitement, then whispering in amazement—recording what she observed. The marvelous constructions within constructions inside the Pyramid of Kukulkan reminded her of a Russian doll—one inside another inside another, each one depleting her stock of adjectives.

Suddenly, in the flashlight beam ahead of her, she saw that the inner walls to her left were of a markedly different color. With a flush of excitement, Cassandra realized she had stumbled upon the inner temple. This must be the original structure on whose foundation the Pyramid of Kukulkan had been erected.

The ancient Maya had often built taller, more impressive temples atop old ruins, because of their belief that certain places concentrated magic as time went by. The glorious ceremonial center of Xitaclan had been the nexus for rituals in this locality. What had long ago begun as an isolated religious center in the thickest jungle had eventually become a magnet for Maya power.

Until the people had abruptly and mysteriously abandoned it . . . leaving it preserved and empty for her to uncover centuries later.

Forcing herself to speak in a slow, analytical voice, Cassandra pressed the microcassette recorder close to her lips. "The stone blocks here are smoother, more carefully cut. They have a glassy finish, like varnish, as if they were vitrified by intense heat." She caught herself with a smile, realizing she had been studying the stone with a geologist's eye, not an archaeologist's perspective.

She ran her hands along the fused stone surface, and in a breathless voice continued to record her impressions. "Normally I would have expected to see fragments of the whitewash or stucco the Maya used to decorate their temples—but I see no remains of paint, not even any carvings. The walls are completely smooth."

Cassandra followed the inner perimeter. The air inside smelled more and more stagnant; no currents had disturbed it in countless centuries. She sneezed, and the sound echoed explosively throughout the catacombs. Trickles of dust rained down from between ceiling blocks, and she hoped the ancient support beams would hold.

"This is clearly the remains of the first temple," she dictated, "the innermost structure that was once the heart of Xitaclan, the first structure on this site."

Very excited now, Cassandra followed the inward spiral, brushing her fingers against the cool slick surface of the stone. She kept to the new wall—actually, it was the oldest wall—wondering what secrets might be contained at the core of the pyramid.

From all the evidence she had uncovered, Xitaclan's glory was no mere stepping-stone in Maya culture. Tales of the legendary city were so deeply implanted in the psyche of the native people that the locals still talked about the curse and the spirits that clung to the place. Many people had supposedly disappeared in the area, too, but Cassandra put that down to local mythology.

What had caused the ancient Maya to place their hub of religious significance here, in an uninteresting portion of the jungle with no roads or rivers, no copper or gold mines nearby? Why here?

Rubble had fallen across the passage ahead, blocking her way. But Cassandra felt her adrenaline pumping. Now that she had reached the center of the pyramid, she needed to see what lay beyond. It was possible that she stood on the brink of a great discovery—but not unless she could go all the way.

Stuffing the tape recorder into her pocket and the scribbled graph paper inside her shirt, she laid the flashlight down and worked with both hands to pull away fallen limestone bricks from the top of the pile. She ignored the clouds of dust and grit raised by her efforts. She had been dirty before.

Digging bare-handed in the rubble, Cassandra managed to make an opening just wide enough to wriggle her slender body through. She clambered up to the opening and thrust the flashlight forward; then, bumping her head as she strained forward to see, she crawled partway into a new corridor that sloped steeply down.

Ahead, the echoing chamber seemed much larger than the numerous other alcoves she had found in the pyramid, large enough to hold dozens of people. A curved shaft led away from it, a spiral ramp that went even deeper. She played her beam around the new room and nearly dropped the flashlight in her surprise. She had never seen anything like this.

Cassandra's white light reflected off walls made of peeling metallic plates, bent girders, crystalline panels. When she moved the flashlight beam away, portions of the newly exposed interior continued to glow with an eerie, pale afterlight.

From her knowledge of ancient history and culture, these bizarre fixtures seemed impossible to her. The Maya had never been known to use any kind of metal extensively, mainly satisfied with obsidian and flint for their needs. But here, unmistakably, she saw smooth, untarnished metal as if it had been made in modern smelters. It was an unusual alloy—certainly not the crude gold and bronze the ancient Maya had used.

Astonished, she stared for a while, still practically facedown in an opening barely large enough for a badger. She drew out her tape recorder, squirming and wedging herself deeper into the opening so she could hold the flashlight in one hand and the tape recorder near her mouth with the other. She pressed the RECORD button.

"This is amazing," she said, then paused for a long, silent moment as she searched for words. "I'm seeing metal with a silvery consistency, but not dark like tarnished silver. It gleams white—aluminum or platinum? But that can't be, since the ancient Maya culture had no access to those metals."

Cassandra recalled reading how some artifacts recovered from Egyptian tombs had gleamed shiny and new despite being locked away for millennia; yet, once exposed to post–Industrial Age air clogged with sulfur-bearing pollutants, the artifacts had tarnished and deteriorated within weeks. "Note—we must explore this chamber with extreme caution," she said. "It seems to be quite an exceptional find."

She desperately wanted to climb all the way inside, to explore to her heart's content. But common sense warned her not to.

"I have decided not to proceed into the chamber yet," she dictated, struggling to keep the dejection out of her voice. "Nothing must be disturbed until the entire team is here to assist me and provide second opinions on questionable items. I'm going back for Kelly and John. They can help me clear the rubble from this opening and support it with overhead beams. We'll need Cait to photograph the objects in state before anyone else goes inside."

After a long pause, she spoke again. "For the record, let me say that I think this is *it* . . . the Big One."

Cassandra switched off the microrecorder, then swallowed hard. After crawling back out, she unenthusiastically brushed herself off, then gave up, leaving the grit and dust. She began to retrace her steps, winding through the labyrinth to reach the exit, forcing herself to be calm. She thought of her wiry old father and imagined how proud he would be to see his daughter making discoveries that rivaled—even overshadowed!—those at the high point of his own career.

She quickened her pace. Her footsteps whispered and echoed through the stone passageways. As she approached the low exit to the pyramid, bright rays from the setting sun shone in her eyes like the light of an oncoming train. She rushed forward and stumbled out of the pyramid into the open air. "Hey, Kelly!" she shouted, "I've found something! You have to get the team, quick. Wait'll you see this!"

No one answered her. She stopped, blinking, and stood outside for a moment in the silence. She held on to the edge of the pyramid doorway for support.

The ruins seemed abandoned again. She heard only the murmur of jungle sounds, nothing else. She looked toward the high levels of the ziggurat, expecting to spot a couple of students on the heiroglyphic stairs . . . but the pyramid stood deserted.

By now the sunset was fading into dusk, the worst time of the day for visibility, when the shadows took on dim colors. Only a thin curve of the retreating sun remained above the treetops in the west, like an orange beacon backlighting the scene with an incomprehensible glare.

Cassandra saw no one, no members of her team, none of the vanished Indian helpers.

"Kelly, John, Christopher!" she called. "Cait, where are you?"

Shading her eyes, she peered out into the open plaza where Cait had earlier erected an easel for her watercolor work. Now the easel lay smashed on the ground. Cassandra could clearly make out a muddy bootprint stomped across one of the new paintings.

Greatly uneasy now, she again scanned the steep staircase that ran up the outside of the ziggurat. There

Christopher and Kelly had painstakingly cleaned the chiseled glyphs and sketched them on pads, translating the chronicle of Xitaclan's mythic history as they went.

No Kelly, no Christopher . . . not a soul in sight.

Across the plaza where young John Forbin had been studying the collapsed ruins of a minor temple, she spotted his case of equipment, his small wooden stakes and colored ribbons marking line-of-sight intersection points—but found no sign of the grad-student engineer.

"Hey! Kelly? This isn't a damn funny joke," she shouted. Her stomach knotted. She felt utterly isolated, engulfed by the surrounding forest. How could the bustling, verdant jungle be so damned quiet? "Hey!"

She heard movement to the side—footsteps coming around the pyramid from the direction of the deep sacrificial cenote. She heaved a sigh of relief. Here were her friends after all.

But then the shadowy silhouettes of strange men appeared—obviously not any members of her team. In the dim light she could barely discern their features, but she did see without a doubt that they carried guns. Rifles.

The men pointed their weapons at her.

One spoke in heavily accented English. "You will come with us, Señorita."

"Who are you?" Cassandra demanded, the old fire within her flaring up enough to burn away her common sense. She gripped her flashlight as if it were a club. "Where is my team? We're American citizens. How dare you—"

One of the other men jerked up his rifle and fired. The bullet ricocheted off one of the pyramid's stone blocks, barely six inches from her face. A spray of needle-sharp stone fragments peppered her cheek.

With a sharp cry, she ducked backward into the temple, seeking refuge in the ancient darkness. She ran down the long tunnel, hearing loud shouts in Spanish outside. Angry curses. More gunfire. Merciful confusion.

Her heart pounded, but she wasted no mental energy trying to guess who the men could be or what they wanted. She didn't dare think of what they might already have done to Cait, John, Christopher . . . and Kelly. She would think about that later—if she survived.

She glanced behind her. The men were barely discernible outside the temple. She saw them appear at the doorway, arguing with each other. One figure cuffed another, then raised a fist high in anger. More shouts in Spanish.

Cassandra ran around a sharp corner. Her flashlight beam bobbed ahead of her. She had forgotten to turn it off when she came out of the pyramid. Perhaps the murderous strangers didn't have lights of their own, but they could see the reflection of her beam on the stone walls. She switched off the light and plunged blindly ahead.

More rifle shots rang out behind her. Bullets bounced along the pyramid walls, whining a high-pitched song of death. Regardless of how poorly these men could shoot, a ricochet could still kill her.

Cassandra had no choice but to keep running headlong into the dark, labyrinthine passages, deeper into the barely explored depths. Rounding one corner, and then another, she finally switched her flashlight on again, although she still heard the sounds of clumsy pursuit behind her. Back in the direction of the opening she saw flickering orange lights splashing against the walls, and guessed that the armed men had taken to striking matches and cigarette lighters to find their way after her.

Cassandra had the advantage—for now. She had been down here before, she had a flashlight, and she had a vague idea of where she was going: back toward the center of the pyramid.

But she had no place to go from there.

Going deeper inside would only drive her more firmly into the trap. She had to think, use her wits to outsmart these men, whoever they were. No problem.

She took out the microcassette recorder and rewound it, hoping that her breathlessly dictated directions and notes could help her to retrace her path to the strange chamber that had remained hidden for centuries. Maybe she could hide there until the men gave up looking for her.

Right. No problem.

The strangers might just post a guard at the outer doorway, then return better equipped to hunt her down. They could search relentlessly until they found her and gunned her down in a corner of the ancient ruin. Worse still, they could just lie in wait for her until she staggered out in a few days, nearly mad from hunger and thirst.

She couldn't think about that. Survive for *now*. She kept moving.

Cassandra pressed the PLAY button, listening for directions on her microcassette. She heard only a faintly crackling hiss. Her words had been erased! Something had blanked her tape.

"Dammit!" She groaned and added another item to the list of things she didn't understand but couldn't think about at the moment. Well, the route was fresh enough in her mind that she could find her way without any other assistance.

She had to.

The corridors of the outer pyramid wound downward on a slope, littered with fallen limestone blocks and rough debris. She stumbled, scraped her hands against the rough walls, but kept moving. Moving. She heard another gunshot. Why did they keep wasting ammunition? The men couldn't possibly have a good shot at her. Maybe they were just spooked by the echoes of their own footsteps. Frightened men with guns were the most dangerous kind.

Finally, Cassandra found the smooth, vitrified walls of the inner temple and knew she had nearly reached her destination—though what she intended to do there was another question altogether.

Casting her flashlight beam ahead, she discovered the small opening she had recently excavated. It looked like an open wound. . . .

No. It was an escape hatch.

Gritting her teeth and panting for breath, Cassandra

crawled onto the pile of rubble and squirmed into the hole like a snake. Before, the opening had seemed too cramped, too constrictive. But now panic propelled her forward. The rocks scraped her elbows, her shoulders, but she didn't care.

She fought her way over the rubble barricade into the isolated chamber and dropped down. Her feet echoed on the floor—a floor that was inexplicably metallic.

The passageways became oppressively silent again.

Her flashlight beam reflected off polished surfaces, curves, and spheres with a geometrical perfection that should have been far beyond Maya capabilities. The light flickered, as if her batteries were rapidly dying.

Another volley of gunfire echoed through the winding labyrinth far behind, separated from her by walls of stone. Then more shouts came, much louder, possibly nearer—but she couldn't be certain due to the reflective rock of the twisting corridors.

Inside the weird chamber, Cassandra was in totally unexplored territory. She rushed ahead to the final descending passage, the spiral ramp at the exact core of the pyramid. The steep tunnel looked as if it burrowed well beneath ground level. Without pausing to think, she hurried down it, moving farther and farther from her pursuers.

A faint wave of hope splashed across her mind. She wondered if this ramp might lead to some unknown exit from the pyramid, perhaps far down the wall of the limestone sinkhole. Maybe she could get out of this after all!

The sharp crack of a gunshot drove a spike of sound through the echoing rooms. Logically, Cassandra knew the shadowy men couldn't be close. She had to be far ahead of them. She *must* have lost them in the twisting and turning passages, but her fear drove her faster and faster down the sloping ramp ... until the passageway opened into a grotto of wonders, glimpsed only briefly.

Glass panels on the walls around her reflected arrays of crystal spheres, gleaming shapes, metal strips laid down in geometric paths along limestone blocks. But she caught only a peripheral blink of everything around her before her flashlight winked out, as if something had consumed its electrical power, sucked its batteries dry, in the same way as her microcassette had been mysteriously erased.

Cassandra swallowed hard, feeling claustrophobic, lost. She staggered forward blindly, sweeping her hands in front of her, searching for a landmark. Her questing hands encountered an opening, a small doorway. She staggered through it, hoping to find some source of light.

A brilliant glare washed around her, and in an instant Cassandra saw that she had crossed into a dead-end room the size of a closet . . . or a coffin. Blazing illumination flooded from behind smooth, glassy walls.

Too late, Cassandra wondered if this fate might not be worse than the men with guns.

Icy, cold light cascaded over her like liquid, freezing hard—and all of her thoughts ceased.

2

X Every time Special Agent Dana Scully ventured into the bowels of FBI Headquarters to see her partner, Fox Mulder, she felt as if she were doing something illicit—or at least unwise.

She remembered the first time she had come here to Mulder's private sanctum, a fresh young field agent inexplicably assigned to the X-Files. "No one down here but the FBI's most unwanted," he had called by way of introduction. At the time, Agent Mulder had considered her a spy for Bureau higher-ups who did not condone his passionate interest in unexplained phenomena.

Now, after three years of working together, Scully and Mulder had investigated dozens of cases and relied on each other's help more times than they could count. Mulder's belief in the supernatural and extraterrestrials remained unshaken, while Scully remained just as steadfast in her search for rational explanations. Though they frequently did not agree on their conclusions, they performed extraordinarily well as a team.

Scully visited her partner's narrow office often enough that its dreary clutter was etched permanently in her mind. She knew exactly what to expect. This morning the room did not disappoint her.

Debris from his unusual research lay strewn about the office: videotapes, DNA records, medical histories, close-up photos of smallpox scars on withered skin, blurry snapshots that supposedly showed evidence of flying saucers. A hunk of twisted shrapnel, purportedly from a crashed spacecraft found in Wisconsin, rested on one shelf. A dozen unsolved mysteries in open folders waited to be put to rest in the nondescript black file cabinets that contained Mulder's raison d'être: the X-Files.

She knocked on the frame of the open door and stepped inside, brushing a hand through her red-gold hair. "I'm not sure I have the energy to face this chaos so early in the morning, Mulder," she said.

Mulder swiveled around in his chair, spat out a sunflower seed, and stood up. "Try eating more presweetened breakfast cereal," he said. "That'll give you the energy to face anything." He grinned at her.

She felt uneasy when he grinned like that, because it usually meant he had focused his attention on some new or unorthodox theory . . . a theory she would most likely have to debunk.

Looking down, she noticed that he had piled his desk with archaeology texts, books on ancient mythology, and detailed maps of Central America. She tried to put all the ingredients together in a flash, because she would have to prepare herself for what her partner would propose for their next investigation.

"Take a look at this, Scully," he said, and held out an object about the size of his fist, intricately carved and polished, made of a buttery, whitish-green stone. "Three guesses."

She took the heavy relic and held it in her hands. The stone's surface was polished so smooth it felt as if it had been oiled. The carving showed a sinuous serpentine form, some kind of viper bristling with large, incongruous feathers. Curved, needle-like fangs protruded from its mouth, giving the creature a ferocious appearance.

The artisan had been a master. The design fit exactly with the irregular contours of the chunk of rock. She ran her fingertip along one of the notches, wondering what sort of test Mulder might be putting her through.

"What do you make of it?" he said.

"I give up." She scrutinized the artifact again, but it remained a mystery. "A Christmas tree ornament?"

"Not even close."

"Okay," she said, taking the question seriously now. "I think I recognize the stone. It's jade, isn't it?"

"Very good, Scully. I didn't know they taught mineralogy in medical school."

"I didn't know they included mineralogy in behavioral psychology courses either," she countered, then turned her attention back to the object. "It looks very old. Some sort of mythological figure, maybe? From the books on your desk, I would guess its origin to be . . . Aztec?"

"Maya, actually," he said. "Best estimates date this piece of work to be about fifteen hundred years old. The Maya people revered jade. It was a sacred stone to them, used for only the most precious of objects."

"As valuable as gold?" Scully asked, playing along, wondering what he was getting at.

"Much more valuable. The Maya used to wear it around their loins as a cure for colic and other maladies. They even placed a piece of jade in the mouths of dead noblemen, because they believed the stone would serve him as a heart in the afterlife."

"Talk about a heart of stone." She turned the piece over in her hand. "It's obvious they put a great deal of effort and intricacy into the carving."

Mulder nodded, pushing one of the books out of the way so he could rest his elbow on his desk. "And it had to be quite a challenge for the carvers, too. Jadeite is exceptionally hard and dense, and so craftsmen couldn't use their traditional flint or obsidian tools." He reached over to tap a fingernail against the carving in her hands. "Instead, they had to use abrasive powders and disposable tools, dozens of them—wooden saws, bone drills, cords drawn repeatedly across the surface to wear down small grooves. Then they polished the whole piece of jade with gourd or cane fibers. Quite a piece of work."

"Okay, Mulder, so this wasn't a simple figure whittled out of wood for amusement. Somebody really wanted to make this particular object. In that case I take it there's some significance to the special design? A serpent with feathers. Did the Mayans revere snakes?"

"Ah," he said. "Not exactly. You'll notice that's no ordinary snake. It's a famous mythological figure associated with the god Quetzalcoatl. That's what the Aztec called him. The Maya used the name Kukulkan, a god of great wisdom. Some sources say Kukulkan taught the Maya about calendars and astronomy."

He offered her a sunflower seed. She shook her head, so he popped it into his own mouth.

"The Maya astronomer-priests were so precise in their calculations that the accuracy of their 'primitive' calendars wasn't surpassed until this very century. They even built interlocking gear-machines to make their calendar computations based on overlapping cycles out to fifty-two years. Kukulkan must have been an exceptional teacher . . . or he knew something the rest of the people didn't.

"Their mathematical abilities were extraordinary, too—in fact, they were the only ancient civilization ever to invent the concept of zero. That's important for balancing your checkbook, of course."

"Not my checkbook," she said.

With some effort, Scully found a place to sit down, moving a cardboard box filled with plaster casts of huge footprints. She glanced down at the casts but decided she didn't want to risk asking about them.

"That's all very interesting, Mulder," she said, "but what does a fifteen-hundred-year-old lump of jade in the shape of a feathered serpent have to do with a case? Have people started seeing feathered snakes in their back yards? Or have you discovered some discrepancy in our calendar that can only be explained by ancient Mayan carvings?"

She handed him back the jade sculpture, and he carefully placed it atop his Central America reference works.

"Under normal circumstances it wouldn't have anything to do with one of our cases," he said, "but this particular relic was recently confiscated at the border of the Mexican state of Quintana Roo, down in the Yucatán. The arrested dealer claims that this artifact came from the archaeological dig of a rediscovered Maya city deep in the jungles, a ruin called Xitaclan.

"According to official Mexican reports, there have been numerous unexplained disappearances in the area, dating back decades. And because the area is so primitive and isolated, you can bet plenty more of them have gone entirely undocumented."

"I'm still not sure I see the connection here, Mulder." She waited, casually crossing one leg over the other.

"Most locals won't go near the place, claiming it's cursed, or sacred . . . depending on which translation you use. Their legends tell of vicious feathered serpents, and the god Kukulkan, and the lost ghosts of sacrificial victims whose blood stained the temple stones."

Scully shifted on the old, government-issue chair. "I doubt that the Bureau would consider sending us to investigate an ancient Maya curse."

"There's more to it than that." His eyes grew bright. "A team of American archaeologists had just begun excavating Xitaclan under the auspices of the University of California, San Diego. According to early reports, this one site is untouched and the key to many mysteries of Maya history. It *could* be the first large-scale construction their civilization attempted. Definitely the site of frequent sacrifices."

He smiled, as if delivering a coup de grace. "Also, my preliminary chemical analysis of this object turned up some interesting anomalies, an odd crystalline structure, unidentifiable impurities that imply that this material did not come from the Yucatán near the ruins. . . ."

She focused on the soft green color of the stone. "You think this thing comes from outer space?"

He shrugged and brushed a pile of damp sunflower-seed shells into his wastebasket, accidentally leaving several behind. "The archaeology team disappeared without a trace a week ago. No signal of distress, no sign of trouble. You and I get to go find them."

"But, Mulder, wouldn't this normally be handled by the Mexican authorities?"

Mulder said, "I also received a call yesterday from the father of Cassandra Rubicon, the young woman who led the UC–San Diego team. It seems her father's an extremely well-known archaeologist himself. He's made a few phone calls, contacted the FBI field office for San Diego. They heard the words 'ancient curse' and 'Maya ruins' and passed the case on to me." Scully met his gaze, and he raised his eyebrows. "I have a meeting with Skinner this afternoon. You and I are going to meet Vladimir Rubicon tomorrow. He's here, in Washington."

Scully glanced at the jade sculpture, at the mythology books, and then at the fascinated expression on Mulder's face. "I don't suppose it'll do me any good to try to talk you out of this?" she asked.

"Won't do you any good at all," he said.

"In that case, I suppose I always wanted to go to Mexico," she answered.

Assistant Director Skinner sat at his desk, ritually tapping his fingertips on the neatly typed forms in front of him. He did not stand when Mulder entered the room.

That's usually a bad sign, Mulder thought. On the other hand, Skinner had thrown him a curve enough times that he decided it would do no good to second-guess him.

The balding man was either a very good friend or the worst kind of enemy. Skinner knew things and passed the information on to Mulder only when he considered it important to do so.

Right now, Mulder needed to stay in Skinner's good graces. He and Scully had to get down to the Yucatán.

Skinner looked at him through wire-rimmed glasses.

"I'm not sure you realize just what a sensitive subject you've stepped into, Agent Mulder."

Mulder stood at attention in front of his superior's desk. Keeping his expression neutral, he looked at the framed photographs of the President and the Attorney General on the wall. "I intend to exercise due discretion, sir."

Skinner nodded, showing that he had already considered this. "See that you do. As far as the Bureau is concerned, this is an important missing-persons case, relating to possible crimes committed upon American citizens. I have obtained for you and Agent Scully the status of LEGATS, legal attachés sent out of the country operating for the United States Embassy in Mexico City."

He held up a finger. "But bear in mind how delicate this situation is, given the current economic and political tensions. The Mexican government is always sensitive to intrusions by U.S. officials on its soil. I don't need to remind you about the number of DEA agents who have been assassinated by drug lords in Central America.

"The area you're heading into, in the state of Quintana Roo, is a political hotbed at this time. The local government is particularly vulnerable because of a violent separatist movement that seems to be growing in force, thanks to an unidentified supply of weapons."

"Are you suggesting that the archaeological team might have fallen victim to political unrest?" Mulder said.

"I find that more likely than an ancient Mayan curse," Skinner said. "Or weren't you going to suggest that?"

"Maybe, maybe not," Mulder said. "We have to examine every possibility."

Skinner picked up a set of travel authorizations and expense vouchers. He passed them across the desk, and Mulder took them, noting that all the signature lines had already been filled in.

"I expect you to strictly adhere to protocol, Agent Mulder," Skinner said. "I would urge you in no uncertain terms to hew the line in this investigation."

"Yes, sir."

"If you offend anyone in high places, you'll have more than just the FBI to answer to; you'll have the State Department as well. That is, unless you get yourself thrown into some Mexican jail first."

"I'll try my best to stay clear of that, sir." Mulder took the forms and tucked them under his arm.

"One more thing, Agent Mulder," Skinner said with an unreadable expression. "Have a nice trip."

3

X "When all else fails, Special Agent Mulder comes to us for the real answers," said Byers, leaning back in his chair. He straightened his suit and tie, ran a finger across his neat reddish beard, and looked up calmly.

Entering alone, Mulder closed the door behind him in the dim offices of *The Lone Gunmen*, a conspiracy exposé publication that purported to know the official truths about a thousand secret plots in which the government was engaged.

Scully had told him once that she considered the oddball characters who produced the magazine to be the most paranoid men she had ever met. But Mulder had found time and again that the esoteric information the three Lone Gunmen had at their fingertips often led in directions that official channels would never have suggested.

"Hi, guys," Mulder said. "Who's taking over the world this week?"

"I think Mulder just likes to keep tabs on us," Langly answered, sauntering across the room with a lazy shuffle that, with a little work, could have been turned into a dance step. Tall and scrawny, inelegantly dressed, he was the type who could easily have fit in with any crowd of computer nerds or roadies for a rock band. "It's for his own protection," he added, adjusting his black-rimmed glasses.

Langly had stringy blond hair that looked as if he washed it in a blender. Mulder had never seen him wear anything other than a ratty T-shirt, usually advertising some fringe rock group.

"I think he just likes our company," Frohike mumbled, working with several pieces of extremely expensive camera equipment on one of the metal shelves at the rear of the office. In the background, Langly switched on the big reel-to-reel tape recorders, getting their entire conversation down on tape.

"Yeah, you three are just my kind of guys," Mulder said with a disarming smile.

Byers always wore a suit and a tie. He was soft-spoken and intelligent, the kind of son any mother would have been proud to have—if not for his vociferous opposition to various government organizations and his obsession with UFO conspiracies.

Frohike, with glasses, close-cropped hair, and rugged features, didn't look as if he would fit in with *any* social group. He had a long-standing crush on Dana Scully, but basically it was all talk. Mulder suspected Frohike would turn into a jittering mass of nerves if Scully ever consented to go out with him. Nevertheless, Mulder had been deeply touched when the short-statured man had brought flowers to Scully's bedside while she lay in a coma after returning from her abduction.

No identifying sign marked the door to the offices of the Lone Gunmen, and they were not listed in any phone book. The three kept their operation very low-profile. They tape-recorded every incoming phone call and took care to cover their own movements in and around Washington, D.C.

Nondescript, utilitarian shelves held surveillance equipment and computer monitors. Wires snaking out of the wall provided hard links to any number of network servers and databases. Mulder suspected the Lone Gunmen had never been granted official access to many of the systems, but that did not prevent the three from hacking into libraries of information closely held by government organizations and industrial groups.

Most of the chairs in the office were filled with boxes of stuffed manila envelopes, preprinted address labels facedown. Mulder knew the envelopes carried no return addresses.

"Your timing is good, Agent Mulder," Frohike said. "We're about to mail out our new issue. We could use some help dispersing them through a couple dozen mailbox drop points."

"Do I get a sneak preview of the contents?" he said.

Langly popped an old reel-to-reel magnetic tape from one of the recorders, labeled the flat metal canister, and installed a new backup system. "This one's a special issue of *TLG*. Our 'All Elvis' number."

"Elvis?" Mulder said in surprise. "I thought you guys were above all that."

"No conspiracy is beneath us," Byers said proudly.

"I can see that," Mulder answered.

Langly took off his glasses and rubbed them on the tail of his T-shirt, which advertised a concert tour by the Soup Dragons. He blinked small eyes at Mulder, then put the black-rimmed glasses back on. "You won't believe what we've uncovered, Mulder. You'll have a whole new take on it after reading our historical retrospective. I did most of the research and writing myself on this one.

"We think that Elvis is being positioned as a messiah figure—by powerful persons unknown to us. You can find similar instances all through history. The lost king who reappears after his supposed death to lead his people again. Could be a strong basis for forming an insidious new religion."

"You mean like legends of King Arthur promising to

come back from Avalon?" Mulder said. "Or Frederick Barbarossa sleeping in a mountain cave until his beard grows all the way around the table, at which point he'll return to save the Holy Roman Empire?"

Langly frowned. "Those two are misfires, because the messiahs in question never did come back, as promised. However, take Russia, for instance—Tsar Alexander II defeated Napoleon and supposedly died . . . but for years the peasants told of seeing a wandering beggar or a monk who claimed to be the real Tsar. It was quite a popular legend. And of course there are the Biblical accounts of Jesus Christ dying and coming back to continue leading his disciples.

"We don't need to remind you how many supposed Elvis sightings occur daily. We believe they have been staged, to provide the foundation for a fanatical new cult."

"Everybody wants an encore," Mulder said. He reached for one of the manila envelopes and slid out the issue to study the photo of Elvis on the front cover. He scanned the first article. "So what you're telling me is that somebody is trying to establish the birth of Elvis was in reality the Second Coming."

"You know how gullible people are, Mulder," Frohike said. "Think about it. Some of Elvis's songs have a very New Testament feel to them. 'Love Me Tender,' for instance. Or 'Don't Be Cruel.' Could almost be part of the Sermon on the Mount."

Byers leaned forward. "And if you think about placing it in a modern context, any hit single reaches far more people than the Sermon on the Mount ever did."

"Ah," Mulder said, "so what was Elvis really trying to say with 'Jailhouse Rock' or 'Hound Dog?'"

"Those took a little more work," Langly said. "Our interpretations will be in the next issue. You'll be surprised."

"I already am."

Byers shrugged and shifted in his chair. "We don't make judgment calls, Agent Mulder, we just report the facts. It's up to our readers to draw their own conclusions."

"About you guys, or about the conspiracies you report?"

Frohike pointed a large camera and clicked a picture of Mulder. "For our files," he said.

Mulder held up the newly printed issue. "Can I keep this copy?"

"Yours should be in the mail," Frohike said.

"Why not go ahead and buy an official subscription, Mulder?" Langly suggested. "Put some of your FBI salary to good use."

Byers smiled. "No, for someone of Mulder's stature, we should make sure he gets a comp copy of each issue. Besides, I'd be uncomfortable having his name and address on our mailing list."

"What, you're afraid you couldn't sell the list of addresses to Publishers Clearing House then?"

"Our readers are a certain type of person, Mulder," Byers said. "The type who might not want their names included among others who are also interested in the conspiracies we expose. We take great efforts to ensure that our mailing list can't fall into the wrong hands. Each of the three of us keeps a third of the names in separate electronic files with separate passwords on separate computer systems. We can't access each other's records. We just bring in the mailing labels, already printed."

Frohike said, "We print them out at the copy shop."

"Can't be too careful," Langly said.

"No, you can't," Mulder agreed.

"Well, we have to get started sealing envelopes," Langly said. "We'd be happy to press you into service, Mulder."

Mulder held up his hand. "No, thanks, I just came here for some information, then I'll be on my way."

"And how can we help save innocent citizens from the nefarious workings of the shadow government?" Byers said. "For this afternoon, at least?"

Mulder moved aside one of the boxes of stuffed envelopes and sat down. "What's the buzz you guys hear on Central America, the Yucatán, particularly some new Maya ruins that are being excavated? Xitaclan. I've got a missing archaeology team and a recovered artifact that may be of extraterrestrial origin."

"Let me think," Langly said, tossing his long blond hair. "I majored in archaeology in college."

Byers looked at him skeptically. "I thought you majored in political science."

Frohike squinted through his glasses. "You told me it was electronics engineering."

Langly shrugged. "So, I had a lot of varied interests."

Byers grew serious, looking back at Mulder. "Central America? I hear a lot of unconfirmed rumors about events in the area. There's been a separatist movement brewing in one of the states in the Yucatán. It's called *Liberación Quintana Roo*. The violence seems to be escalating—car bombs, threatening letters—and of course, you know about the U.S. military complex supplying arms at an exorbitant price to the freedom fighters."

"Why would they do that?" Mulder said.

"To create political instability. It's a game to them," Byers said, passion flickering behind his normally calm eyes. "And don't forget about some of the more powerful drug lords in the area who have become arms merchants themselves. Buying up technology. Serious stuff that we never would have dreamed about a decade ago."

"I dreamed about it," Frohike said.

"And how does this tie in with your particular interest, Mulder?" Langly asked.

"As I said, an American archaeological team disappeared there a week ago. They had unearthed new artifacts in the ruins—artifacts that are now turning up on the black market. The locals won't go near the place. Apparently there's a long-standing curse on the city. It was abandoned a thousand years ago, and now I've been hearing talk about the revenge of Kukulkan and his ferocious guardian feathered serpents."

"Knowing you, Mulder, I'm surprised you're not out chasing ancient astronauts," Langly said.

"I'm keeping an open mind," he answered. "There are plenty of mysteries connected with Maya culture and history, but I'm not necessarily ready to adopt any of them yet. With ancient astronauts and the Maya curse . . . not to mention the drug lords and military operations and revolutionary movements Byers was talking about, the Yucatán really sounds like a happenin' place."

"So are you and the lovely Agent Scully going down to investigate?" Frohike said, sounding hopeful.

"Yeah, we leave for Cancún tomorrow."

"Our tax dollars at work," Langly snorted.

"I'd love to see Agent Scully with a healthy tropical tan," Frohike said.

"Down, Frohike," Mulder said.

Mulder turned to leave. It was late in the afternoon, and traffic on the Beltway would be horrendous. He thought he might go back to the office and do more research. "Thanks for the information."

As he stood by the door, Byers called after him, standing up and straightening his tie. "Agent Mulder," he said, "if you do find anything interesting, be sure to let us know. For our files."

"I'll see what I can do," Mulder said.

4

Private villa of Xavier Salida,
Quintana Roo, Mexico
Tuesday, 5:01 P.M.

X The old Mexican police cruiser with official state markings rolled along the tree-lined driveway, working its way uphill. The walled fortress of one of Quintana Roo's most powerful drug lords stood like a citadel in the dense forest.

The car rode low on the damp driveway made of packed limestone gravel. Blue-gray exhaust belched in oily clouds from its tailpipe. The police car had been painted recently, but so unevenly, that it did not look as new as it should have.

In the front passenger seat reclined Fernando Victorio Aguilar, feigning a calm and ease that he had learned always helped him to do better business. He rubbed his fingers along his slick cheeks. He had shaved only an hour before, and he loved the delicious, glassy-smooth feel of his skin. The sharp but pleasant scent of his cologne filled the car, masking other less pleasant aromas that Carlos Barreio, the chief of Quintana Roo's state police, had collected during his daily work.

Barreio drove slowly, easing around muddy puddles

in the driveway. He wore his clean police uniform as if he were a military general, pleased with his position and flaunting it in a way he thought was subtle. Aguilar didn't find many things about Barreio to be subtle.

In the back seat rode young Pepe Candelaria, Aguilar's assistant, a steadfast young Indian who felt compelled to do everything Aguilar told him. Pepe sat protectively beside the precious object packed in its crate as if he were a common criminal under arrest in the back of Barreio's police cruiser.

While Aguilar and Pepe might have deserved to be arrested under the national system of laws, they both knew beyond the shadow of a doubt that Police Chief Barreio would never take them into custody. He had too much to lose.

The cruiser pulled to a stop outside the ornate, imposing wrought-iron gates that closed the access way through a stone wall. Barreio rolled down his window, grunting as he turned the door crank. He waved at the heavily armed private guard, who recognized him immediately.

Aguilar stared out the windshield, gazing appreciatively at the thick wall that surrounded Xavier Salida's huge fortress. Slabs of stone covered with ornate glyphs, Maya writing and sculptures, designs of jaguars and feathered serpents, images of priests wearing quetzal-feather headdresses and loincloths studded with beaten gold plates. Some of the carved panels were genuine, uprooted from forgotten and overgrown ruins out in the jungle. Others were clever forgeries Aguilar had commissioned.

Xavier Salida never knew the difference. The drug lord was a self-deluded, if powerful, fool.

"Tiene una cita, Señor Barreio?" the guard said in rapid Spanish. Do you have an appointment?

Carlos Barreio frowned. A heavy mustache rode on his upper lip like luggage, and his dark hair was slicked back under his police cap. His hair was thinning, receding with a pronounced widow's peak, but the bill of his official cap covered those details.

"I shouldn't need an appointment," Barreio boomed. "Excellency Salida has told me I'm always welcome in his home."

Aguilar leaned across to the driver's side, eager to divert an annoying and time-wasting confrontation. "We have another one of the ancient treasures Excellency Salida so fervently desires," he said out the window. "You know how much he enjoys them—but this item is even more precious than most."

He tossed a meaningful glance to the back seat, where the crate remained covered, hiding its contents. Whip-thin Pepe Candelaria slid a protective arm over its top.

"What is it?" the guard asked.

"It is for Excellency Salida's eyes only. He would be very upset if his guards were to get a look at the merchandise before he has a chance to assess its value." Aguilar tugged on his floppy ocelot-skin hat and flashed a hopeful smile.

The guard fidgeted, shifted his rifle from one shoulder to the other, and finally opened the wrought-iron gate, swinging the barricade inward so Barreio could drive the police cruiser through.

The police chief parked the car in the broad, flag-stoned turnabout inside the walled courtyard. Dogs barked and howled from their kennels: Salida kept half a dozen purebred Dobermans, which he used for intimidation whenever necessary. Imported peacocks strutted around the grounds, clustering near the cool mist of a fountain that splashed into the hazy air.

Aguilar turned to look at both the driver and the passenger in the back seat. "This is a complex deal, so let me do the talking. When we meet with Salida, I'll handle the negotiations. Since this object is rare and unusual, we have no way of determining its true value."

"Just get the most you can," Barreio growled. "Weapons cost money, and *Liberación Quintana Roo* needs them."

"Yes, yes, your precious revolutionaries." Aguilar smoothed down the front of his khaki vest and then adjusted his spotted hat, making certain that his long dark hair was still in its neat ponytail that hung beneath the ocelot skin. Then he looked up at the broad expanse of Salida's whitewashed adobe villa.

It had taken a great deal of effort to smuggle Xitaclan artifacts from under the watchful eyes of the American archaeology team—but now that had all been taken care of. The foreigners would cause no further problems. This particular artifact was one of the last large relics taken from the pyramid, a "chamber of wonders" the Indian had called it in an awed voice . . . just before he had disappeared back into the jungles, never revealing where he had discovered the treasures.

But now his people had the run of Xitaclan again and plenty of freedom to explore . . . and exploit. For all of them who had risked so much, the time had come to reap the rewards.

Aguilar and Barreio got out of the car, while Pepe hauled the crate containing the artifact with him, lurching awkwardly under its bulk. The mysterious object was surprisingly lightweight for its size, but the young man had short arms and legs. Neither Aguilar nor Barreio offered to help.

Salida's second-floor balconies were decked with flowers, splashes of color that trickled between the railings and across the clean adobe surface. A hammock hung on one small balcony. Wicker chairs sat empty on another.

A guard at the door came forward, also armed with a shoulder rifle. "Hola!" Aguilar said, flashing his well-practiced smile. "We are here to see Excellency Salida."

"I'm afraid he is not having a good day," the guard said. "If you see him, you must accept the risk of upsetting him."

"He will see us," Aguilar said, again smiling. "If you wish to improve his day, you'll let him see what we've brought for him, eh?"

The guard looked at the box and stiffened, instantly suspicious. Before the man could ask, Aguilar said, "Another prize for your master. Even more breathtaking than the feathered serpent statue we delivered. And you know how highly he prized that carving."

Outside in the courtyard one of the peacock males set up a racket, a raucous squawking that sounded like a chicken being slowly crushed by a cement truck. Aguilar looked around and saw the large bird spread its amazing plumage. It sat on top of a tall stela, a stone pillar carved on all sides with Maya glyphs and pictures surrounding a ferocious-looking jaguar head.

The stela was ten feet tall and weighed many tons. It had begun to tilt, though Salida's landscaper had anchored it firmly in the ground. Dozens of sweating workers had labored for hours to bring the artifact in secret up the gravel driveway and into the drug lord's fenced courtyard.

The peacock squawked again, flaunting its feathers. Aguilar considered yanking them out, one by one.

The guard ushered them inside to a cool hallway and then up a curving grand staircase to the second level, where Xavier Salida kept his offices and his private withdrawing rooms. Sunlight drifted in through narrow windows, glistening on dust motes that fell through the air.

Their footsteps echoed with a hollow sound. The house seemed silent and sleepy . . . until they reached the second level. They could already hear Salida shouting as they approached down the hallway.

The guard looked wryly at the three visitors. "I told you, Señor Salida is not having a good day. One of our small cargo planes was shot down near here. We lost a pilot as well as many, many kilograms of product."

"I had nothing to do with this," Barreio said, suddenly defensive. "DEA?"

The guard looked back at the police chief. "Señor Salida has his own suspects."

They approached the largest withdrawing room, where two ornately carved mahogany doors stood mostly closed, leaving a gap of only a few inches between them. The drug lord's shouts carried through, only slightly muffled.

"Grobe! It must be Pieter Grobe. No one else would have the audacity!" Salida paused for a moment as if listening. "I'm not afraid of escalating our rivalry," he said. "We must take out twice as much in retaliation—but make no comment, no threats. Just do it." He slammed the phone down with an echoing clang, and silence fell on the rooms like a smotherer's pillow.

Aguilar swallowed, adjusted his floppy cap, and made to step forward. By smiling and taking the initiative, he hoped he could cheer the drug lord. The guard remained in place, blocking their way, his rifle on his shoulder. He shook his head in warning. "Not yet. It is not wise."

A moment later the strains of an opera emerged from a large stereo system inside the room. A shrieking soprano voice that sounded, if anything, worse than the peacock's cries outside in the courtyard, sang of some unimaginable human misery in a language Aguilar could not comprehend.

He knew the drug lord couldn't understand the words either, but Salida loved to put on airs, to wear the mask of cultured enlightenment. The opera went on for five nearly unbearable minutes, and then it was abruptly switched off to be replaced by a much more relaxing classical piece with orchestral instruments playing rich and complex melodies.

Hearing the change in music, the guard nodded and gestured for them to enter. He pulled open the heavy mahogany door on the right side.

Aguilar and Carlos Barreio entered side by side, but Aguilar knew that he had the upper hand. Behind them, Pepe struggled to carry the crate containing the precious and exotic artifact.

Xavier Salida turned to look at them, folding his hands in front of him and smiling a patient smile with a warmth that looked almost genuine. Aguilar was amazed at how rapidly the drug lord had transformed his mood from the shouting fury they had heard only moments before.

"Greetings, my friends," Salida said. His clothes were fine, his shirt made of white silk, his pants precisely tailored. He wore a nice vest with a gold watch chain dangling from its pocket.

Aguilar nodded and took off his ocelot-skin cap, holding it in front of him in the posture of a supplicant. "We are pleased you would see us, Excellency," he said. "We have another fine artifact to show you. Something so marvelous you have never seen anything like it."

Salida chuckled. "Fernando Victorio Aguilar, you say that every time you bring something to my home."

Aguilar smiled. "And aren't I usually correct? Don't you usually buy what I offer you, eh?" He gestured for Pepe to come forward and set the crate down on a glass table near the drug lord's desk.

Carlos Barreio stood at attention, trying to look imposing in his police uniform, while Aguilar glanced around the room: the familiar collection of fine art prints, professionally matted with heavy gilt-covered frames, the Maya sculptures on pedestals, some examples of pre-Colombian art in glass cases, others sitting on windowsills. Salida showcased the ones he liked the most, since he had no idea which were truly valuable and which were merely gaudy trinkets. A wine rack filled with the most expensive wines sat in one corner of the room.

Aguilar knew that although Xavier Salida flaunted his wealth and power, the drug lord had been illiterate until he became wealthy and powerful. The story was told of how he had brought in a tutor to teach him to read. The man had done a good enough job at it, but unfortunately the hapless tutor, after consuming too much tequila in a local cantina, had joked about the drug lord's lack of education ... and so Salida had had him removed.

There had been a succession of other tutors who had taught Salida courses in art and music appreciation, transforming him into a fine upstanding citizen. He ate his expensive Sevruga caviar. He drank his fine wines.

He played his old music on the newest stereo systems. And he pretended to know what he was doing when he collected expensive art objects.

Aguilar had taken advantage of this, fawning on him, playing on the drug lord's lack of expertise. Rather than admit he didn't know what he was doing, Xavier Salida nearly always bought the objects Aguilar offered.

But this time the prize was indeed something special. No question about it.

Pepe stood back from the glass table, sweating, swallowing, shuffling his feet. He wiped his palms on his pants, and waited for further instructions.

The drug lord gestured to the crate. "Well, go on, Fernando—open it, let me see what you have found this time."

Aguilar impatiently turned to Pepe, waving his hands. The young helper went to the crate and dug his nails in so that he could pry the tacks free. The lid popped open. He lifted aside the packing material, then carefully withdrew the magical artifact. Aguilar smiled magnanimously.

The drug lord caught his breath and stepped forward, compelled and fascinated. Aguilar's heart pounded. This was exactly the reaction he had hoped for.

Pepe set the object on the table and stepped back, wiping his sweaty hands on his pants again. The artifact was a completely transparent rectangular box a little more than a foot on each side. It gleamed with prismatic colors in the light, as if the workings inside were really sheets of thin diamond plating.

The components within were strange and exotic, interlocked components, connections made of glass fibers, glinting crystals. Aguilar thought it looked like the world's most complicated clock, made entirely of lead crystal. Tiny holes had been drilled in the side of the clear case. Other movable squares marked the corners and part of the top. Etched symbols not unlike some of the incomprehensible Maya glyphs marked portions of the clear glass faces. None of it made sense at all.

"What is it?" Salida said, touching its side and withdrawing his fingers quickly, as if burned. "It's cold! Even in this heat it's cold."

"This object is a great mystery, Excellency," Aguilar said. "I have never seen such an artifact before, even with all my archaeological expertise." In fact, Aguilar had very little archaeological expertise . . . though it was true enough that he had never encountered such an item before. Xitaclan was home to many unusual things.

The drug lord leaned toward the strange object, his mouth partly open. "Where did it come from?" He was entranced—and Aguilar knew the deal was assured. A high-priced deal.

"This artifact came from a secret new dig called Xitaclan, a pristine site. We are in the process of removing many of the most valuable pieces now. Before long, though, I am certain a new archaeological team will arrive to remove more of the objects."

Carlos Barreio's face became stormy. "They want to steal them from Quintana Roo," he said, "and take them from the land where they belong." Aguilar hoped the police chief wouldn't get distracted and plunge into one of his interminable political lectures.

"Yes, but we will 'preserve' what we can before that happens, eh?" Aguilar said, smiling. "And you, of course, are one of our foremost citizens, Excellency Salida."

Fernando Victorio Aguilar had grown up on the streets of Mérida. His mother was a prostitute. While he was still young, she had taught him how to steal so they could live in relative comfort. But he had quickly learned that stealing was stealing, whether he stole a piece of fruit from the market or a Mercedes-Benz car. His philosophy, he had said with a laugh one night while sharing a bottle of mescal, was that if you are going to steal a mango, you may as well steal a diamond watch from a tourist and use the money to buy yourself a lifetime supply of mangoes. Stealing was stealing. Why not take the best?

Despite his upbringing, though, Aguilar had always felt uncomfortable about the thievery. He allowed himself a touch of guilt after seeing the anger, grief, and fear on the faces of the tourists he mugged and the shopkeepers from whom he stole.

But Aguilar had discovered to his delight that stealing expensive artifacts was a completely different prospect. That was stealing from people who didn't care, people who were long dead. He could make more money at it, and it wasn't as risky as robbing a tourist in Cancún.

Unless, of course, a meddling American archaeology team happened to be in the wrong place at the wrong time . . .

When Xavier Salida offered to buy the relic, his opening price was already far more than Aguilar had hoped to get. Carlos Barreio could barely restrain himself, but Aguilar still managed to increase the offer by another fifteen percent.

When the guard led them back out to the parked police cruiser, everyone was happy. The drug lord had brightened visibly after acquiring his new objet d'art, while Aguilar and Barreio were more than satisfied with the agreed-upon price.

The police chief drove his cruiser back out through the wrought-iron gate and down the long gravel drive. When they reached the dirt road at the bottom of the hill, Aguilar ordered Barreio to stop the car. He turned to talk to his young helper in the back seat.

"You'll get out here, Pepe. I want you to return to Xitaclan right away. You saw how much money we earned for this one artifact. There must be more. I trust no one but you. See what you can find at the ruins—and hurry."

Pepe climbed uneasily out of the rear passenger door. He reached under the seat to retrieve an old machete he frequently carried with him. "But . . . you want me to walk there?"

Aguilar scowled. "You can get there in a day. Two days if you're slow. Hitch a ride for part of the way, but hurry! Or are you afraid? There's a big bonus in it for you."

Pepe swallowed, then shook his head. "I will do as you ask, Señor Aguilar."

"You know where to find me," Aguilar said. He reached into his case and drew out a stack of pesos. "Here, this is for your family," he said. "There will be much more, but you shouldn't carry it all alone. Tell your lovely mother and your sisters hello for me. Perhaps I'll come and visit them again sometime soon."

Pepe stammered his own promises, then fled into the jungle beside the road. Aguilar tugged his floppy-brimmed ocelot hat hard against his head again, then loosened his ponytail, letting his dark hair fall free. He lounged back in the police car's seat, immensely pleased with himself. He might even reward himself with another shave.

"Off to Cancún," Aguilar said. "Let's spend some of our money, eh?"

Carlos Barreio wore a hard, satisfied grin on his face. "Spend your own share," he said.

"I intend to," Aguilar answered, and they drove off down the narrow dirt road through the thick trees.

5

Museum of Natural History,
Washington, D.C.
Wednesday, 10:49 A.M.

The stone jaguar stared at the spectators with eyes that were disks of polished green jade. Fangs of sharp flint were embedded in its open mouth; the scarlet paint on its stylized body of sinuous curves had weathered and faded over the centuries. A placard identified the statue as a relic from the tomb of a Maya high king in the city of Uxmal.

"Reminds me of a cat my neighbors used to have," Mulder said.

A crowd of third grade schoolchildren led by a harried-looking teacher bustled through the Pre-Colombian Treasures exhibit room, yelling and playing tag despite the teacher's strenuous efforts to keep them quiet and respectful.

Mannequins dressed in bright feathered headdresses and ritual loincloths stood in front of colorful backdrop paintings that showed squarish ziggurats and the encroaching jungle. In another mural, Spanish Conquistadors arriving from the eastern sea looked like spacemen in their gleaming silvery armor.

Speakers mounted within the dioramas pounded out

tinny recorded drumbeats, flute calls, and Indian chanting, as well as the sounds of jungle birds and insects. Tinted lights simulated Central American sunsets.

In the middle of the exhibit hall a carved limestone stela—or at least the plaster reproduction of one—towered nearly to the ceiling rafters. Bright spotlights shone down on the high-relief glyphs and exotic carvings that depicted the Maya calendar and astronomical markings.

Scully bent over to scrutinize a strange stone sculpture within a rectangular Plexiglas case: a squatting scarecrowish figurine with a long chin and hooked nose, wearing what appeared to be a charcoal brazier on his head. Scully glanced at her watch, then at her partner, and raised her eyebrows.

"Archaeologists deal with centuries at a time," Mulder said. "You can't expect a guy like this to even notice if he's five minutes late for a meeting."

As if on cue, a thin weathered man appeared behind them, peering over Scully's shoulder to look at the sculpture of the hooked-nose man. "Uh, that's Xiuhtecuhtli, the Maya fire god. He is one of the oldest deities in the New World."

The man's wide, strikingly blue eyes carried an owlish expression of unintentional surprise, as if he was on the verge of knowing what to say but hadn't yet figured out how to articulate it. A pair of reading glasses dangled from a chain around his neck. He continued his lecture.

"This fellow was the lord of passing time. Ceremonies in his name were particularly important at the peak of a fifty-two-year cycle. On that night the Maya would put out their fires in the entire city, making it dark and cold. Then the high priest would kindle a brand-new blaze." The old man's eyebrows went up, and his thin lips curled in a devilish smile. "That special fire was kindled on a prisoner's breast. The victim was tied to an altar, and the fire blazed, consuming his still-beating heart. The Maya believed that the ceremony kept time moving forward."

"Of course," Scully said.

The man extended his hand. "You must be the FBI agents. Uh, I'm Vladimir Rubicon. Sorry I'm late."

Mulder shook the proffered hand, finding the old archaeologist's grip strong and firm, as if from a lifetime of moving heavy stone blocks. "I'm Special Agent Fox Mulder. This is my partner, Dana Scully."

Scully shook his hand, while Mulder studied Rubicon's demeanor and the details of his features. The old archaeologist had a narrow chin accentuated by a thin goatee. Unkempt hair hung long about his ears, its whiteness tinged with brownish yellow where blond had not yet turned entirely gray; it looked as if he had spilled coffee in his hair and beard.

"Uh, I thank you for meeting with me." He fidgeted nervously, as if he didn't know how to come to his point. "If there's anything you can do to help find my daughter Cassandra and bring her back, I would be forever in your debt."

"We'll do our best, Mr. Rubicon," Scully said.

He gestured toward the exhibit, looking tired, and sad, and worried. He seemed to be avoiding a conversation he dreaded. "I volunteer at the museum in the afternoons, since my courseload is light this semester. I don't really have time for it, but it's an investment in our future to keep new students interested in archaeology. It's the only way we old diggers can maintain job security." He forced a laugh, and Mulder got the sense it was a joke he used often.

"We'll need to find out more information about your daughter, Dr. Rubicon," Mulder said. "Can you tell us what exactly she had discovered at this new site? What was she looking for, in particular?"

"Of course. Uh, let's see . . ." Rubicon's eyes widened again. "Xitaclan is a magnificent city, judging from the photographs Cassandra sent up. The find of the decade for pre-Colombian artifacts. I wish I could have been there."

"If it was such an important find, Dr. Rubicon, why was such a small team assigned to it?" Scully asked. "The

UC–San Diego expedition doesn't appear to have been terribly well equipped or funded."

Rubicon sighed. "Agent Scully, you overestimate the importance universities place on unlocking the past. Would it surprise you to learn that there are an estimated one thousand sites still unexcavated in the Yucatán, Guatemala, and Honduras? That area of the world was the center of Maya culture where, uh, the greatest cities of the New World were built.

"Think of the Yucatán as ancient Greece, but barely scratched, abandoned in place. In Greece the land has been exploited for thousands of years. Old-hat stuff. In much of Central America, though, the jungle still reigns supreme. The encroaching rain forest has swallowed up all the old cities like a protective blanket, covering them from the eyes of man."

Mulder cleared his throat. "Dr. Rubicon, I understand that the Indians in the area have some strange legends and superstitions about the old abandoned city. I've heard talk about Maya curses and supernatural warnings. Do you think it's possible that your daughter in her excavations has perhaps discovered something . . . unusual? Something that might have gotten her into trouble? Are you aware of the numerous reports of missing persons in that area of the Yucatán?"

Scully sighed and kept her comments to herself, but Mulder looked at the old archaeologist with intense interest.

Vladimir Rubicon swallowed, but raised his chin, as if searching for strength. "I am fully aware of the numerous disappearances—and it terrifies me that my Cassandra has fallen prey to some awful fate. I have seen many strange things in this world, Agent Mulder, but, uh, I'm more inclined to believe Cassandra ran afoul of black market artifact smugglers. There's quite a brisk trade in selling off antiquities to private owners. Since my daughter and her team were uncovering an unexploited archaeological site, I think it would have drawn the black marketeers like parasites."

He scratched his goatee and looked at Mulder with a

concerned expression. "I'm more afraid of men with guns than I am of any myth."

Near the Conquistador mural, one of the children on the field trip pushed open a side door marked "Emergency Exit Only," setting off the fire alarm. The teacher hurriedly dragged the wailing boy away as sirens screeched through the room. The other children scurried like panicked chicks around a mother hen. A security guard came running.

"Sometimes I think it would be more peaceful for an old archaeologist to be back out in the field again," Vladimir Rubicon said, toying with the glasses hanging around his neck. He forced a smile, turning first to Scully, then to Mulder. "So, uh, when do we leave? How soon can we expect to be at Xitaclan? I'm anxious to find my daughter."

"We?" Scully said.

Mulder put a hand on her arm. "I've already cleared it, Scully. He's an expert in the geographical area, as well as the field in which Cassandra was working. He knows Maya ruins as well as any guide we could find."

"I've got money saved. I'll pay my own way." Rubicon's bright blue eyes took on a desperate look. "Can you really feel what I've felt since Cassandra's disappearance . . . not knowing whether she's alive or dead, where she might be?"

Mulder looked at Scully, who was staring back at him. Suddenly it became clear to her how much her partner empathized with the old man and his search for his lost daughter. Years ago, Mulder too had lost someone very close. . . .

Mulder swallowed. "Yes, Dr. Rubicon," he said. "You may not believe me, but I can understand exactly what you're going through."

6

Vladimir Rubicon made a fuss, insisting that it would be no trouble, no trouble, as he graciously offered to take the center seat between Mulder and Scully. His form was lanky, but he seemed good at folding it up to fit into tight places. Probably, Mulder thought, because of an early career filled with squeezing through tight openings, sleeping in cramped tents, or huddling under trees in the rain while he worked in the field as an archaeologist.

As passengers filed onto the airplane, Mulder took the window seat as usual, hoping to catch a glimpse of something interesting outside. He scanned the rows of other passengers on the specially chartered flight and saw shimmering rows of blue-white hair and musty suit jackets that had been out of style for so long they were bound to come back in fashion any day now.

But instead of being primly nervous elderly people who sat quietly in their seats as if waiting for church services to begin, this group of retirees was as rowdy as kids on a school bus. Each one wore a self-adhesive "Hi! My Name Is:" tag.

Thinking back on all the cases he and his partner had

worked on together, Mulder leaned over to the aisle seat to speak to her. "Scully, I'm not sure we've ever encountered a situation as frightening as a senior citizens chartered flight to Cancún." He buckled his seatbelt, ready for a wild ride.

After they were airborne, the flight took them away from Florida's clear and sunny skies, past the Keys, heading southwest across the Caribbean toward a horizon decorated with cloud cover over the Yucatán. Scully sat back and closed her eyes, snatching a moment of quiet relaxation.

Mulder remembered their very first case, flying out to Oregon to look into the mysterious deaths of high school students who, Mulder was convinced, had been abducted by aliens. During their flight, the plane had lurched and lost altitude. He had remained confident and calm, while Scully gripped the arms of her seat.

Sandwiched between them, Vladimir Rubicon slid his half-glasses onto his nose and squinted at a notepad. He scribbled names, places, people he remembered from previous expeditions. "It's been a long time since I've worked down in Central America, but Maya work is one of the cornerstones of my career," he said. "Perhaps some of my old contacts will be able to help us get out to Xitaclan. Uh, it's not on any map, you know."

"Tell me a little bit about your former work, Dr. Rubicon," Scully said. "Anything I would have heard of? I'm afraid I'm not as familiar with archaeology as I'd like to be."

The old archaeologist smiled at her and tugged at his yellow-gray goatee. "Those words are music to an old man's ears, my dear Agent Scully!

"My primary research interest lies in the American Southwest, particularly the Four Corners area of northern Arizona, New Mexico, southern Utah, and Colorado. The pueblo-building Indians there had a spectacular culture, which still remains quite a mystery." His half-glasses slid down his nose, and he nudged them back into place.

"Like the Maya, the Anasazi Indians had a vibrant and thriving civilization along with other cliff dwellers in the Southwest—but they inexplicably dwindled from a thriving, burgeoning culture to become pueblo ghost towns. Other groups around the area had extensive trade—the Sinagua, the Hohokam, the Mogollon—and left behind significant ruins you can see in many national monuments, especially Mesa Verde and Canyon de Chelly.

"I made my own fame—if you can call it that—unearthing and reconstructing sites in northern Arizona around Wupatki and Sunset Crater. Most of the tourists in that part of the country just head out to the Grand Canyon and ignore all the historical areas ... which is good news for us archaeologists, since tourists tend to have sticky fingers, wandering off with fragments and souvenirs." He cleared his throat.

"I was personally fascinated by Sunset Crater, a large volcano near Flagstaff. Sunset Crater erupted in the winter of 1064 and virtually wiped out the bustling Anasazi civilization, knocking it to its knees—sort of like Pompeii. Their culture never fully recovered, and when extreme droughts ruined all their crops another century later ... well, that was all she wrote for the Anasazi. If memory serves me correctly, I believe the place was finally turned into a national monument because some Hollywood filmmaker wanted to fill the crater with dynamite and blow it up for a movie."

Scully folded down her tray table as the flight attendant came by with a cart of beverages.

"The Native Americans scattered around the Southwest after Sunset Crater erupted nine hundred years ago ... but on the positive side, the volcanic ash made the surrounding area much more fertile for the farmers. Until the drought came, at least."

As Mulder had dreaded would happen, once the pilot turned off the seatbelt light, the senior citizens tour group got up and began to exchange seats, gossiping, walking up and down the aisles, waiting in long lines at the coffin-sized lavatories.

To his horror, some vile ringleader got it into her head to start singing "family favorites"—and to his even greater surprise, most of the passengers actually knew all the verses to "Camptown Races" and "Moon River."

Vladimir Rubicon had to shout to be heard over the singing. "My little girl Cassandra accompanied me on some of my later digs. Her mother left us when she was ten, didn't want to deal with a crazy man who spent his time digging in the dirt in uncivilized portions of the world, playing with bones and reassembling broken pots. But Cassandra was just as fascinated as I was. She went with me happily. I suppose that's what sparked her desire to follow in my footsteps."

Rubicon swallowed and removed his half-glasses. "Now I'll feel guilty if something terrible has happened to her. She focused more on Central American civilizations, following the Aztec and Olmec and Toltec southward as they swept into Mexico, one culture overtaking and adopting the best parts of another. I never could tell whether Cassandra was doing it for the love of the work itself, or if she was trying to impress me and make me proud of her . . . or if she just wanted to compete with her old man. I hope I get the chance to find out."

Mulder frowned solemnly, but said nothing.

About an hour into the flight, the senior citizens performed an act that Mulder considered tantamount to a highjacking. One old man wearing a golfing cap stood up at the flight attendants' station and commandeered the telephone handset used for the plane-wide intercom.

"Welcome, everybody, to Viva Sunset Tours!" the grinning man said with a tip of his golf cap. "This is your entertainment director, Roland—are we having fun yet?"

The senior citizens let out a loud cheer that rattled the inner hull of the plane. Someone whooped, while other scattered individuals made rude catcalls.

"Think of it as a second childhood," Scully murmured. Mulder just shook his head.

Then Entertainment Director Roland announced that the flight crew had graciously agreed to allow them to use the intercom so they could spend the remaining hour of their flight playing a few rounds of Bingo.

Mulder felt his stomach sink. Looking amused, the long-suffering flight attendants marched down the aisles, handing out stubby golf pencils and index cards printed with numbers.

Entertainment Director Roland seemed to be having the time of his life.

After a while, the intercom chatter ceased being entirely annoying and became instead a background drone, easy to ignore ... except when a plump old woman literally leaped out of her seat, waving her card and yelling "Bingo! Bingo!" as if she were being mugged.

Mulder stared out the window, seeing nothing but the blue ocean and tattered white clouds. "I wonder if we're anywhere near the Bermuda Triangle," he muttered, then smiled to show he had just been joking.

If Scully had been sitting next to him, she might have elbowed him in the ribs.

Vladimir Rubicon munched on one of the bags of pretzels the flight attendant had distributed, sipped from his paper cup of coffee, and cleared his throat, turning to get Mulder's attention.

"Agent Mulder," he said, his words difficult to decipher above the roaring background noise of coach class, "you seem to carry a deep sadness yourself. A lost loved one? You still wear the pain like an albatross around your neck."

"The Rime of the Ancient FBI Agent," Mulder said. But the humor didn't work, and he looked seriously into Vladimir Rubicon's cornflower-blue eyes. "Yes, I lost someone." He didn't elaborate.

Rubicon placed a strong, blunt-fingered hand on Mulder's arm. To his credit, the archaeologist did not probe any further. Mulder was reluctant to describe his memories about the bright light, the alien abduction, how his sister had floated up in the air, drifting out the window as he glimpsed the spindly, otherworldly silhouette that beckoned from the glowing doorway.

Mulder had buried those thoughts himself for a long time and had only reconstructed them through intense sessions of regressive hypnosis. Scully suspected that Mulder's memory of the event might be unreliable, that the hypnosis sessions had only reinforced images he himself wanted to believe.

But Mulder had to trust his memory. He had nothing else to go by—except for his faith that Samantha must be alive and that he would find her again some day.

"It's the not knowing that's the worst," Rubicon said, interrupting his thoughts. "Waiting and waiting, hearing nothing."

Someone else in the back squealed "Bingo!" and Entertainment Director Roland set to work, meticulously checking the numbers off. Apparently the winner of each game received a free tropical drink at their tour group's resort in Cancún.

Mulder fervently hoped that the entire group would board a double-decker luxury bus and drive off to a hotel—any hotel—far from where he, Scully, and Rubicon had made reservations.

Finally, the plane began its gradual descent, and Mulder could see the distant coastline of the Yucatán Peninsula, a curve that sliced across the azure waters of the Caribbean.

"At least you can do something to find your daughter," Mulder said to Rubicon. "You have a starting place."

Rubicon nodded and folded his notepaper, tucking it into his pocket. "Traveling again feels good—to get out and around, I mean," he said. "It's been a long time since I did, uh, field work. I had thought my days of Indiana Jones excitement were long gone."

He shook his head, looking very tired, very sad. "I've wasted far too much time teaching, lecturing about artifacts that somebody else discovered and brought to a museum. I've been reduced to an old fart who lives on his lost glory, doing nothing but puttering around." He said the word with derision. "I just wish it hadn't taken such an extreme event to wake me up."

Scully leaned over. "We'll do everything in our power to find your daughter, Dr. Rubicon. We'll find the truth."

7

Yucatán jungle, near Xitaclan
Thursday evening

The jungle at night held a thousand noises, a thousand shadows, a thousand threats. . . .

The big silvery coin of the moon cast its watery light like rain, barely penetrating the clenched fists of branches above. Pepe Candelaria felt as if he had been transported into another universe, all alone.

He stopped to get his bearings. He could see the stars, but was barely able to discern the trampled path through the underbrush. Even without the path, though, he knew his way back to the Xitaclan ruins. His unerring sense of direction was an innate skill, common among his Indian ancestors.

Thornbushes snatched at his pale cotton sleeves like desperate beggars, holding him back. With his father's machete, he hacked them away and moved onward.

He felt greatly honored that his friend and employer Fernando Victorio Aguilar had such confidence in him. Pepe was Fernando's most trusted guide and helper—although such an exclusive level of trust often meant Pepe had to accomplish his tasks without the luxury of assistance. Sometimes it seemed that his work could not be done by one man, that Fernando was taking advantage of him, pushing him too far—but Pepe could not refuse. Fernando paid him well enough.

Pepe Candelaria had four sisters, a fat mother, and a dead father. On his deathbed, sweating and moaning from a fever that coursed like lava just beneath his skin, Pepe's father had made him promise to take care of the family.

And now Pepe's mother and sisters took him at his word. . . .

He ducked under a low-hanging tangle of gnarled branches. As he jiggled the twigs, something small and many-legged dropped down on his shoulder. Pepe briskly swiped it away without taking the time to identify the creature. In the jungle, spider and insect bites were often poisonous, or at least painful.

The moon continued to rise, but shed little light through the gauze of high clouds moving swiftly across the sky. If he was lucky, and worked hard, he might be able to get back home before dawn.

Pepe followed his instinct through the forest, making his way along the old paths, the uncharted roads used for centuries by descendants of the Maya and Toltec who had made their civilization here, before losing it to the Spaniards.

Unfortunately, all the customary roads led away from the sacred site of Xitaclan, and Pepe had to chop his own path with the machete. He wished he had taken the time to sharpen the blade.

His father had died from an infected wound, a sting from a deadly fire-colored scorpion. Father Ronald at the mission had called it the will of God, while Pepe's weeping mother had pronounced it to be a curse from Tlazolteotl, the goddess of forbidden loves, an indication that her husband had been unfaithful to her.

Because of this, Pepe's mother had refused to stay in the same room with her husband as he died—and then, according to tradition, she had demanded that he be buried beneath the dirt floor of their home. Then the family had no choice but to abandon their small dwelling ... and Pepe was forced to secure a new house for them.

Building a new home had merely been the first of the new financial burdens Pepe had endured. Now, to atone for his father's disgrace and fulfill his own grief-driven promise, the family counted on Pepe to take care of everything.

And he did. He had to. But it wasn't easy.

The money he received from Fernando Victorio Aguilar kept them all fed, kept the new home repaired, and had even allowed him to buy his little sister Carmen a parrot. She adored the bird and had taught it to say his own name, much to his delight ... except when it squawked "Pepe! Pepe!" in the middle of the night.

A palm tree scraped dry fronds together with a sound like a rattlesnake. Now, as he fought the dangling vines, Pepe longed to hear the parrot, longed to hear his sisters breathing softly in sleep and his mother's deep snores. But he had to get to Xitaclan first, in order to keep his friend Fernando happy.

He understood the task well enough. So long as Excellency Xavier Salida was interested and anxious to buy, Fernando must have more artifacts from the ancient ruins. Fernando needed Pepe to help him take advantage of the timing.

The ancient city was deserted, the American archaeological team now gone. He was particularly glad that the foreigners no longer rooted around in the ruins— Fernando couldn't allow outsiders to make off with more of his treasures, while Pepe just didn't want them touching the precious objects, cataloguing them, analyzing the pieces as amusing debris from a lost civilization. At least Fernando's customers prized the treasures for what they were.

Without Fernando's help, Pepe's family would certainly have starved. His sisters would have been forced to work the streets of Mérida as prostitutes, even little Carmen. He himself might have become enslaved in the marijuana fields of Xavier Salida or Pieter Grobe or one

of the other drug lords. Recovering precious Maya artifacts from long-abandoned ruins seemed safer, more
honorable.

Pepe's mother adored Fernando, flirted with him,
praised his cologne and his ocelot-skin hat. She claimed
that Fernando's patronage had come to her son as a gift
from the gods, or God, depending on whether she was
thinking of the old images or the Catholic religion at the
time. Pepe didn't complain—he would accept such luck,
whatever its source.

In their church gatherings on Sundays, when the
entire village came together to celebrate Mass, Pepe was
entertained by some of the fanciful tales Father Ronald
told from the Bible, but he doubted their relevance to his
life here. Singing angels and white-robed saints might
have been fine for people living comfortable lives and
attending air-conditioned churches, but here in the thick
jungle, in the primeval womb of the Earth, the older ...
more primal beliefs seemed to hold a greater credence.

Especially at times such as now.

A branch cracked overhead, settling into other twigs.
Leaves whispered together as something moved unseen
across the treetops ... a snake, a monkey, a jaguar.

Pepe splashed across a narrow stream, placing it in
his mental map of the area, knowing indisputably where
he was, how close he had come to his destination.
Xitaclan lay just up ahead.

In a thicket of fragrant hibiscus shrubs on the bank of
the stream, the underbrush rustled. Something heavy
splashed into the water. He recognized the reptilian eyes,
the sleek form of a night-hunting cayman—large, and
hungry, judging from the ripples that arrowed through
the water toward him. Pepe quickly slogged through the
mud, climbing the bank and rushing into the underbrush
to get safely away from the crocodile-like creature.

Above, he heard more movement, crashing branches,
falling leaves. He hoped it wasn't a night-prowling cat,
ready to drop down on him to rip him apart with curved
claws and powerful feline muscles—then he heard the

scolding of a group of awakened monkeys, disturbed by his flight from the cayman. He sighed, feeling a shiver tingle through him. The old religion had revered jaguars, but he would not have felt blessed to encounter one of the jungle panthers alone in the night.

For centuries, the Catholic priests had done their best to squash continued practice of the old beliefs. In the village Father Ronald railed with stories of hellfire and eternal damnation whenever he found evidence of ritually shed blood, of scars from self-scourging, even missing fingers or toes cut off with razor-sharp obsidian knives in personal mutilation.

The villagers apologized, did their penance, behaved with meek shame in front of the priests . . . but altered none of their thinking. Their hearts had not changed since the coming of the Spaniards five hundred years earlier. Sometimes pure sacrificial blood washed away stains the frequent jungle rains could never obliterate.

Pepe remembered quite vividly, while his father lay dying of the scorpion sting, his mother kneeling outside the door of their hut. She drew a thorny vine through her mouth, ripping her tongue open so that she could spit bright, fresh lifeblood onto the earth in her own sacrifice.

The sacrifice had not worked, though. Pepe wondered if the old gods had demanded more blood than she was willing to give.

In the golden past, the Maya gods had feasted on blood, on hearts torn out of willing victims, on sacrificed prisoners hurled to their deaths into the sacred limestone wells beside the great temples.

Now only ruins and artifacts remained of all that glory. Perhaps the gods had tired of blood after all. . . .

Finally, after another hour of trying to slip like a thief through the jungle's night, Pepe arrived at the forgotten metropolis of Xitaclan.

Parting the wide, slick leaves of a banana tree, he gazed into the moonlit clearing, the rough hummocks of fallen temples, the sculpture-laden walls showing the hook-nosed masks of the rain god Chac, the numerous feathered serpent motifs now defaced by moss and vines, the impressive Pyramid of Kukulkan tall in the night, but smothered with vegetation.

Some of the thick trees had been chopped down and hauled away as the archaeological team had worked on their initial excavations, clearing the site of the densest foliage to remove the blanket of undergrowth deposited by undisturbed time. The trenches and shorn tree stumps stood like raw wounds in the earth.

The American team had been gone for only days, but the jungle had already begun to reclaim its territory.

In the center of Xitaclan's plaza, the stepped pyramid dominated the scene. The regularly spaced platforms had partially crumbled on one side, huge blocks tugged free by the strength of roots and vines. But at the ziggurat's apex the temple to Kukulkan, the god of wisdom, flanked by his feathered serpent guardians, remained intact.

Pepe would have to go inside the pyramid, rummage around the narrow passages until he found a few more alcoves containing jade artifacts, intact pots, glyph-painted tiles. Fernando Aguilar would make up a fanciful story or legend for whatever Pepe found, increasing its potential worth. Pepe had merely to bring back the treasures, for which he received his share of the money.

With a lightness to his step, he started forward into the plaza clearing—then Pepe looked up as he noticed a flash of movement, mysterious independent shadows gliding down the pyramid's crumbling steps, like hot oil trickling across water.

He held still, but the shadows kept moving . . . toward him.

Above, the branches rustled again with a slithering sound. On the ground, the tall feathery ferns waved as something large crawled through the leafy underbrush.

Narrowing his eyes, Pepe flicked his gaze from side to side. Smearing cold perspiration away from his face, he held up the gleaming arc of his father's machete, ready to fight an attacking jaguar or wild boar. He drew a long breath, his senses fully alert, then took another step away from the trees, glancing up to make certain that no huge predator could drop down on him from above.

The moon slipped behind a cloud, hiding its weak but comforting light. Pepe froze, listening—and the jungle seemed to become alive with movement, creatures slipping toward him with imperfect silence. In the renewed darkness, he saw a faint glow limning the edge of the Pyramid of Kukulkan, like a luminous mist that seemed to rise from the dark mouth of the cenote well.

Swallowing hard, Pepe stepped away from the dangling branches of a tall chicle tree, wishing he knew where he could find shelter. He was far from any village, from any help. Could he hide inside the pyramid or one of the other temples? In the debris-littered ball court where Maya athletes had played a violent sport in front of cheering crowds? Should he run back into the forest, away from Xitaclan? Pepe didn't know where to go.

With daybreak, the low jungle would be a much safer place. But not now, not at night. Never at night—he should have known.

Then he saw two long, supple forms coming over the piled rocks, the stone blocks of another fallen temple covered by moss and time. The creatures glided with reptilian, liquid motions mixed with a bird-like grace, jerky yet somehow delicate movements: the two shadows he had seen descending the steep pyramid steps. He found it entirely unlike the ominous, sluggish advance of the scaly cayman he had seen in the jungle stream.

At the edge of the ball court stood a glyph-adorned stela, a stone monolith used by the Maya to record their calendar, their conquests, their religion. A third shadow separated from the side of the stela, slithering toward him.

Pepe slashed his father's machete in the air, hoping the threat would frighten the creatures off. Instead, they came at him faster.

The high, thin clouds drifted apart, and the moonlight

returned, spilling details into the murk of the excavated plaza. Pepe's heart pounded, and he gasped his amazement in the ancient language his mother and father had spoken. In the plaza before him, he saw monsters that emerged from the myths and legends he had heard since he was a boy.

The feathered serpents moved with the speed of dancing lightning—larger than crocodiles but with a power and intelligence that surpassed any other predator. They came at him from three sides, stalking, confident.

"Kukulkan!" he cried. "Kukulkan, protect me!"

The three feathered serpents hissed with the sound of water spattered on fire. They reared up, flashing long fangs as sharp as any sacrificial knife.

With bright clarity Pepe knew what he had to do.

In awe even greater than his terror, Pepe used the edge of his machete to slash open his arm, feeling the warm gush of blood, yet experiencing no pain whatsoever. He extended his arm, offering them his blood as a sacrifice, hoping to appease the benevolent Kukulkan's servants with what he knew of the ancient rituals, the old religion.

But instead of satisfying them, the scent of the fresh warm wetness drove the creatures into a frenzy. The feathered serpents charged toward him with the sound of rushing water, crackling leaves. In the moonlight, feathered scales gleamed . . . bright teeth . . . long claws from vestigial limbs.

Tonight, Pepe thought, the old gods would get their sacrifice. His machete dropped to the dirt. The feathered serpents fell upon him.

8

Cancún, Mexico
Thursday, 4:21 P.M.

With some amusement, Scully watched Mulder heave a sigh of relief as the crowd of partying senior citizens filed off the chartered airplane and ambled toward the baggage claim area and customs station in the Cancún airport. They waited by a row of stations where uniformed men took their tourist cards and stamped their passports, before turning them loose to retrieve their luggage.

The man at the counter stamped Mulder's passport and handed it back.

"If I ever start wearing plaid pants, promise me you'll stop me before I buy a ticket for the Love Boat," Rubicon said, as if forcing a joke. "I'm never going to retire."

Dozens of people hawking tour packages swarmed among the tourists, stuffing brochures into every empty hand. After conquering their luggage, the senior citizens tour group descended upon the bus aisle outside and climbed aboard their specially chartered Luxury Coach like lost chickens being rounded up and ushered back to the coop. Young men—certainly not airport employees—bustled about to help with the baggage, hoping for a tip.

Scully led the way through immigration to the baggage

pickup area where they grabbed their luggage, passed through customs without incident, and went to find the courtesy van that would take them to their hotel. Though neither she nor Mulder spoke Spanish, nearly all signs and shops around them catered to English speakers. The moment any one of them looked confused, two or three Mexicans appeared, smiling warmly and offering their assistance. Rubicon made a show of employing his linguistic abilities to get directions and exchange their money. The old archaeologist seemed delighted to be useful as part of the expedition.

On the way to the Caribbean Shores hotel, they rode in the small van with a newlywed couple who were entirely preoccupied with each other. The driver played brassy disco music on the car stereo; he hummed along, tapping his fingertips on the steering wheel, the dashboard, or his leg.

Mulder sat next to Scully, flipping through a handful of colorful brochures the various tour representatives had forced upon him. "Listen to this, Scully," he said. "Welcome to Cancún, 'where the beautiful turquoise Caribbean Sea caresses the silky sand beaches.' The waters are 'filled with romantic coral reefs or mysterious and exciting sunken Spanish galleons.' Somebody must have a good thesaurus to concoct those descriptions."

"Sounds charming," she said, looking out the window at the bright sun, the vibrant colors. Thick trees lined both sides of the road. "At least this is better than an Arctic research station or an Arkansas chicken-processing plant."

He flipped through other pamphlets, including a map of the hotel zone, a narrow spit of land between the Caribbean Sea and Nichupte Lagoon. Bright letters proclaimed, "Nearly every room with an ocean view!"

Rubicon sat with his duffel across his bony knees. He seemed either to be listening to the disco music or preoccupied with his own thoughts. His blue eyes blinked rapidly against a sheen of dampness. Scully's heart went out to him.

The van driver honked his horn and muttered curses in Spanish as he swerved to avoid an ersatz old-fashioned motorized buggy that took up more than its lane in the road down into the hotel zone. The laughing American driver of the buggy waved and then honked his horn in return, a loud cartoonish *ahooogah*. The driver of the van forced a smile at the tourists and waved back, then cursed again under his breath.

In the back of the van, the newlywed couple giggled and continued kissing.

Rubicon held on to the half-glasses hanging from a chain on his neck and turned to Mulder. "One of the hotels even brags about the golf course they designed so that the ninth hole is constructed around the ruins of a small Maya temple." His astonished-looking eyes now carried a look of weariness and dismay.

"It's sad that they should be allowed to do that," he said. "They've exploited their history and culture, cheapened it. You should see the Hollywood-style extravaganza at Chichén Itzá. They charge a lot of money for their 'spectacular temple show' with lights and sounds, multicolored spotlights blazing across the pyramids every night, cheesy folk dances by professional actors wearing plastic feathered capes and gaudy costumes. The drumbeats pound out through stereo systems."

The scorn in the old archaeologist's voice surprised Scully. Rubicon gave a defeated sigh. "The Spanish Conquistadors were only the first devastating invasion of the Yucatán—next came the tourists." He forced a smile. "At least some of the tourism income goes toward funding restoration of the archaeological sites . . . like Xitaclan."

Their stucco-faced hotel boasted modern construction with a pseudo-Aztec design, gleaming windows, sun decks with palm-thatched umbrellas, and direct beach access. The curling waves were as jewel-tone blue and the sand as powdery white as the brochures had promised.

They sent their bags off with the bellman while Mulder and Scully waited in line to check in.

Rubicon murmured to himself, taking out his hand-written notes, anxious to make phone calls and track down potential guides for their expedition deep into the jungles. He did not want to waste a moment in the search for his daughter. The old archaeologist wandered around the lobby, looking at cast-plaster jaguar sculptures, bogus bas-reliefs, and stylized Maya glyphs.

"Welcome to the Caribbean Shores Resort!" The desk clerk handed them room keys and cheerily began his memorized spiel of the evening's planned events. "Señorita, you cannot pass up your chance to go on a fun-filled party boat for an evening dinner cruise." He waggled his eyebrows.

Scully shook her head politely. "No, thank you. We're here for business, not pleasure."

"Ah, but there is always time for pleasure," he said. "We have a fine selection of lobster cruises or disco boats, even an adventure with the real pirates of the Caribbean." He continued to sound hopeful.

"Thank you, but I still have to say no." Scully took the keys and turned away.

The clerk called after them one last time. "Señor, surely you cannot pass up our famous limbo party tonight."

Mulder took Scully's arm and leaned close, whispering in her ear, "The limbo could qualify as calisthenics for the Bureau's physical fitness requirement."

Scully glanced over at the old archaeologist. "Let's hold off on the vacation until we find Cassandra Rubicon."

After showering and changing, they met in one of the hotel restaurants for dinner. The maitre d' showed Mulder and Scully to a table with a centerpiece of tropical flowers that showered the air with heady perfume. While the waiter held the chair for Scully, Mulder sat down. He glanced at his watch, knowing that Rubicon would join them at any moment.

Mulder had dressed down in a comfortable cotton shirt and slacks, leaving his usual suit and tie behind. Scully finally noticed his change of outfit and raised her eyebrows, hiding a small smile. "I see you're already getting into the casual Mexican spirit," she said.

"It's the Caribbean," he answered. "We're supposed to be undercover, so we ought to look like tourists, not FBI agents."

Unbidden, another server brought them each a lime-laden margarita, the glass rims crusted with salt. Scully settled down to study the menu, a mouthwatering list of local fare—fresh lobster, lemon-and-cilantro grouper, chicken with spicy chocolate molé sauce. Mulder sipped his margarita, smiled, then took another drink. "Love those ancient Mayan beverages," he said.

Scully set her menu down. "I called the consulate to check in. The Bureau has filed all the appropriate clearances and notified local law enforcement, but apparently they weren't too helpful. So the next step is up to us."

"As soon as we figure out what the next step is," Mulder said. "I think we can rent a car and drive toward the area where the team disappeared. Maybe we can find a guide to take us through the jungles."

Before Rubicon even arrived, the waiter came by to take their order. Mulder was famished after eating only snacks on the charter plane from Miami. He chose chicken cooked with bananas and a side dish of lime-and-chile-pepper soup, while Scully ordered fish marinated in annato-seed sauce and baked in banana leaves—supposedly a Yucatán specialty.

Scully opened her briefcase and drew out a folder. "I've been going over the background information we have on the members of the archaeological expedition," she said, "the other missing American citizens. You never know where we might find a lead."

She spread the folder and took out several dossiers on the UC–San Diego grad students, along with photographs. She held up the first one. "In addition to Cassandra Rubicon, another archaeologist was instrumental in getting this team put together: Kelly Rowan, twenty-six years old, six feet two inches, athletic, an honor student with a specialty in pre-Colombian art. According to his course advisors he had nearly finished writing a thesis that traced the connections in Central American mythologies between key stories of the Mayans, Olmecs, Toltecs, and Aztecs." She passed the paper over to Mulder, and he picked it up to study it.

"John Forbin, the youngest of the group, twenty-three, first-year graduate student. Apparently he planned to be an architect and structural engineer. According to this, he was chiefly interested in primitive methods of large-scale construction, such as the Central American pyramids. It seems likely that Cassandra Rubicon took him along to suggest methods for restoring the fallen buildings." She passed the paper over.

"Next, Christopher Porte, from all reports a well-respected . . . *epigrapher*. Are you familiar with that term?"

"Just from what I've read recently," Mulder answered. "It's someone who specializes in translating codes and glyphs. Much of the Maya written language is still unknown and is very context sensitive."

"So they brought Christopher along to translate any hieroglyphics they found," Scully said, then shuffled to the last piece of paper. "And finally, Caitlin Barron, their historian and photographer. Also an aspiring artist. It says here Ms. Barron has even held a few minor exhibitions of her watercolor work in one of San Diego's student art galleries."

She handed Mulder the photographs, and he glanced at each one in turn. Then, checking his watch again, Mulder scanned the room just in time to see Rubicon at the entrance to the dining room, newly shaven and dressed in an evening jacket. Most of the other patrons of the restaurant wore shorts, sandals, and loud shirts. Mulder held up a hand to catch his attention, and the old archaeologist came over, walking as if already exhausted.

The waiter hovered beside Rubicon as he took the empty seat at the table. He ignored the margarita the waiter placed at his right elbow.

"No luck," Rubicon said. "I've called all the contacts I still have. Of course, some of them in the outlying areas don't have ready access to telephone service, but the ones in Cancún and Mérida were unavailable. One is retired. I tried to talk him into accompanying me for one last field expedition, uh, until I found out he's confined to a wheelchair. Another of my old friends—a man who saved my life during an expedition in 1981—has been killed in some sort of drug-related shooting. I set his wife to weeping when I asked for him." Rubicon cleared his throat. "I had no luck reaching the three others."

"Well," Mulder said, "we may be forced to rely on our own ingenuity to find someone who can take us to the site. It's a long drive just to get to the right geographical area."

Rubicon slouched back in his chair and pushed the menu aside. "There's one other possibility," he said. "In the last postcard I received from Cassandra, she mentioned a man who had helped her. A local named Fernando Victorio Aguilar. I have tracked down someone with that name and left a message, uh, that we are interested in being guided into the jungles. The man who answered the telephone seemed to think Señor Aguilar might be willing to help us. If so, I hope we can connect with him either tonight or tomorrow."

He threaded his fingers together and squeezed his hands as if trying to massage arthritis out of his knuckles. "Sitting around at some glitzy tourist resort makes me feel so helpless . . . so guilty, not knowing what my Cassandra could be going through at this very moment."

Mulder's and Scully's meals came, breaking the mood. Rubicon quickly chose a selection of his own from the menu and sent the waiter off.

Looking at the forlorn expression on the old man's face, Mulder remembered the days after Samantha had disappeared. Though he had teased her mercilessly—as any brother teases a sister—he had longed for her, desperately trying to think of what he could do to help, how he could find her. He took it as his personal responsibility, since he had been with her when she disappeared. If only he had done something different on that night. If only he had faced the bright light. . . .

As a twelve-year-old boy he had limited resources but endless drive, a drive that had stayed with him all his life. He remembered riding his bike around the hometown neighborhood of Chilmark, Massachusetts—population 650—ringing doorbells, asking everyone if they had seen Samantha. He knew deep in his heart, though, that no simple explanation could possibly account for what he had seen.

He had worked for days, making "Missing" posters that described his sister, begging for information as if he were putting up notices for a lost dog. And that had been in the days before accessible photocopy machines, so he had handwritten each one individually with a black marker, the pungent fumes of the solvent drifting up into his nose and making him sniffle even more than he already had for his lost sister. He had taped up his paper notices on store windows, tacked them to utility poles and bus stop signs.

But no one had ever called except to offer sympathy.

His mother had been devastated by her grief, incoherent with tears, while his father remained stony and stoic through it all. Possibly, Mulder now knew, because his father had had some dark knowledge about what had really happened. His father had been given some warning, had known something regarding Samantha's danger—and he had done nothing.

For years now Mulder had seen an echo of Samantha in every little dark-haired girl. She had disappeared long before the days of the "Have You Seen Me?" pictures of missing children on milk cartons or bulk-mail flyers. All Mulder's efforts to put up posters or knock on doors had ultimately been useless, helping not in the least. But he'd felt he had to do something. It had been his mission.

Now he watched Vladimir Rubicon going through a similar process, coming to the Yucatán, calling his old contacts, insisting on accompanying the FBI agents on their investigation.

"We'll find her," Mulder said, reaching across the table, forcing confidence into his voice. In the back of his mind he again saw an image of his sister being dragged off into the light.

Mulder looked into Rubicon's eyes. "We'll find her."

But he wasn't sure to whom exactly he was making his promise.

9

Caribbean Shores Resort, Cancún
Thursday, 9:11 P.M.

Scully had just settled in for the evening, satisfied from a delicious meal and finally comfortable after removing her shoes and panty hose. Knowing the lack of amenities and jungle hardships they were bound to encounter in the coming days en route to Xitaclan, she planned to get a good rest.

Her hotel room displayed a colorful, if typical, painting of a sunrise over the Caribbean, complete with calm surf and silhouetted palm fronds. Her private balcony looked out over the powdery white beach and the ocean. She smelled the evening salty breeze, listened to the rumble of the waves, and watched couples stroll along the sand beneath bright electric torches posted above the tide line. The thought of swimming and relaxing sounded wonderful—but she reminded herself that they were here on a case.

With a weary sigh, Scully flopped back onto the bed without turning down the sheets, hoping that the moment of peace would last for more than two minutes.

The pounding on her door was sharp and strident, like cannon blasts from a warring Spanish galleon.

She hadn't ordered room service, and she became instantly on guard as she got up off the bed. The pounding didn't stop. "All right, coming," Scully called out in a voice devoid of enthusiasm.

She glanced over at the half-open connecting door to Mulder's room, feeling a cold chill—the insistent thudding knock was not the polite request for attention that room service would ever use. This pounding sounded bold and impatient. Cautious, she picked up her own weapon from the courtesy table.

Upon opening the door she found a barrel-chested man clad in a police chief's uniform, his hairy-knuckled fist raised to continue the insistent knocking. Before she could blink back her surprise enough to speak, the man planted his foot in the door to prevent her from shutting it in his face.

"I came as soon as I learned of your arrival," the man said beneath a thick black mustache. "You are FBI Agent Scully—and the other one's Mulder." His police cap rested firmly on his head, and sweat glistened on his cheeks. His shoulders were broad, his chest wide, his arms muscular, as if he juggled bags of cement mix for exercise.

"Excuse me?" Scully said, making sure he saw her 9-mm pistol. "Who are you, sir?"

He waited for her to invite him into her room, ignoring the weapon. "I'm Chief Carlos Barreio of the Quintana Roo Police Force. I am sorry I could not meet you at the airport. Please pardon my rudeness. I have many cases, but few men."

"We were told you had been contacted," Scully said, "but that you offered no help in our investigation."

The connecting door opened, and Mulder stepped into her room, his hair tousled, his shirt untucked and hastily buttoned. She noticed that he had missed his buttonholes by one, but at least he had taken a moment to tug his shoulder holster in place.

Seeing the burly policeman, Mulder said, "We sure must have upset that hotel desk clerk by not going on one of his disco cruises."

"With your heavy case load, we're glad to focus our own efforts on this particular investigation," Scully said, straightening her blouse and running her hands down her skirt and hips. Despite his outwardly polite manner, she sensed an antagonism buried deep within him. "We have obtained all the proper clearances and authorizations."

"Yes, I cannot spare the manpower," Barreio said. "You understand." His complexion was ruddy, his face calm, but his posture remained stiff and on guard. He removed his cap, and she noted that his thinning hair had been slicked into a pronounced widow's peak. "I'm afraid I have little to report on the disappearance of the American archaeological expedition."

Scully, trying to remain polite, said, "We have a long-standing tradition of cooperation with local law-enforcement agencies, Mr. Barreio. We both have the same goal, after all—to find our missing people. We are anxious to proceed and happy to add our expertise to your own."

Barreio, his eyes still cold, said, "Of course I will cooperate. I have been informed by the Federal Bureau of Investigation satellite office in Mexico City that you two have been assigned here as legal attachés. Your inspector in charge at the Office of Liaison and International Affairs has graciously requested that I provide you with copies of all information I have currently compiled. My own superiors have passed along this request."

"Thank you, Mr. Barreio," Scully said, still cautious, still sensing his antagonism. "Please be assured that we are not trying to infringe upon your jurisdiction. The State of Quintana Roo is the area in which the crime was committed—"

"Alleged crime," Barreio interrupted, letting his composure slip. "Allegedly committed, to use your legal terms. We have no confirmation as to what actually happened."

"Allegedly committed," Scully conceded. "You have jurisdiction. Mexico is a sovereign country. As agents of the Federal Bureau of Investigation, my partner Mulder and I are empowered only to offer our assistance."

Mulder cleared his throat. "However, we do have the right to investigate crimes perpetrated upon American citizens." With one hand he smoothed his hair back, standing beside his partner. "The FBI has as its mandate investigations into terrorism, arms dealing, drug trafficking—as well as possible kidnapping of American citizens. Until we know additional information about Cassandra Rubicon and her companions, we must operate under the assumption that someone may intend to hold them as potential hostages."

"Hostages!" Barreio smiled. "I'm sorry, Agent Mulder, but I think it's more likely they just got lost out in the jungle."

"I hope that proves to be the case," Scully said, keeping herself between Mulder and the burly police officer.

Outside, an imperious-looking room-service waiter strode down the hall carrying a tray loaded with fruit-garnished tropical drinks that looked like Dr. Jekyll's chemistry experiments gone awry. As he walked past, the man studiously ignored the conversation taking place in the doorway of Scully's room.

Barreio sighed, shaking his head slightly. "You'll forgive me if I don't entirely trust the FBI." Barreio's eyebrows bunched like black caterpillars on his forehead. "My former counterpart in Mexico City—Arturo Durazo—was the target of one of your sting operations. He's now rotting in an American jail."

Scully frowned. The name was completely unfamiliar to her.

"The FBI claimed Durazo was selling millions of dollars of drugs to the United States," Barreio said. "They lured him outside our borders to the Caribbean island of Aruba, where they could 'legally' arrest him—he was never extradited, as far as I know. It was a setup."

Scully tossed her red-gold hair, looking calmly at the police chief. "I assure you, Mr. Barreio, we have no interest in the police force in your state or its internal activities. We're only looking for our missing citizens."

Two men hurried down the hall, and Scully looked

past the police chief to see Vladimir Rubicon, his yellow-white hair unkempt, his reading glasses landed haphazardly on his sharp nose. He hustled along, leading another man who was deeply tanned and wiry, with long hair bundled in a ponytail under a floppy wide-brimmed hat made from the skin of a spotted cat. The long-haired man reeked of aftershave.

"Agent Scully! Guess who I found," Rubicon called, then stopped upon seeing the police chief. "Excuse me. Is anything wrong?"

Barreio looked at the two men, his eyes blinking in recognition as he saw the man with the floppy spotted hat. "Señor Aguilar," Barreio said, "are these people part of an expedition you are mounting?"

"Yes, yes indeed," the other man—Aguilar—said. "I have just entered into arrangements with this gentleman here. Quite satisfactory arrangements. Dr. Rubicon is a most eminent archaeologist. Carlos, you should be impressed to have a man of his stature come to Quintana Roo! Perhaps you will be pleased to receive positive international publicity instead of those unpleasant stories about revolutionary activities and illicit arms sales, eh?" Aguilar's voice carried a barely hidden threat. Barreio bristled, his skin darkening.

Scully looked over at Dr. Rubicon, who was flushed with excitement. Grinning, he paid little attention to the uniformed police chief.

"Agent Scully, Agent Mulder," he said, popping his head into her room. He swept his hand in a welcoming gesture to the man behind him. "Allow me to introduce Fernando Victorio Aguilar. He's the person I was, uh, trying to contact . . . a—what did you call yourself?—an expediter, yes, that's it, a man who can promptly arrange for helpers and guides and equipment to take us out to the site of Xitaclan. My daughter was indeed in touch with him, and he helped put together her party originally, though he hasn't seen her since she departed. He can take us out there."

"That should help our case," Scully said, then she

turned with forced pleasantness to the police chief. "I believe Mr. Barreio here was about to offer us the maps and notes from his ongoing investigation, everything he has compiled so far about the missing team members." She raised her eyebrows. "Isn't that correct, Chief Barreio?"

The ruddy-faced man frowned, as if he had just remembered an important detail. "If you are about to mount an expedition, have you obtained the proper permits, the entrance passes, the work release forms? Have you paid your appropriate state fees?"

"I was just about to take care of all that," Fernando Aguilar interrupted. "Carlos, you know you can trust me." The man removed his floppy hat and looked from Scully to Mulder, back to Vladimir Rubicon. "In order to make certain portions of our expedition move more smoothly through political channels, we require clearances and taxes and fees. An unfortunate complication, but it cannot be helped."

"How much will all that cost?" Scully asked, immediately suspicious.

"It varies," Aguilar said, "but a thousand American dollars should allow us the complete freedom for our expedition to depart as early as tomorrow morning, eh?"

"Tomorrow! That's wonderful!" Rubicon said, rubbing his hands together in delight.

"A thousand dollars?" Mulder said. He looked over at her. "Is your per diem higher than mine, Scully?"

"The Federal Bureau of Investigation does not engage in bribery," Scully said, her voice firm.

Rubicon seemed exasperated and impatient. "Nonsense," he said to Scully, "you don't understand how things are done."

He untucked his shirt and withdrew his own money belt. Yanking out a wad of hundred-dollar bills, he counted out ten and stuffed them into Aguilar's outstretched palm. He looked back at the FBI agents. "Sometimes you have to make concessions, and I don't want to get into a bureaucratic head-butting contest for weeks while my Cassandra remains lost."

Aguilar nodded deeply, hiding a grin, as if he had just stumbled upon an unexpectedly easy mark. "It will be a pleasure doing business with you, Señor Rubicon," he said. He pocketed two of the hundred-dollar bills and extended the remaining eight to Barreio, who snatched them quickly, scowling at Mulder and Scully.

"That'll be enough for the standard government fees," he said. "I'll contact the office and see if it is possible to copy our case files for you by morning. Check at the hotel desk. I make no promises. I have such limited help in my offices." The police chief turned and marched off down the hall, turning the corner toward the elevators, where he deftly sidestepped another room-service waiter bearing drinks served inside hollowed pineapples and coconuts.

Vladimir Rubicon stood in the hall outside Scully's door, flushed with the urgency of his mood. Fernando Aguilar placed the spotted hat back on his head and extended a hand. "I'm very pleased to meet you, Señorita Scully." He nodded to Mulder. "We'll be seeing much more of each other in the coming days."

He released her hand and stepped back, bowing his head. "Be sure to get a good night's rest, and take the time to enjoy a relaxing bath. I assure you, your accommodations for the next few nights will be much less . . . comfortable."

10

X The fire crackled in the hearth, burning hot as it consumed the aromatic wood, sending curls of perfumed smoke into the upstairs drawing room. Xavier Salida stood in front of the blaze, his hands clasped behind his back as he drew deeply of the bay and nutmeg scent, the peppery oils that made the smoke heady, almost a drug by itself.

He turned away from the warmth and went over to the thermostat on his wall, turning up the air conditioning so he could enjoy his fire, yet keep the room from getting unpleasantly warm. There weren't many things in life that one could enjoy both ways. But Salida had reached the point where he could do anything he wanted.

From the rack of brass-handled fireplace implements, he selected the cast-iron poker and jabbed the flaming wood, watching the sparks fly. He liked to play with fire.

Salida stepped back and strutted around the room with the poker as if it were a walking stick, practicing his moves, reveling in his personal grace—though newly acquired, he expected the grace would remain with him for the rest of his life. Education and culture were an investment, an intangible wealth that went beyond mere baubles and art objects.

Salida went over to the stereo system on the wall and casually flipped through his collection of phonograph records, LPs of the best classical music, performances memorable as well as pleasing to the discerning ear. He selected a symphony by the great Salieri, an obscure eighteenth-century composer. The man's very obscurity meant his works must be rare and therefore precious.

As the bold overlapping strains of violins overwhelmed the old album's scratchiness, Salida went over to the bottle on the table, twisted off the cork with his fingers, and poured himself another glass of the purplish red wine, a 1992 Merlot. It was well aged and smooth, he thought, not as young as some of the Cabernet Sauvignon he had in the wine cellar. He had been told this label was from one of the best California vineyards. He held up the glass, swirled it, and allowed the firelight to shine through its rich garnet color.

Salida stepped out to his open balcony, taking a deep breath of the moist night air. The hammock hung, suggesting thoughts of lazier days, relaxing afternoons ... but this past week had been very difficult. A thousand stressful challenges, each one dealt with decisively.

As he gazed beyond where the lights shone, he saw the monolithic silhouette of the ancient Maya stela in the middle of his courtyard. Starlight trickled down on the prized monument, and he could make out the lumpy form of that damned male peacock perched on top.

A foolish peacock. Much like his rival, Pieter Grobe, a showy, blustering man who was ultimately insignificant ... just an amusing piece of coloration.

Salida had attempted to get even with the Belgian expatriate, requiring revenge for Grobe's ill-advised tactic of shooting down one of Salida's private courier planes. Salida had demanded that his men eliminate one of Grobe's planes in retaliation, but that had not proved possible.

Grobe had tightened his own security procedures, allowing no vulnerabilities around his own aircraft—and so Salida had had no choice but to take an alternative vengeance. Not as full of finesse, but ultimately as satisfying: a large truck filled with fuel oil had "accidentally" exploded in the middle of one of Grobe's marijuana fields. The resulting fire and caustic smoke had damaged a great portion of the crop.

With the score evened again, Salida had no desire to escalate events into a full-scale war. He suspected that Grobe was just bored and needed to blow off pressure every once in a while. Done is done.

Now he could relax and enjoy life, culture, the finer things. As the symphonic strains of Salieri's first movement built to its crescendo, Xavier Salida walked back into his withdrawing room.

He took another sip of the wine, rolling the taste in his mouth, identifying the nuances he had been taught about. He sniffed the "bouquet," judging the "dryness," appreciating the "finish."

In private, however, Salida allowed himself to long for the days when he could sit back with his local compadres, drink too much tequila, laugh out loud, and sing raucous songs. That was in the past . . . he was beyond such things now. He had become a powerful man.

He paused to inspect his magnificent private collection of historical artifacts, pre-Colombian objects any museum would have been proud to own. But these items would never appear in any dusty display cases, because they belonged to him and him alone.

He saw the delicate, translucent green sculptures of jade, the writhing, otherworldly forms of the feathered serpent companions of Kukulkan, a small stone figure of the great god of wisdom himself. Salida collected pots and carvings from all Central American peoples, the Toltec, the Olmec, as well as the Maya, and later the Aztec. He made a point of glancing at the engraved label on each artifact, refreshing his memory to make sure that he recalled every name and every detail exactly. It wouldn't do to embarrass himself in polite conversation by not knowing the items in his own collection!

Finally, like a boy creeping forward at dawn on Christmas morning, Salida went over to his new prize, the amazing crystalline artifact Fernando Victorio Aguilar had brought to him from the ruins of Xitaclan. He already knew he must place this item in a protective glass case, displaying it but never allowing other visitors or any of the servants to touch it. It must be valuable.

Setting his glass of wine next to the shimmering transparent box, Salida reached out with both hands, one on either side, gently touching its slick, cold surface with his manicured fingertips.

Because of all the distractions and headaches caused by Pieter Grobe, he had not been able to spare the time to admire his new prize for the past two days—but now he would reward himself. With Grobe appropriately punished, and the rest of Salida's operation running smoothly, now he could stare at the strange Maya box with a childlike sense of wonder. His fingers touched some of the finely detailed glyphs that had been etched into its diamond-hard surface. He touched one of the sliding squares, and it moved as if gliding on a pool of oil.

The relic hummed.

Startled, Salida drew away, felt the deep cold tingling on his fingertips. But then he bent over again, pressing his hands, feeling the faint vibrations within the artifact. The inner tremors seemed to be gaining strength, building in power.

Salida laughed in amazement. In the back of his head, somewhere beyond the range of his hearing, he sensed a high-pitched sound, a throbbing noise that eluded him as he tried to concentrate on it.

Outside, in the fenced-in kennels, his prized Dobermans set up a howl in unison, barking and baying. The peacocks in the courtyard squawked and shrieked.

Salida hurried over to the balcony and looked out. One of the guards had switched on the mercury lamp to spill white light out into the courtyard. Two other guards strode out with rifles leveled at the shadows. Salida scanned the area within his walled enclosure, expecting to see the flitting shadow of a jaguar or an ocelot, some nighttime predator that had dared to cross the fence for a meal of peacock. The dogs continued to bark—but Salida saw nothing.

"Silencio!" he hollered out into the night, and then turned back to the drawing room—astonished to see that the crystalline ancient box now glowed with a silvery light.

As he bent over the shimmering box, the humming turned into a clear vibration. The diamond-like walls throbbed and pulsed. The bone-chilling cold had vanished from the oily surface, which now radiated a prickling warmth, a sunny richness that flowed through him like melting butter.

Salida pressed some of the glyphs, trying to stop the frenzied activity—but instead he saw the tiny jewel-like components inside the glass case whir to life.

It seemed to him more amazing to know that this artifact had been constructed by the ancient Maya at the dawn of history. They had used gears and primitive machinery to develop their calendars ... but this device seemed amazingly sophisticated, even for modern construction, without any recognizable gears, levers, buttons. . . .

At the core of the gadget, light began to grow, cold yet searingly bright . . . as if a pool of mercury had flared into incandescence.

Salida stepped back, now frightened and anxious. What had Aguilar given him? What had he done? How could he stop it?

Outside, the dogs and the peacocks set up such a racket, it sounded as if they were being flayed alive.

The light within the crystalline object became blinding, reaching an unimaginable peak. The last thing Salida could make out was his glass of wine rattling next to the artifact.

The dark red liquid rolled in a furious boil.

Then the light reached its critical point and leaped to another level. Its intensity increased a thousandfold. The heat and energy washed over Salida so rapidly he never had time to register the immense explosion ... or even a second of pain.

11

Gentle white clouds rode high against the sunshine, and the sea gleamed as turquoise as a Beverly Hills swimming pool. Tour groups flocked out of the hotels along the thin strip of land between the ocean and the lagoon, waiting in courtyards and traffic turnarounds to catch scheduled buses departing for the famous Maya ruins at Chichén Itzá, Tulum, Xcaret, and Xel-Há.

Marble fountains filled with Mexican coins sprayed next to the lobby courtyard of the Caribbean Shores Resort. A battered Jeep bearing three people approached, swerving around old taxicabs, vans, and the diesel-belching tour buses before it pulled up to the hotel entrance. The driver blared the horn, waved his hand, and honked again impatiently, offending the white-uniformed bellmen who stood in the open doorway. They scowled down at the Jeep, but the driver pulled closer to the curb, parked, and honked again, ignoring the stares from the staff.

Waiting just inside the lobby next to other tourists ready to go on day trips, Mulder grabbed his duffel and turned to Scully. "I'll bet that's our ride."

She set down her Styrofoam cup of coffee next to a sand-filled ashtray and picked up her own bag. "I was afraid of that."

Vladimir Rubicon followed with his backpack and his own duffel, flushed and eager. "I'm sure everyone else enjoys their vacation here in glitzy Cancún—but to me this just isn't, uh ... isn't the Yucatán. Might as well be Honolulu."

Inside the Jeep, Scully recognized Fernando Victorio Aguilar by his floppy ocelot-skin cap and his long dark ponytail. Aguilar waved at them, flashing white teeth in a grin. "*Buenos días*, amigos!"

Mulder took Scully's bag and threw it with his own in the back, while Rubicon stuffed his personal equipment in the crowded compartment. Two dark-haired, brown-skinned young men rode in the vehicle with Aguilar, ready to help. Rubicon took the strangers in stride and crowded into the back seat. Mulder slid in beside him.

Aguilar patted the passenger seat for Scully. "For you, Señorita—beside me, where it is safer, eh?" He turned around, looking at Mulder and Rubicon. "Are you ready to be off? You are properly dressed, ready for the jungles?"

Rubicon fingered his thin goatee. "They're prepared enough," he said.

Mulder leaned forward. "I even brought my hiking boots and bug repellent."

Scully looked over at her partner in the back seat. "Yes, the essentials."

The lanky "expediter" looked freshly shaved, his cheeks and chin glassy smooth. Scully could smell his aftershave. He rubbed his fingers along his face. "It will take many hours to get to where we must leave the roads and brave the jungle."

"And who are our new companions?" Mulder asked, gesturing to the other two squashed with him and Rubicon in the back of the Jeep.

"Helpers," Aguilar said. "One will drive the Jeep

back, while the other will accompany us into the jungle. He's worked with me before on such expeditions."

"Only one helper?" Rubicon said, leaning forward. "I expected we'd require, uh, much more assistance, more supplies. I paid—"

Aguilar cut him off with a nonchalant wave. "I already have guides and workers waiting for us at the rendezvous point with supplies, Señor. No need to shuttle them all down to the end of the Yucatán."

Aguilar tugged the brim of his cap and shifted the Jeep into gear, roaring off and squealing around a lumbering tour bus that tried to pull out at the same time. Scully squeezed her eyes shut, but Aguilar honked the horn and wrestled the Jeep to the left, running two wheels onto the damp grass before he screeched around the bus and increased acceleration toward the main road.

Aguilar took the Jeep southwestward, toiling through the crowded hotel zone and following the coastal highway, whipping around curves, dodging buses, mopeds, bicycles ridden by careful but unhurried people.

They passed weed-overgrown ruins beside the road, small temples and eroded limestone pillars, some covered with illegible graffiti, none highlighted in any way, not even so much as a roadside marker. The jungle had swallowed them up. Scully found it amazing that artifacts a thousand years old weren't treated with more reverence.

The drive continued, with Aguilar paying more attention to Scully than to the road. He roared along like a madman or a professional, depending on how much credit she wanted to give him. Aguilar managed to cover as many miles in an hour as a scheduled tour bus would do in three.

At first they followed the coast, heading southwest on Mexico 307, passing the popular seaside ruins of Tulum, then continuing inland, past small, poor towns bearing names such as Chunyaxché, Uh-May, Limónes, and Cafetal filled with tiny white-washed homes, log shacks, gas stations, and supermarkets the size of Scully's kitchen.

Scully unfolded a tattered, grease-stained roadmap she found jammed between the dashboard and windshield. With a sinking heart, she saw that no roads, not even dirt tracks, marked the area where they were headed. She hoped it was a misprint, or an old map.

The low jungle sprawled out endlessly on either side of the highway. Women walked on the wide, powdered-limestone shoulder wearing brightly embroidered white cotton dresses, the traditional garment that Vladimir Rubicon identified as a *huipil*.

As they continued inland, the curves got sharper, and the flatlands gradually gave way to hills. Mulder pointed out small white crosses and fresh-cut flowers beside the road at certain points. He raised his voice to be heard above the wind rattling through the flimsy windows of the battered vehicle. "Mr. Aguilar, what are those for?" he said. "Religious sites? Roadside shrines?"

Aguilar laughed. "No, those mark locations where loved ones died in traffic mishaps."

"There seem to be quite a lot of them," Scully pointed out.

"Yes," Aguilar said with a snort, "most other drivers are quite inept."

"I can see that," Scully agreed, looking directly at him.

From the back Mulder sat forward. "We'd better take particular care around those two-shrine curves."

After eating an early lunch at a roadside cantina that was little more than a table and an awning, they set off again, driving at breakneck speed for two more hours. Scully found herself feeling queasy and roadsick, especially after the stuffed chiles she had eaten. The cafe's menu had been quite limited, though Mulder had enjoyed the fresh, thick tortillas and the chicken stew.

"How much farther?" Scully asked Aguilar in the middle of the afternoon. She eyed the thickening gray clouds.

He squinted through the windshield and flicked on the wipers to smear smashed bugs across his view. He peered intently, looking alongside the road, but remained silent for a long moment. "Right here," he finally said and slammed on the brakes.

Aguilar pulled off the side of the road onto the powdery white shoulder, where a little mud track emerged from the thick jungle. The Jeep slewed from one side to another, fishtailing across traffic. Behind them a bus blatted its horn and casually passed them in the opposite lane without bothering to look for oncoming vehicles.

Aguilar climbed out to stand beside the groaning vehicle, while Mulder popped the back door, stretching his legs. Scully emerged, drawing deep breaths of the humid air filled with the damp aromas of the surrounding rain forest.

Overhead, the morning's cottony clouds had metamorphosed into thicker cumulus clouds, the kind likely to become thunderheads before long. Scanning the low jungle they were about to enter, though, she wasn't sure if rainfall could even penetrate the thick vines, weeds, and undergrowth.

The other two passengers in the back seat climbed out the driver's side of the Jeep and opened the rear, hauling out Mulder and Scully's bags. They handed the backpack to Vladimir Rubicon, who bent over, massaging his stiff, bony knees.

Mulder looked at the tall grass, thick vines, palms, creepers—an impenetrable mass of foliage. "You've got to be kidding," he said.

Fernando Aguilar laughed and then sniffed. He rubbed his cheeks, where stubble had already begun to bristle. "Well, amigo, if the Xitaclan ruins were right beside a four-lane highway, it wouldn't exactly be an untouched and unexploited archaeological site, eh?"

"He's got a point," Rubicon said.

As Aguilar spoke, a group of dark-skinned, dark-haired men suddenly appeared out of the jungle, as if from a cheap movie special effect. Scully saw a clear difference in these people from the Mexicans she had encountered in Cancún. They were shorter, not well nourished or well clothed: descendants of the ancient Maya, who lived far from the cities, no doubt in small, unmapped villages.

"Ah, here is the rest of our crew, ready to work," Aguilar said. He gestured for the other Indians to take the supplies and the backpacks, while Aguilar himself removed several canvas bags from the Jeep. "Our tents," he said.

Mulder stood with his hands on his hips, scrutinizing the jungle, sniffing the humid air. "It's not just a job, Scully—it's an adventure." Mosquitoes flew around his face.

When the Jeep was completely empty, Aguilar pounded on the hood to signal that he was ready for the replacement driver to go. One of the dark-haired young men scrambled into the driver's seat without saying a word. He simply grabbed the shift lever and roared off, swerving the Jeep back onto the road without pausing to look for traffic. With a belch of oily exhaust, he proceeded down the highway.

"Let us be off, amigos," Aguilar said. "Onward, to adventure!"

Scully took a deep breath and adjusted the laces on her boots. Together, the group plunged into the jungle.

Slogging through the underbrush, fighting with both hands against the branches and weeds and creepers and vines, Scully soon longed to be back in the Jeep, no matter how bad Fernando Aguilar's driving.

The Indians ahead of them were a flurry of activity, hacking away the most obtrusive debris with stained machetes, grunting with the effort but making no complaint. Beautiful hibiscus and other tropical flowers splashed rainbow colors on either side of the path. Water stood in puddles on the rocky ground. Thin mahogany trees with twisted trunks and smooth bark protruded in every direction, swallowed by thorny shrubs and flowering weeds. Ferns brushed Scully's legs, sprinkling droplets of water from frequent rainstorms.

They paused to rest beside a tall gray-barked "chewing gum," or chicle tree, its trunk slashed and scarred from the sap the locals had harvested over the years. Scully noticed that their helpers chewed diligently on wads of chicle sap. Aguilar allowed them to stop for only a few minutes, then they trudged on, wielding their machetes.

Before long Scully was hot and sweaty and miserable. She had half a mind to write the manufacturer of their commercial bug repellent to complain about its ineffectiveness. It had been late afternoon before they even started on the path, which allowed them no more than four hours of hiking before they would have to stop and set up camp.

Scully asked about it, and Aguilar simply laughed. He patted her on the back, and his touch made her uncomfortable. "I am trying to ease you into the long march, Señorita," he said. "It would be impossible to reach Xitaclan within a day, so this way we take the drive and several hours walk, then we camp. After a good night's sleep, we press on tomorrow, refreshed and ready to conquer the distance, eh? By midafternoon on the next day, we should reach the ruins. From there, perhaps, you will find your missing friends. Maybe their radio is just broken."

"Maybe," Scully said doubtfully.

The heat was incredible, the air moist and thick like a steam room. Her hair hung in stringy wet strands, clinging to the sides of her face. Dirt and smashed bugs covered her skin.

Overhead, howler monkeys chattered and shrieked, charging through the treetops. They leaped from branch to branch, creating an incredible chaos. Parrots screamed rough-throated calls, while jewel-toned hummingbirds flitted silently in front of her eyes. But Scully concentrated only on plodding along, avoiding the murky puddles and limestone outcroppings, stomping down the undergrowth.

"I'll make you a deal, Scully," Mulder said, wiping

perspiration from his forehead. He looked as miserable as she did. "I'll be Stanley and you be Livingstone, okay?"

Vladimir Rubicon trooped along without complaining. "We've only traveled two hours off the road," he said, "and look where we are! See how easily there could be immense ruins yet undiscovered in the Yucatán? Once the people abandoned them, the jungle rapidly covered them up—and they live only in, uh, local legends."

"But Xitaclan was special?" Mulder asked. "More than just another set of ruins?"

Rubicon drew a deep breath and paused to lean against a mahogany tree. "My Cassandra thought so. It existed for a long time, from pre–Golden Age through the Toltec influence and later human sacrifices."

Through her own misery and weariness and sticky perspiration, Scully looked in the archaeologist's intense blue eyes—to her surprise she saw that the old man did not look at all uncomfortable in the jungle. He seemed more alive and animated than she had seen him since the first day back in the pre-Colombian exhibit in Washington, D.C. Doing field work, the old archaeologist seemed in his element, on his way to rescue his daughter and also to explore uncatalogued Maya ruins.

When the shadows grew long in the jungle, Aguilar's native workers proved their worth yet again. They labored quietly and vigorously to set up camp, selecting a low clearing near a spring. They hacked away shrubs and weeds to open a sleeping space, then set up the tents where Mulder, Scully, Rubicon, and Aguilar would spend the night, while they themselves found other places to camp, presumably in the trees nearby. Scully watched the Indians moving with precision, using few words, as if they had done the task many times before.

Rubicon pressed Aguilar for more information about when he had accompanied Cassandra and her team out to the ruins, two weeks earlier.

"Yes!" the guide said. "I brought them out here—but because they intended to stay for many weeks doing their excavating, I left and went back to Cancún. I am a civilized man, eh? I have work to do."

"But she was fine when you left her?" Rubicon asked again.

"Ah, yes," Aguilar said, his eyes shining. "More than fine. She took great pleasure in encountering the ruins. She seemed very excited."

"I look forward to seeing them myself," Rubicon said.

"Day after tomorrow," Aguilar answered, nodding enthusiastically.

They sat down on fallen trees and rocks to eat a cold dinner of rolled tortillas, chunks of cheese, and fresh unidentifiable fruit the native guides had harvested out in the jungle. Scully drank from her canteen and ate her meal, slowly relishing the taste, happy for the opportunity just to sit down.

Mulder shooed gnats away from his red banana. He spoke to Scully around a mouthful of fruit. "Quite a bit different from last night's four-star restaurant." He stood up and went into her tent, where the bags had been stowed, rustling around in the packs and clothes.

Scully finished her own meal and sat back, drawing a deep breath. Her legs throbbed with weariness from fighting her way along each step of the path.

Mulder came out of the tent, holding something behind his back. "When I was doing preliminary research on this case, I remembered the story about Tlazolteotl." He glanced at the old archaeologist. "Am I pronouncing it correctly? Sounds like I'm swallowing a turtle."

Rubicon laughed. "Ah, the goddess of guilty loves."

"Yeah, that's the one," Mulder said. "A guy named Jappan wanted to become a favorite of the gods—sort of a midlife crisis. So he left his loving wife and all his possessions to become a hermit. He climbed a high rock in the desert, spending all his time at religious devotions." Mulder looked around at the jungle. "Though where he found a desert around here, I'm not sure.

"Naturally, the gods couldn't turn down a challenge like that, so they tempted him with beautiful women—

but he refused to yield. Then Tlazolteotl, the goddess of guilty loves, appeared to him as a real knockout. She said she was so impressed with Jappan's virtue that she just wanted to console him. She talked him into coming down from his rock, whereupon she successfully seduced him—much to the delight of the other gods, who had been just waiting for him to slip up.

"The gods punished Jappan for his indiscretion by changing him into a scorpion. From shame at his failure, Jappan hid under the stone where he had fallen from grace. But the gods wanted to rub it in, so they brought Jappan's wife to the stone, told her everything about his downfall, and turned her into a scorpion, too."

He smiled wistfully at Scully, still hiding something behind his back. "But it's a romantic story after all. Jappan's wife, as a scorpion, ran under the rock to join her husband, where they had lots of little baby scorpions."

Vladimir Rubicon looked up at him, smiling. "Wonderful, Agent Mulder. You should, uh, volunteer to work at the museum, just like I do."

Scully shifted her position on the fallen tree, then brushed crumbs from her khaki vest. "Interesting, Mulder—but why tell that story now?"

He brought his hand from behind his back, holding out the ugly smashed remnants of an immense black scorpion, its many-jointed legs dangling in jagged directions. "Because I found this under your pillow."

12

Yucatán jungle
Saturday, early morning, exact time
unknown

As they prepared to break camp in the morning, Mulder noticed that his watch had stopped. His first automatic thought was that sometime in the night their group had experienced an unexplained alien encounter. Then he realized that the time stoppage probably had more to do with the jungle muck than any extraterrestrial phenomena.

Shucking his outer layer of wet and dirty clothes, he pulled on another set that would get just as filthy during the day's trek. Mulder decided to wear his New York Knicks T-shirt, the one with the torn sleeve, since it didn't matter if it stained or tattered further.

Scully emerged from her tent, slapping at bug bites, her eyes droopy and half-closed from too little sleep.

"Good morning, Sunshine," Mulder said.

"I'm considering being reassigned to the Records Section," she said, yawning and stretching. "At least those people have a clean, dry office and a vending machine down the hall."

She took a drink from her canteen, then dribbled

water in the palm of her hand, splashing it on her face, rubbing it across her eyes. She blinked until her eyes cleared up, then waved away a cloud of mosquitoes. "I never truly appreciated the wonders of a bug-free work environment."

Fernando Aguilar stood by a tree, staring into a small shaving mirror. He held a straight razor in one hand. His ocelot-skin cap dangled from a broken branch within arm's reach. He turned around to grin at them, his cheeks soaped up. "*Buenos días*, amigos," he said, then went back to stroking his cheeks with the blade, his eyes half closed with pleasure. "Nothing like a good shave in the morning to make one feel clean and ready for the day, eh?"

He flicked soapy stubble off the razor's end with the precision of a professional knife thrower, splattering a white pattern across the ferns. "A secret, Señor Mulder: I mix my soap with bug repellent. It seems to help."

"Maybe I'll try that," Mulder said, rubbing the stubble on his chin. "Which way to the nearest shower?"

Aguilar laughed, a loud, thin sound that reminded Mulder of the squabbling cries of howler monkeys that had kept him awake through the night.

The local workers took down the camp, rolling up clothes and supplies into duffel bags, knocking down the tents and folding them into compact packages. They moved with remarkable speed, packed up and ready to go in no time.

Vladimir Rubicon bustled about, pacing impatiently as he munched from a small bag of raisins. "Shouldn't we be off soon?" Mulder saw bloodshot patterns around the old archaeologist's bright blue eyes and knew that Rubicon hadn't slept well, though he was apparently accustomed to such conditions.

Aguilar finished shaving and wiped his now-glistening face with a bandanna, which he tucked into his pocket. He spun the ocelot-skin cap on one finger, showing off, then settled it firmly on his head. "You are right, Señor Rubicon—we should be off to find your daughter. It's a long walk yet, but if we keep up a good pace, we can reach Xitaclan before nightfall tomorrow."

They set off again through the jungle. The quiet and solemn locals took the lead, hacking with their machetes, with Aguilar right behind to guide them.

A flock of butterflies, a cloud of bright color and fluttering wings, burst from a clear pool beside a fallen tree. They looked like a spray of jewels flashing into the air, as bright as the numerous brilliant orchids that dotted the trees around them.

Snakes dangled from branches, looking at them with cold eyes. Mulder wished he had taken more time to study the poisonous species in Central America. For safety reasons, he chose to avoid all the snakes.

They had been on their way for no more than an hour before rain began to sheet down, warm and oddly oily. Rivulets trickled and pattered like streams from the scooped banana leaves, washing away spiders, insects, and caterpillars from above. The wet air seemed ready to burst with its newly released lush scents.

Aguilar pinched the brim of his spotted hat so the water ran off in a spout. His wet ponytail dangled like a limp rag between his shoulder blades. He flashed a grin at Mulder. "You asked for the showers, Señor. It seems we have found them, eh?"

Wet leaves, moss, and rotted vegetation clung to them. Mulder looked at Scully and Rubicon, whose clothes were spattered with green streaks, brown smears of mud, and clinging yellowed fern leaves. "We've certainly managed to camouflage ourselves," he said.

"Is that what we were trying to do?" Scully answered, brushing her khaki pants. Ever-present mosquitoes swarmed around her face.

"I certainly wouldn't be inspired to build towering temples and pyramids in an environment like this," Mulder said. "It's amazing to me that the Maya could have created such an enormous civilization here."

"At least the temples would have been dry inside," Scully said, flinging water from her hair.

Rubicon's face showed a dreamy look. "Human ingenuity always surprises us when we look back through history. It would be so wonderful just to have five minutes in the past to ask, 'Why did you do this?' But we have to make do with tiny clues. An archaeologist must be like a detective—uh, an FBI agent of the past, to unravel mysteries where the suspects and the victims turned to dust a thousand years before any of us were born."

"I was impressed with the scientific and astronomical achievements the Maya made," Mulder said, "though some people think their civilization may have had some help."

"Help?" Rubicon asked, distractedly pushing a leafy frond away from his face. "Uh, what kind of help do you mean?"

Mulder took a deep breath. "According to Maya legend, their gods told them the Earth was round—quite an observation from a primitive people. They apparently knew of the planets Uranus and Neptune, which weren't discovered by Western astronomers until around the nineteenth century. Must have had great eyesight, considering they had no telescopes.

"The Maya also determined the Earth's year to within *one five-thousandth* of its actual value, and they knew the exact length of the Venusian year. They calculated other astronomical cycles out to a span of about sixty-four million years."

"Yes, the Maya were fascinated by time," Rubicon said, not rising to the bait. "Obsessed with it."

"Mulder," Scully said, "you're not going to suggest—"

He swatted away a biting fly. "If you look at some of their carvings, Scully, you'll see figures that are unmistakable—a towering form sitting in what has to be a control chair, just like an astronaut in the shuttle cockpit. Fire and smoke trail from the vehicle."

Amused, Rubicon countered with a story of his own. "Ah, yes. 'Chariots of the Gods.' Interesting speculations. I'm required to know all such tales and legends. Some of the stories are, uh, quite amazing. This is one of my favorites—you know that Quetzalcoatl, or Kukulkan as the Maya called him, was the god of knowledge and wisdom?"

"Yes," Mulder said, "he supposedly came down from the stars."

"Uh, supposedly," Rubicon said. "Now, Kukulkan's enemy was Tezcatlipoca, whose mission in life was to sow discord." Rubicon slipped his glasses on his nose, though they were perfectly useless in the jungle rain. It seemed to be a habit of his, a required action for the telling of a story.

"Tezcatlipoca came to an important festival disguised as a handsome man and called attention to himself by dancing and singing a magic song. The people were so captivated that a multitude began imitating his dance— uh, sort of like the Pied Piper. He led them all onto a bridge, which collapsed under their weight. Many people were hurled into the river far below, where they were changed into stones."

Rubicon grinned. "In another city Tezcatlipoca appeared with a puppet magically dancing on his hand. In their wonder to see this miracle, the people crowded so close that many of them suffocated. Then, pretending to be dejected at the pain and grief he had caused, Tezcatlipoca insisted that the people should stone him to death because of the harm he had done. So they did.

"But as Tezcatlipoca's corpse rotted, it gave off such a dreadful stench that many died from smelling it. At last, in sort of a commando mission, a series of brave heroes, one after another, succeeded in dragging the body out of town, like a relay race with a stinking cadaver, until finally their city was free of the pestilence."

They continued to slog along through the jungle. Rubicon shrugged his bony shoulders. "They're all just legends anyway," he said. "It's up to us to listen to the stories and learn what we can from them. I'm not going to tell you which to believe."

"Everybody else seems to," Mulder said quietly, but he did not bring up the subject of ancient astronauts again that day.

13

Striding down the corridor of the East Wing of the Pentagon, Major Willis Jakes fell into his typical routine of spotting landmarks, memorizing the route so he could trace his path back under any circumstances.

Normally he would have noted a broken tree, a rock outcropping, or a gully in the barren highlands of Afghanistan, tromping through the fever-infested swamps of Southeast Asia, slipping into Kurdish territory in the northern mountains of Iran. Now, though, instead of wearing a camouflage outfit or a survival suit bristling with small weapons and resources, Major Jakes sported his full military dress uniform, neatly pressed and smelling of laundry detergent.

Despite the amenities of civilization, he felt less comfortable this way.

The halls of the Pentagon provided as difficult a challenge as any highland wilderness, though, because each corridor in the labyrinthine headquarters was symmetric and unmemorable. The giant building's geometric shape made it easy to become disoriented and lost. One could emerge from a familiar-looking doorway out to a parking lot . . . only to find oneself on the wrong side of the immense fortress.

But Major Jakes did not find it an insurmountable tactical obstacle. He looked at the succession of office doors, most of them closed, the interior lights shut off. On Saturday the Pentagon offices closed down, the civil servants and military personnel sent home for their routine weekend activities. Normal civilians worked their regular forty-hour weeks, filling out the appropriate forms, passing them from office to office for the appropriate stamps, signatures, and file copies.

But for a career officer like Major Willis Jakes, the civilian timeclock meant nothing. He did not punch in or punch out when he went to work. His services were available on demand, all day long, all year long, whenever duty might call. He took his vacation and his relaxation time when circumstances permitted. He would have had it no other way.

The fact that he had been called here on a Saturday for a high-level briefing meant that an important mission must be in the works. Before long, Jakes would find himself in some other far-flung corner of the world, performing another series of tasks clearly defined by his superiors. Serving rules he had sworn by, the major unquestioningly took actions his country would almost certainly deny.

Jakes was tall and lean, clean-shaven, his skin the color of mahogany from deep Egyptian blood. His features were angular and Semitic, never rounded and soft.

Jakes followed the office numbers to the end of the corridor and turned left, passing door after door until he reached another darkened room, nondescript, closed—apparently as vacant as the other rooms. He did not hesitate, did not double-check the number. He knew he was right.

He precisely rapped three times on the wire-reinforced glass window. The name on the door said "A. G. Pym, Narratives and Records." In the regular day-to-day activities of the Pentagon, Major Jakes doubted other workers ever called to visit the office of Mr. Pym.

The door opened from inside, and a man in a dark suit stood back in the shadows. Jakes stepped into the dim room. His expression remained stony, emotionless—but his mind spun at hyperspeed, seeing details, sensing options, scanning for threats.

"Identify yourself," the suited man said, his voice disembodied in the shadows.

"Major Willis Jakes," he answered.

"Yes, Major," the shadowy man answered, remaining out of sight. He extended his hand, holding a silver key. "Use this to unlock that door in the rear of the office," he said. "Take the key and close the door behind you. It will lock by itself. The others are waiting for you. The briefing is about to begin."

Major Jakes didn't thank him, simply followed the instructions, opening the back door to find a half-lit conference room. Banks of fluorescent lights alternately flickered white or remained dark. At one end of the wall hung a white projection screen.

Three men dressed in suits and ties sat in chairs, while another man fiddled with the carousel of a slide projector. Major Jakes had never seen any of the men before, nor did he expect ever to see them again.

A man in a charcoal-gray suit with wire-rimmed glasses said, "Welcome, Major Jakes. Right on time. Would you care for some coffee?" He gestured to an urn in the back of the room.

"No, sir," Jakes said.

Another man with a maroon tie and a jowly face said, "We have some Danishes, if you'd like those."

"No, thank you," Jakes answered the man.

"Okay, we're ready, then." A young man fiddled with the projector. A glare of yellow-gold light splashed in a square across the screen, unfocused.

While curiosity was not part of his duty, sharp attention to details and an unfailing memory remained crucial to his work.

The last man, who had steel-gray hair and a white dress shirt, leaned back in his chair, rumpling the brown suit jacket draped behind him. "Show the first slide," he said.

"Major Jakes, please pay attention," said the man with the maroon tie. "All of these details may be important."

The slide-projector operator focused quickly to show a satellite image of a dense jungle, in the middle of which a circular area had been absolutely flattened, a crater excavated with almost perfect symmetry. The ground around it looked like slag, glassy and molten, as if someone had stubbed out a gigantic cigarette there.

"This used to be a private ranch in Mexico. Do you have any idea what might have caused this, Major Jakes?" the man in the charcoal suit asked.

"A daisy cutter?" Jakes suggested, citing one of the fragmentation bombs used to knock down trees in the jungles for the purpose of clearing helicopter landing pads. "Or a napalm burst?"

"Neither," said the man with steel-gray hair. "The scale is half a kilometer in diameter. Our seismic sensors revealed a sharp pulse, and our distant radiation detectors pinpointed a significant rise in residual radioactivity."

Major Jakes perked up. "Are you suggesting this is the result of a small nuclear strike?"

"We can think of no other explanation," the second man said, straightening his maroon tie. "A tactical nuclear device, such as an atomic artillery shell, could provide such a precise yield. This type of ordnance was recently developed by our nation and, we presume, by the Soviets, in the final years of the Cold War."

"But who could have used such a weapon in Central America, sir? What would have been the provocation?"

The man with steel-gray hair, who seemed to be the leader of the meeting, laced his fingers behind his head and leaned back against his suit jacket. "There is no small amount of political turmoil in this portion of the Yucatán. We know of numerous terrorist acts, minor squabbles with a small group of militant separatists—but we feel that an action such as this would be beyond their meager capabilities. There are also many rival drug lords in the area whose tactic of choice has been to eliminate their rivals through the use of assassination—car bombs and the like."

"This is no car bomb, sir," Major Jakes pointed out.

"Indeed not," said the man in the charcoal suit. "Next slide, please."

The slide-projector operator clicked to a higher-resolution image that showed the trees knocked down, the edge of the crater almost perfectly circular, as if a fireball had arisen so quickly that it vaporized the forest, turned the ground to glass, and then faded before the surrounding forest fires could propagate.

"Our working assumption is that at least one and possibly many more of these tactical nuclear warheads have trickled out following the collapse of the former Soviet Union. In the chaos of the breakup of the socialist republics, many of the sovereign states laid claim to the nuclear stockpiles left behind by the central Communist government. Many of those warheads have been . . . misplaced. That ordnance has been on the open market for international thugs and terrorists. It's the only thing we know of that could have come close to that kind of high-energy devastation. Such a device could have come from Cuba, for instance, across the Caribbean Sea to the Yucatán Peninsula, and from there to the drug lords in this area of Mexico."

"So, you suspect this may only be the first strike. There could be more."

"It's a possibility," said the man with steel-gray hair. "If other such weapons exist."

The next slide displayed a map of the Yucatán showing the states of Quintana Roo, Yucatán, and Campeche, as well as the small Central American countries of Belize, Honduras, El Salvador, and Guatemala.

"We need you to take a team in and find the source of these weapons, then confiscate or destroy them. We cannot allow nuclear terrorists to run free, even if they are just murdering each other."

The man with the maroon tie smiled, and his jowls jiggled. "It sets a bad example."

"My usual commandos?" Jakes said.

"Whatever you desire is at your disposal, Major Jakes," said the man with steel-gray hair. "We know our investment in your efforts will be worth every penny."

"Or every peso," said the slide-projector operator.

The others ignored the joke.

"I presume this will be a covert insertion, a search and destroy mission? But how am I to locate the target? What intelligence do we have that there are additional tactical warheads?"

"We have a strong suspicion," said the man in the charcoal suit. "There seems to be a military base located in one of the more isolated portions of the Yucatán. We've picked up a powerful transmission, encoded with an encryption scheme unlike any we have ever seen before. The signal suddenly appeared a little more than a week ago, so powerful it could not be hidden. We suspect the transmitter indicates a secret military base there."

"Does the target correspond to any known location?" Major Jakes said, leaning forward, drinking in the image on the screen.

The slide-projector operator clicked to the next image—a high-resolution satellite photograph with the lines and contours of a map overlaid upon it.

"It is apparently the site of isolated Mayan ruins. When we cross-referenced our records with those of the State Department, we found that a team of American archaeologists disappeared there at about the same time the signal began, and only a few days before this detonation occurred.

"We suspect our enemies have taken over the ruins as their own secret military base. As no ransom demands or hostage threats have been forthcoming, the status of our American citizens remains unknown . . . and, for the purposes of your mission, low priority."

"I understand," Major Jakes said. He squinted to see the site on the map. He saw nothing that even remotely resembled a road anywhere in the vicinity.

The slide-projector operator twisted the focusing ring around the lens to bring the photo into crystal clarity.

"Xitaclan," Major Jakes muttered, reading the label.

At least it sounded better than the cold mountains of Afghanistan.

14

The diligent trailblazers began to mutter quickly and quietly among themselves in their own language, excited or uneasy— Scully couldn't tell which. For the past two days her entire energy had been focused on taking step after step, proceeding deeper into the jungle . . . farther from civilization, comfort, and safety.

Fernando Aguilar picked up his pace. "Come quickly, amigos," he said and spread ferns aside. He leaned against a tall ceiba tree and gestured. "Behold—Xitaclan!"

Sweaty and exhausted, Mulder stood beside Scully, his eyes suddenly bright with interest. Vladimir Rubicon sprang forward with renewed energy, as if he had been jump-started.

Catching her breath, Scully shaded her eyes and looked out at the ancient, decaying city that might have cost the lives of Cassandra Rubicon and her team. Gray clouds hung in the sky, casting the site in a cool gloom, but the broken edifices still towered like hulking shapes in a storm.

The shadow of the vast ancient city could be easily seen, like an afterimage on the eyes. In the center of a broad plaza, spindly trees pushed up through cracks in the flagstones. A towering, stair-stepped pyramid dominated the abandoned metropolis, overgrown with vines. Smaller shrines and elaborately decorated stelae lay collapsed, unable to withstand time and natural forces. Intricately carved glyphs poked out from the moss and vines.

"This is astounding," Rubicon said, pushing past Fernando Aguilar. He stepped out into the broad plaza, scratching his yellow-white goatee. "Look at the size of the place. Imagine the number of people who came here." He turned to look at Scully, then Mulder, desperate to explain.

"Maya slash-and-burn agriculture never could have supported a large population center like this. Most major cities such as Tikal or Chichén Itzá were probably inhabited only during, uh, religious ceremonies, ball games, and seasonal sacrifices. For the rest of the year, the cities were abandoned, left to the jungle until it was time for the next festival."

"Sounds like an Olympic village," Mulder said. He and Scully came out to stand next to the old archaeologist, while the native guides hung back, talking nervously with Aguilar in some Indian dialect.

"You said ball games, Dr. Rubicon?" Scully asked. "You mean they had spectator sports?"

"There, I believe, was their stadium." He gestured across the clearing at a broad sunken space walled in with carved bricks. "The Maya played, uh, sort of a cross between soccer and basketball. They hit a hard rubber ball with their hips, thighs, and shoulders—they were not allowed to touch it with their hands. The object was to knock it through an upright stone ring on the wall."

"Cheerleaders, pennants, and everything," Mulder said.

"The losers of the tournament were usually sacrificed to the gods," Rubicon continued, "their heads cut off, their hearts cut out, their blood spilled on the ground."

"I suppose you couldn't say it was an honor just to make the playoffs," Mulder said.

A deeply troubled look crossed Rubicon's face as he walked forward, turning from side to side. He tugged at his grimy goatee, leaving a mud-streaked fingerprint across his chin. "I don't see much sign of Cassandra and her team here, no ambitious excavation work." He looked around, but the jungle seemed very vast, very oppressive. "I suppose I should give up hope that her problem was something so innocuous as a broken radio transmitter."

Scully indicated where the trees and underbrush had been hacked away. Piles of discarded branches and uprooted creepers lay in a mound half burned, as if some of the missing team had tried to make a bonfire to get rid of the debris . . . or to send some kind of desperate signal.

"They were here not long ago," she pointed out. "I would imagine all scars of their work would be obliterated and swallowed up by new growth within a month."

Aguilar said, grinning at them, "Perhaps they got lost in the jungle. Maybe jaguars ate them, eh?"

"You're not being helpful," Scully chided him.

"Cassandra's team would have been more careful than that," Rubicon said, as if trying to convince himself. "Unlike the old days of amateur diggers coming on a lark, professional archaeologists must proceed with caution, prying up every stone, uncovering the fine details."

He blinked his blue eyes, staring at the weathered stone structures. "Some of the worst amateurs thought they were doing good for history. They came to the old temples at the turn of the century, shoveled away the fallen blocks from walls, and dumped all the discarded potsherds and glyph stones down into mounds of rubble—things we now call GOK piles, for God Only Knows . . . because God only knows what's in them."

They stepped cautiously, tiptoeing and whispering, as if afraid they might offend the ancient ghosts of Xitaclan. The limestone paving bricks formed a once-level surface to the plaza, but now the flagstones had been buckled and hummocked by protruding roots.

Rubicon said, his voice hoarse and husky, "I can imagine why Cassandra was so excited here. This is an archaeologist's dream come true—all the stages in Maya history. Everything we see is a new discovery. Every place we visit, every new glyph we find is something never before catalogued. Any one relic could be the long-awaited Rosetta stone for Maya writing. It could be the secret to why this great people abandoned their cities and vanished centuries ago . . . uh, so long as other people don't ransack it for souvenirs before the scientific teams finish their work."

With her imagination Scully erased the green tufts of the lush overgrowth. Few outsiders had ever seen this place or known of its existence. "Xitaclan must have been a breathtaking spot."

Standing like gateposts, two impressive stelae displayed rows of incomprehensible Mayan writing, calendrical symbols; a great coiled snake bristling with feathers, wrapped around each obelisk. She recalled the feathered serpent symbol on the jade artifact Mulder had shown her.

"Is that supposed to be Kukulkan?" Scully said, indicating the sculpture. "The feathered serpent?"

Rubicon studied the stelae, slipping his half-glasses on his nose while the chain dangled on his neck. "Yes, and very vividly rendered, too. This one seems larger and more fearsome—as realistic as some of those jaguar statues on exhibit back in my museum. Uh, quite unlike the stylized glyphs and symbolic drawings we normally see on Maya stelae. Most interesting."

"Almost as if the sculpture was drawn from life," Mulder suggested.

Scully gave him a look, and he offered a faint smile in return.

"The afternoon light is already fading," Aguilar said. "Perhaps we should make a quick inspection of the site and then set up our camp, eh? Tomorrow you can begin your real work."

"Yes, that's a good idea," Rubicon admitted. He seemed torn between his dejection at not finding his daughter there waiting for him . . . and his other goal of studying this marvelous uncatalogued site.

"It is quite a treat to see a place like this before it is defaced by tourists. The most famous ruins have been corrupted by thousands of visitors who know nothing about history and come there only because a colorful brochure tells them to." He placed his hands on his hips. "Once a new site is opened up, somebody usually manages to destroy it before long."

The four of them went through the plaza alongside the ball court, and then skirted the spectacular central pyramid. The underbrush had been cleared away from two sides, and Scully spotted a narrow entrance passage at the ziggurat's bottom level that had been forced open—a doorway leading into the dark catacombs of the ancient monolithic structure.

"Looks like someone went exploring," Scully said.

Mulder went ahead of them, around the path at the base of the pyramid, and then called for them to come. She found him standing at the rim of a circular well at least thirty feet across that plunged down into the limestone as if it had been drilled there by a giant rig.

"A cenote," Rubicon said. "A sacred well. It's a very deep limestone sinkhole. They're, uh, scattered all over the Yucatán Peninsula. Perhaps that explains one reason why Xitaclan was built at this location."

Scully stepped up to a crumbling platform that must have been like a gangplank over the edge of the deep hole. They stood at the edge, and Scully peered over to see a mirror-smooth pool of murky green water. The depths seemed fathomless. Stained limestone outcroppings ridged the cenote walls like the turns of a screw. Mulder tossed a pebble into the water, watching the ripples spread out like shock waves.

"These natural sinkholes were considered to be sacred wells, water from the gods rising from the earth," Rubicon said. "You can be sure this one contains a treasure trove of relics and bones."

"Bones?" Scully asked. "From people that fell in?"

"Uh, were thrown in," Rubicon said. "The cenotes were sacrificial wells. Perhaps they would club the victims to death, or just tie them up and weight them down so the bodies would sink.

"Other times, for special sacrifices, the victim was chosen as much as a year in advance. He led a life of pleasures and indulgence, food and women and fine clothes—until the day when he was drugged and led to the edge of the cenote, then thrown into the sacred waters."

"I thought the Maya were primarily a peaceful people," Scully said.

"That's an old belief, a false story promulgated by an archaeologist who admired the Maya beyond all common sense—and so he slanted his findings to downplay the bloodshed evident in the writings and carvings."

"An archaeological spin doctor," Mulder said.

"The Maya culture was quite violent, shedding a great deal of blood, especially in later periods, due to Toltec influences. They considered it beautiful to scarify themselves, to hack off fingers and toes in self-mutilation ceremonies.

"In fact, the most bloodthirsty cult belonged to the god Tlaloc, whose priests would prepare for great festivals by approaching mothers to buy their young children. At a great ceremony the children were boiled alive, then eaten with great pomp and splendor. The priests took special delight if the infants cried or wailed while they were tortured to death, uh, because they thought the tears promised a year of plentiful rain."

Scully shuddered as she stood on the edge of the sinkhole, looking down into the murky cenote, thinking of all the secrets the bottom of that deep, dark well might hold.

"I'm sure nobody practices that religion anymore, though," Rubicon said, as if that might comfort her. He brushed his hands on his pants. "There's nothing you need to worry about. I'm sure it has nothing to do with all those missing-person rumors . . . or Cassandra."

Scully nodded noncommittally. Yes, here they were, isolated, two days from the nearest major road, at an

abandoned site of ancient ruins where the Maya had performed countless blood sacrifices. A place where an entire
team of American archaeologists recently disappeared. . . .

Of course, she thought. She had nothing to worry
about.

15

Xitaclan ruins
Sunday, 6:38 P.M.

Standing near the broken-brick sacrificial platform at the edge of the limestone sinkhole, Mulder stared downward, feeling the depths beckon him. The air smelled sour and mildewy, hinting of decay. He wondered what secrets lay beneath the murky waters, how deep the well went, how many skeletons it held in its gullet.

A tingle traveled up his spine, a brooding uneasiness—but he could not pinpoint its source. The colored rays of the setting sun and the dim amber light cast long shadows. Mulder thought he saw dark shapes swirling like oil in the cenote, and he felt a slight tremble beneath his feet . . . a vibration as if from deeply buried engines, generators entombed beneath the earth. He thought of H. G. Wells's novel, *The Time Machine*, the evil Morlocks laboring in subterranean tunnels, working their machines . . . hungry for the flesh of surface dwellers.

The water in the cenote began to stir and froth. Suddenly large bubbles belched to the surface, each as wide as a barrel, spewing gas from the depths.

"What's going on?" Scully said.

Mulder backed away from the rough edge as the

vibration grew stronger beneath his feet. A wave of stench struck him, sour and sulfurous like a thousand rotten eggs made into a giant omelet. He covered his nose, choking. Scully, who was accustomed to smelling cadavers and decay under even the most horrendous autopsy circumstances, wrinkled her nose and gasped.

"What a stink!" Fernando Aguilar said.

"Maybe it's the legendary corpse of Tezcatlipoca," Vladimir Rubicon suggested, unbothered by the event. "That's a stench bad enough to kill off half the population."

Scully took a cautious sniff and shook her head. "No, that's sulfur—sulfur dioxide, I think. It's a volcanic gas."

"Maybe we should talk about this a little farther from the edge," Mulder said.

The four of them hurried back around to the front of the large pyramid. "My knees are still shaking," Scully said. "Wait, that's not my knees—it's the ground. It hasn't stopped."

Mulder saw the trees swaying, the ground jumping and bucking. In the back of his skull, in the rumbling subsonic range below his ability to hear, he experienced a loud tremor . . . growing in power as a deep subsurface event gained strength.

Aguilar's hand-picked Indian guides stood next to the half-erected tents, talking quickly among themselves. One stocky man fled into the forest, shouting back at the others.

"I wonder what their problem is?" Mulder said. "Haven't they ever experienced angry gods before?"

"That's seismic activity," Rubicon said, his voice sounding out-of-place, analytical. "Uh, how can there be earthquakes, volcanic action? The Yucatán Peninsula is a high, stable, limestone plateau—it is geologically impossible to have volcanic activity here."

Seemingly to disprove him, the ground shuddered as if someone had struck it with a giant sledgehammer. Plaza flagstones bucked. A group of spindly mahogany trees beside an old temple tipped, their roots pulling out of the wet powdery ground like a dirt-encrusted mat of tentacles.

One of the ancient, half-fallen facades collapsed the rest of the way with an explosion of crumbling stone blocks. Bricks from the sides of the stair-stepped pyramid popped loose and pattered down, bouncing, gaining speed.

At the edge of the jungle, the stressed ground split apart like a newly broken scab, bleeding foul gases from beneath the earth's surface. Mulder grabbed Scully's arm to help her keep her balance.

"We better get away from these large structures," Scully said. "One of them could collapse and bury us."

Together they helped the old archaeologist stagger out into the middle of the open plaza while the ground swayed and shook beneath them. The trees thrashed about like gnashing teeth.

From his vantage Mulder could see the ziggurat rocking from side to side like a Chicago skyscraper in a windstorm. He grabbed Scully's shoulder. "Better hang on!"

But then, before the quake seemed ready to reach its peak, the tremors subsided, dampening to a faint vibration that might well have just been Mulder's nerves misfiring with fear.

Rubicon smeared his goatee flat, occupying his shaking hands with some nervous gesture. "Uh, I could be wrong about that seismic stability," he said.

Aguilar pointed to the half-fallen tents and the scattered supplies. The campsite lay empty, abandoned. "It looks like we have lost our assistants for now," he said, his face ashen. He fumbled in his vest pocket to find cigarette papers and tobacco.

"They'll be back tomorrow, amigos. They are good workers. But we are on our own to prepare this evening's dinner and to recover from our adventure, eh?" He forced a laugh, which made Mulder feel decidedly uneasy.

Rubicon found an awkward seat on one of the upraised flagstones. He hung his head. "One of the reasons this area interested Cassandra was because of its, uh, very localized and unusual geological instability. Her first love was geology, you know. My little girl collecting rocks, studying how they were made, igneous, metamorphic, and sedimentary. She had a large collection, knew them all, labeled them all.

"Then Cassandra allowed her interests to shift to digging not just for the rocks themselves but for what lay hidden in them—the marks of human impact and the history trapped between layers of deposited sediment and dust. She seemed very excited about certain seismic readings she had obtained in this area—just as excited as she was about leading the first team out to Xitaclan."

The old archaeologist shook his head. "But it still seems impossible such violent activity would occur here." He gestured toward the tall central pyramid, where a few loose pebbles continued to rain down the exaggerated steps. "You can *see* that the area is thoroughly stable—if seismic tremors occurred frequently, these ruins would have been leveled centuries ago. The mere fact that Xitaclan remains standing provides incontrovertible evidence that this land is phenomenally stable."

"It didn't feel stable a moment ago, Señor," Aguilar said, standing with his feet braced far apart, as if he expected the ground to begin rocking and shaking again at any moment. He finally succeeded in rolling and lighting his cigarette.

Mulder sifted through the scattered information he kept stored in his brain, the enormous amounts of trivia and tidbits gleaned from encyclopedias and reports he had studied over the years. He always tried to remember items that had the slightest unexplained or mysterious flavor to them.

"Most of the major volcanoes in Central America are in the highlands of Mexico, right down the backbone of the country—but volcanoes are unusual things. One called Parícutin suddenly appeared in 1943 . . . right in the middle of a Mexican cornfield that was as flat as a tortilla. A farmer was out plowing his field when the ground began to smoke and shake. For nine years afterward the volcano continued growing, dumping over a billion tons of lava and ash. It buried two entire towns."

"Mulder, are you saying a volcano just sprang up in the middle of nowhere?" Scully asked.

Mulder nodded. "And as it grew, Parícutin was watched by geologists from around the world. Within the first twenty-four hours, the volcano had made a twenty-five-foot-tall cinder cone. In eight months it grew to about fifteen hundred feet . . . quite a vigorous little event. In all, Parícutin covered about seven square miles of the surrounding area with lava and volcanic ash. Its maximum height topped nine thousand feet—and that was only half a century ago. No telling what else might just pop out of the ground."

He looked from Scully over to Rubicon and then to Fernando Aguilar. "I'd sleep lightly tonight and be ready to make a run for the jungle if a volcano starts erupting underneath our feet."

"An excellent suggestion, Señor," Aguilar said, puffing on his newly rolled cigarette.

But Scully looked at Mulder with concern, and he knew what she must be thinking, because he was bothered by the same question. What large energy release, what sharp aftershock could have triggered the burst of volcanic activity around Xitaclan? And why now?

Something had happened here. Mulder didn't know if it had anything to do with the disappearance of Cassandra Rubicon's team, or if it was just a coincidence.

He believed in many unlikely things . . . but Mulder had a difficult time believing in coincidences.

16

X Removing his policeman's cap at the doorway to the castle-like fortress of Pieter Grobe, Carlos Barreio waited while the guard made a telephone call to his master. Barreio used the meaty palm of his right hand to slick back his thinning dark hair, then brushed his thick black mustache in place. He felt like a supplicant at the gate of a powerful baron, but he would swallow his pride if need be—for the freedom of his land.

In his scuffed leather satchel he held carefully wrapped pieces of Maya jade, ancient relics scavenged from the lesser temples around the Xitaclan site. He had never before tried to sell historical items on his own, and he did not know what price such jade carvings should fetch—but he needed the money ... and the *Liberación Quintana Roo* movement needed the weapons and the supplies it would buy.

Aguilar's unreliable assistant Pepe Candelaria had never returned from his mission the week before. The wiry little man seemed to have abandoned his mother and sisters, running off somewhere without ever delivering more treasures from Xitaclan, as he'd been instructed to do. Barreio could not tolerate any additional delay, so he had taken the remaining small pieces he kept in his possession, and decided to do with them whatever he could.

Fernando Victorio Aguilar excelled in selecting discerning customers for the most expensive sculptures, but Aguilar did not sell the art objects frequently enough, and Barreio had his own needs. Besides, now with the recent death—no, the complete obliteration—of Xavier Salida, Barreio had to find new customers, even if it meant cultivating them himself.

The guard hung up the black telephone and grunted, unlatching the steel-reinforced wooden door that led into the limestone block walls of Pieter Grobe's home—it looked more like a fortress than even some of the largest Maya ruins.

"Master Grobe will see you for fifteen minutes," the guard said. "I am to accompany you."

Barreio cleared his throat and nodded. "Thank you." He brushed down the front of his white uniform, still holding his policeman's cap in one sweaty hand. It seemed deeply ironic for him to be waiting at the pleasure of a drug lord when Barreio was one of the men ostensibly in charge of law enforcement in the state of Quintana Roo, under corrupt Mexican law.

But Barreio understood the games he had to play in order to accomplish his main goal. The descendants of the Maya had long memories. They had waited for centuries to be free again, able to recreate their lost golden age.

Freedom and independence. The people of Quintana Roo would thank him for it, once the turmoil and bloodshed and political upheaval had faded into memory. After all, during the great Mexican Revolution of 1910, wasn't it true that one in every eight citizens had been killed? All those martyrs had paid the price for freedom—and oftentimes that price was high indeed.

When the guard slammed the massive front door behind them, the echoing boom sounded like a cannon shot on the Spanish Main.

Inside, Grobe's fortress looked even more Germanic and imposing, smelling of wood smoke from poorly ventilated fires and mildew in the stone cracks. Ceiling fans twirled from rafters above. The hall arches and narrow windows let in only fragments of light. Shafts of afternoon sun played across the tiled floors, illuminating faded tapestries on the walls. The room felt clammy, heavily air-conditioned, cold as a tomb.

Barreio felt the guard walking close beside him, shouldering his automatic rifle. The Belgian expatriate certainly acted paranoid—and with good cause, since rival drug lords killed each other off so frequently that Barreio's police forces had little time to investigate their criminal activities.

Surprisingly, the guard had allowed him to keep his police-issue revolver in its side holster; Barreio decided that must reflect on the guard's confidence and skill, an utter certainty that the automatic rifle would cut him down much faster than Barreio could ever draw and fire his pistol. He hoped he would never have to test that assumption.

The police chief walked along, holding the satchel of jade artifacts in one hand, his cap in the other, wondering if the clock on his fifteen-minute audience had begun ticking when he entered the door of the fortress, or if he would be able to talk for the full time once he actually met the drug lord face-to-face.

The burly guard led him through the main fortress and out to a screened-in back porch, a lavish patio area that contained a kidney-shaped in-ground Jacuzzi. Doors led off to other rooms, perhaps a sauna, perhaps a shower.

Pieter Grobe sat alone in a canvas chair, reveling in the silence, listening to the fine buzz of the jungle outside the walls of his home. He played no music, listened to no distractions.

Barreio stood at the entrance to the patio, waiting to be noticed. A black telephone rested on a round glass table beside Grobe's chair. A transparent pitcher sat looking cool and refreshing, filled with a pale green liquid and garnished with round slices of lime; the pitcher gleamed with droplets of perspiration. Like nylon cobwebs, a protective covering of mosquito netting draped the windows, the chairs, and a rocking swing that hung from chains.

Grobe himself, thin and scarecrowish, sat within one such cocoon of netting. He held a long black cigarette holder with a smoldering, pungent clove cigarette. Grobe took a long puff, exhaled bluish-gray smoke. His hand slipped out between the folds of mosquito netting, reaching toward the table. He grasped the handle of the pitcher and poured a long, languid stream of limeade into a glass. He curled his skeletal hand around the glass and drew it inside the mosquito webbing.

Unable to contain his impatience, Barreio cleared his throat—earning himself a sharp glare from the guard.

Pieter Grobe sighed and then turned from his contemplation, showing a gaunt face seamed with deep lines. His chocolate-brown hair was thick and carefully styled, laced with frosty wings at his temples. Droplets of perspiration stood out on his cheeks and forehead; he looked sticky and uncomfortable in a baggy, cream-colored cotton suit.

"Yes, Señor Barreio?" he said. "Your fifteen minutes have begun. What is it you wish to discuss with me?" The Belgian drug lord's voice was quiet, patient, and firm. Barreio already knew that Grobe spoke excellent English and Spanish without the slightest trace of an accent—a skill that not many diplomats ever acquired with such precision.

"I have some items I was hoping might interest you, Excellency," Barreio said. He drew a deep breath, swelling his already broad chest as he stepped forward to another low table and set the leather satchel down before placing his policeman's cap beside it. The guard stiffened, ready for treachery.

"Don't overreact, Juan," Grobe said, not even looking at the guard. "Let us observe with an open mind what has compelled our friend the police chief to visit us."

"Jade sculptures, Excellency," Barreio said, "priceless Maya artifacts. If you agree to purchase them, they will never become lost in museums, where they would be squandered for the benefit of the public, their true artistic value lost."

Barreio opened the satchel and withdrew the pieces of Xitaclan sculpture. "Instead, these items will be yours to enjoy in private, as you wish."

Each artifact showed the predominant feathered serpent motif, fanciful drawings of plumed reptilian forms with long fangs and round intelligent eyes, legendary creatures the Maya had worshipped in times long past.

Grobe leaned forward, pushing his gaunt face against the mosquito netting that surrounded his chair. He stubbed out his clove cigarette and exhaled again. In the thick smoke Barreio could smell a pungent sweet burning scent, not entirely unlike marijuana.

"And what makes you think I am the slightest bit interested in purchasing contraband antiquities, Señor Police Chief Barreio?" Grobe said. "Is this perhaps a . . . 'sting operation,' as the Americans call it? Are you trying to tempt me into an illegal act, so that you can arrest me red-handed?"

Barreio stood back, appalled. "That would be the height of folly, Excellency Grobe," he said.

"Yes," the Belgian agreed, "yes, it would."

Barreio continued. "The state of Quintana Roo operates on nuances of power. I know my place in this society, Excellency, and I also know yours. I would never attempt something so foolish."

He swallowed. "If I might add, we have seen the results of tangling with you, Excellency. I myself have been to the devastated ruins of Xavier Salida's villa. It is inconceivable to me exactly what you did to retaliate against him, but the threat of your supreme power is absolutely clear, and I have no intention of crossing you."

Grobe actually laughed, a long, dry series of chuckles that might have been misinterpreted as a cough. "I am glad you fear me so, Señor Barreio. It is true that the . . .

squabbles between myself and Xavier Salida had escalated over the past few weeks. But I assure you I had nothing to do with the devastation that occurred at his household. I wish wholeheartedly that I knew how to create such destruction, because then all of my rivals would fear me as much as you do."

Barreio reeled, off-balance with the information. If not Grobe, then who had destroyed Salida? Who had that kind of power in all of Mexico?

The Belgian continued. "I have been given to understand that you and that parasite Fernando Aguilar had also sold artifacts to Salida—ancient Maya artifacts from a newly excavated ruin called . . ." Grobe placed a slender finger to his lips as he searched for the name. "Xitaclan, I believe. Many of my Indian servants, including our friend Juan here"—with a gaze cast over his shoulder, he indicated the rigid guard, who still had not lowered his rifle—"believe that such items are cursed and should never have been taken from their resting place. The gods are angered and will exact their vengeance.

"Xavier Salida has already paid for the indiscretion of stealing those antiquities. Now, I trust these jade artifacts you intend to sell to me are also from Xitaclan? Señor Barreio, I have no wish to incur the wrath of the ancient gods."

Barreio forced a laugh and shifted uneasily, toying with one of the jade feathered serpent carvings. His mind whirled as he tried to think of another tack, a new way to open negotiations.

He had to sell some of this jade. He had to raise money. He had already donated what cash he could spare from his salary, but it was difficult for him to work as the police chief and also to hide his real passion—the fight for the independence of Quintana Roo.

It seemed only fitting to use the fallen glory of the Maya, the people who had created civilization in this corner of the Yucatán. Their precious artifacts would finance the struggle for freedom, help Barreio and his group of revolutionaries to conquer a new and independent land, help them win their struggle against the corrupt, bankrupt central government of Mexico. If they succeeded, *Liberación Quintana Roo* would proclaim a new homeland where the glory of the lost Maya could rise again.

"You must be joking, Excellency," he said. "Such superstitions! Surely a sophisticated European like yourself places no stock in ancient curses?" He raised his dark eyebrows. His thick mustache bristled, tickling his nose.

Grobe took another patient drink of limeade, glanced at his wristwatch, then blew out a long sigh before he answered. "My own feelings are irrelevant in this situation, Señor Police Chief Barreio. If the locals believe the artifacts are cursed, then I am unable to get anyone to work for me. My household servants are afraid. They disappear in the night, and I have a terrible time finding others to replace them. The quality of my life diminishes."

He tapped his empty cigarette holder on the edge of his chair. "I enjoy my lifestyle as it is, without further complications. I don't even want to consider the possibility that certain followers of the ancient Maya religion might try to get their revenge on me if I were to flaunt these old artifacts."

Grobe leaned forward, finally thrusting his narrow, well-lined face out of the protective netting. His brown eyes bored into Barreio. "With all of my money, I can install defenses against attacks from rival drug producers—but a suicidal religious fanatic is a threat against which few people can defend."

He slipped the netting back around him again and glanced at his watch. "Your time is up, Señor Barreio. I'm sorry we could not accommodate your needs."

Deciding against further negotiation, which would at this point sound like pleading or wheedling, Barreio returned the items to their case and snapped shut the leather satchel. He placed his cap back on his head and, shoulders slumping, he turned to the door that led into the thick-walled fortress.

The Belgian drug lord called after him, "Wait a moment, Señor Barreio."

Barreio spun around, his heart beating fast, hoping that Grobe had been only toying with him, searching for a better deal. But then the Belgian said, "Let me offer you something else of value. I have no interest in your relics, but I will give you this information for free—for now. I'll trust you to remember me if anything else should come up where you might repay me in kind."

"What is it, Excellency?" Barreio said.

The Belgian removed the stub of the cigarette from his holder, fished in his suit pocket for a dark brown box, and inserted a new clove cigarette. He lit it, but let it smolder for a few seconds as he answered.

"I have learned through international sources that a covert U.S. military team is coming to infiltrate Quintana Roo. It is a search-and-destroy mission. The commandos intend to find some weapons cache or military stronghold deep in the jungles. Perhaps you know about it? Perhaps it has something to do with the guerrilla revolutionary group known as *Liberación Quintana Roo*?" He smiled thinly. "Since you are the police chief in these parts, I thought you might wish to be informed of this development."

Barreio froze, feeling the color drain from his face. A knot of ice in his stomach made him desperately uneasy, while at the same time a flush of anger surged through his veins. "The U.S. military is coming here—in secret? How dare they! Under what pretext?"

"The commando team is landing across the border in Belize, I believe. With a little snooping around I'm sure you can get more detailed information."

"Thank you," Barreio said, stunned and startled. "Thank you, Excellency."

The jade relics nearly forgotten, the leather satchel heavy in his numb hand, Barreio stumbled behind the footsteps of the guard.

His mind spun, no longer worried about the short-term solution of raising money by selling artifacts, but wondering what the U.S. military had discovered, what they could be up to—and if his own plans for state independence might be threatened.

17

Hours after the bizarre volcanic tremors, the ground had settled back down to relative peace. The noxious sulfurous odors had cleared from the air, to be replaced by the heady scents of the jungle: the perfumes of flowers, the sharp spice of decaying mulch, and the crackling resin of dry branches consumed in their campfire.

Fernando Victorio Aguilar came up to them, smiling, a loose satchel dangling at his side. "Instead of your American junk food, I have secured a repast from the arms of the forest." He reached inside to withdraw a handful of bulbous mushrooms mottled with gray-green. He brushed loose strands of moss and leaf debris from their caps. "We shall roast these to start—delicious mushrooms, eh? They taste like nuts when they've been cooked."

Mulder's stomach growled, but Scully shifted uneasily. "These are safe to eat?"

Aguilar nodded vigorously. "These are local delicacies, used in many traditional Maya dishes."

Rubicon reached out to take one of the mushrooms

from Aguilar's hand, holding it close to the firelight. Blinking his surprised-looking blue eyes, he hauled up his reading glasses and set them on his perspiration-slick nose. "Yes, I've eaten these before," he said. "Delicious." He skewered the mushroom on a twig next to the fire and held it in the flames, roasting it like a campfire marshmallow.

"At least he didn't bring us beetle grubs to eat," Mulder said. Other bugs swarmed around the firelight.

"Yes, grubs!" Aguilar said, clapping his hands in surprise. "I can go find grubs—there are many delicious kinds! Or, if you would like a true feast, I could shoot us a monkey."

"No thanks," Scully said.

"A little different from dinner last night," Mulder said.

Darkness surrounded them like an oppressive blanket. Their crackling campfire stood as an island of warm light in the middle of the Xitaclan plaza. In other circumstances, Mulder might have suggested they all begin a chorus of "Row, Row, Row Your Boat." But not here, not now.

Bats flew about, swooping silently through the air, their high-pitched chirps beyond the edge of human hearing, though Mulder could feel the sounds in the fillings of his teeth. Large night moths flew in graceful spirals, pale splashes against the darkness. Farther out in the jungle they could see the eyes of predators flickering with reflected gleams.

Scully plucked one of the mushrooms from her stick, looked at it smoking in her fingers, and popped it into her mouth. She chewed, about to comment on its taste, when suddenly a bat swooped in front of her face, chomping one of the large moths. The bat swooped off before she could do anything but reel backward, startled.

When Mulder commented about the Indians who had fled from the rumbling eruptions and now refused to come closer to the ruins, Aguilar snorted. "They are superstitious cowards," he said. "Their respect for their religion outweighs their common sense. They claim this place still holds the spirits of their ancestors sacrificed to appease the gods, not to mention the old gods themselves."

Rubicon stared into the shadows, listening to the buzz of insects, the symphony of night birds, the dance of predator and prey. He wore a pinched, concerned look on his narrow face. Mulder knew the old archaeologist must be imagining his daughter lost and alone in the deep jungle filled with stalking jaguars and poisonous snakes . . . or murderous treasure-seekers.

Mulder cocked his head as he heard something large stirring in the trees, saw the thick ferns swaying as an unseen creature moved through the undergrowth outside the edge of firelight. The others didn't notice the disturbance.

"Things haven't changed so much in a century," Rubicon muttered, far away in his thoughts. "When I think of Cassandra and her team exploring here, I can't help but remember some of the first amateur archaeologists in this region. They suffered hardships unlike any we are likely to encounter."

Rubicon settled the reading glasses on his nose. *Story time*, Mulder thought.

"Two of the first white men to explore the Maya ruins were Stephens and Catherwood. They were veteran travelers, confident they could make their way through any rough country.

"They had read some obscure books that mentioned great cities buried in the rain forest, uh, 'ruined and desolate without a name'—I think those were the exact words . . . I've read their travel diaries.

"Stephens and Catherwood went into the rain forests of Honduras in 1839. After days of trudging through the jungle, they finally reached the ruins of Copán, where they encountered fallen buildings, stone staircases covered with vines or trees. Stephens and Catherwood knew nothing of Maya history, and when they asked the local Indians who had built the ruins, the Indians simply shrugged.

"These two gentlemen returned to Central America on several trips, visiting dozens of ruined cities. Together they published bestselling accounts of their adventures, Stephens with his eloquent journals, Catherwood with his beautiful illustrations. Their books ignited a huge interest in archaeology—uh, for better or worse.

"But it didn't come easy—especially not for Catherwood. He seemed to be under a curse. He contracted malaria and suffered from the recurring fever. He went lame from swollen and infected insect bites. His left arm became almost paralyzed. He had to be carried on the shoulders of Indians, since he was unable to walk.

"But he did recover and made his way back to set up his paintings in New York. Then a fire broke out, and one of their greatest exhibitions was destroyed—Catherwood's drawings as well as spectacular artifacts brought back from Maya country."

Scully shook her head. "What a loss."

Rubicon stared into the campfire. "Years later, when Catherwood was on his way back to the States from yet another expedition, he drowned at sea when his ship collided with another. Bad luck, or a Maya curse—depends on what you believe."

Squatting by himself, Aguilar chewed on something that seemed inordinately crunchy. Mulder caught a glimpse of flailing black legs as the guide popped another morsel into his mouth.

"A good story, Señor," Aguilar said around a mouthful. "But the curse was not strong enough to stop the flood of white adventurers such as yourself, eh?"

"Or my daughter," Rubicon said.

Scully stood up to stretch, brushing her legs. "Well, we should go to bed and try to get some sleep," she said. "Any minute now you'll start telling ghost stories just to give us the creeps."

"Good idea," Rubicon said. "We'll want to get up at

dawn so we can start our detailed investigations, search for traces of my daughter."

Mulder said dryly, "I guess the story about teenagers necking on Lover's Lane will have to wait for another night."

Mulder woke in the middle of the night to the sound of rustling and creeping noises. Close, too close. He blinked, then sat up, listening intently.

He definitely heard something moving outside across the plaza ... perhaps a large predator stalking them, searching for easy prey. The flimsy fabric walls of his tent seemed weak and unprotective.

He leaned forward cautiously, parting the folds of mosquito netting to reach the opening flap of the tent. He accidentally rustled the cloth and froze, listening intently—but he did not hear the sound outside again.

He pictured some large carnivorous monster from the jungle, a prehistoric denizen lost in time, sniffing the air, looking toward the sound he had made. Swallowing, Mulder gradually eased his tent flap open, pushing his head out into the open night air.

The bright gibbous moon had just begun to rise like a half-closed eye, spilling pale watery light across the tree-tops as thick clouds scudded across the sky.

The tents had been erected next to one of the weathered stelae around which the feathered serpent wrapped itself like a vicious protector. The tall stela tilted at a slight angle, its shadow blurred and indistinct on the buckled flagstones of the plaza.

Out in the jungle the line of skeletal trees and tangled blackness seemed quiet and still. This late in the core of night, even the nocturnal creatures hung back, waiting.

Mulder heard the rustling sound again, a rattling growl. He scanned the darkness, trying to find its source, but he saw nothing, only shadows, no movement. He waited, breathing shallowly, his attention entirely focused.

Finally, just when he had convinced himself that he

had heard nothing more than his overactive imagination, Mulder caught a writhing flash, something stirring in the moonlight at the edge of the jungle.

He turned, trying to see clearly in the uncertain illumination. In the tall, matted trees and the dangling creepers, he spotted a huge serpentine body moving sinuously, slithering, plowing its way through the underbrush with incredible stealth.

He gasped—and the thing turned toward him. He saw a flash of flaming eyes, a glint of impossibly long scales—feathery scales, like cloth mirrors overlapping, reflecting a dazzling sequence of moon images back at him.

Then, with a flick of its lissome body, the thing vanished into the midnight shadows. Mulder saw no further sign of it, though he waited for many minutes. Once, he thought he heard a cracking branch deep in the jungle— but that could have been from anything.

Eventually he went back to bed, crawling inside his tent and replaying the scene over and over in his mind. He needed to understand just what—if anything—he had seen.

Sleep was a long time coming for him.

18

Xitaclan ruins
Monday, dawn

The local helpers returned at daybreak, just as Fernando Aguilar had predicted. The guide sat over the cooling campfire, smoking one of his hand-rolled cigarettes, scowling at the Indians who crept into the plaza, heads down as if in embarrassment.

Mulder crawled out of his tent, watching the locals, who looked for all the world like a blue-collar crew showing up for the morning shift. Vladimir Rubicon was already up, scrutinizing the nearest feathered serpent stela, using a pocketknife to pry loose lumps of moss to get a better look at the glyphs.

"Ah, Agent Mulder, you're up!" Rubicon said. "Today we're sure to find some sign of what my daughter and her team were doing. She must have uncovered a secret in these ruins. If we can find the same secret, we'll discover why her team vanished."

Hearing their voices, Scully also crawled out of her tent. "Good morning. Mulder, are you cooking breakfast?"

"Just cereal and milk for me, thanks," he replied.

Aguilar tossed away the stub of his vile-smelling cigarette. He looked freshly shaved. Seeing his employers awake and about, Aguilar turned to berate the Indians in a language Mulder couldn't understand, his voice filled with disgust.

"What's he saying?" Scully asked. "What did they do?"

Vladimir Rubicon listened a moment before shaking his head. "It must be a Maya language derivative. Many of the locals still speak the old tongue." He shrugged. "Uh, I suspect they didn't do anything wrong, other than running off into the night. Aguilar's just trying to impress us with his authority."

"I had a boss like that once," Mulder said.

Aguilar came over, grinning at them as if he had just learned what they were getting him for his birthday. "Good morning, amigos," he said. "Today we shall discover the mysteries of lost Xitaclan, eh? We shall learn what happened to the lovely Señorita Rubicon and her companions."

"Have you asked the locals?" Scully said, gesturing to the Indians who appeared appropriately cowed after the long string of beratements.

Aguilar said, "They claim the spirit of this place has taken Señorita Rubicon. The old gods are hungry for blood after so many years. That is why the natives camp away from the ruins. They are not civilized people, like you and I. They don't even try to pretend."

"But did any of these workers remain to assist the archaeologists?" Scully said, her voice harder, pressing for an answer. "Somebody must know."

"Señorita Scully, I guided the archaeology team to Xitaclan, for which they paid me a lot of American money—and I am very grateful. These Indians, descendants of the Maya, say there were many loud noises, strange activities, after I had left. Señorita Rubicon and her friends laughed at them for their foolishness, but the Maya helpers all ran to safety. Now they say the gods have shown who is foolish and who is wise."

"Sort of like failing a supernatural IQ test," Mulder muttered.

Aguilar rummaged around in his pocket for paper

and tobacco to fashion himself another cigarette. A beautiful green-feathered bird flitted across the plaza from one tall tree to another, singing out a thin musical call. The Indians stopped their work, pointing up and chattering to each other in amazement.

"Look, the quetzal bird," Aguilar said, nodding. He took off his ocelot-skin hat to shade his eyes in the slanted morning light. "Very precious. The Maya used quetzal feathers for many of their ceremonial dresses."

Rubicon frowned and looked around as if he might see some sign of his daughter, while Mulder turned back to Aguilar, exasperated. "Do they know what happened to Cassandra, or not?"

Aguilar shrugged. "All I know is that Señorita Rubicon was safe and quite happy with the work awaiting her when I left her to return to Cancún."

"Let's get busy looking for her, then," Scully said.

"These ruins may extend for a mile or so," Rubicon said, stretching out his arm, "with separate sites or temple buildings blocked off from each other by the dense trees and vegetation."

"Tell the locals what we're searching for," Scully suggested. "Maybe they can help us comb the site."

Aguilar passed on the information, and the Indians dispersed to the jungle, diligently scouring the fallen ruins, talking excitedly with each other. Some looked uneasy, some confused, others eager, as they undertook the exploration.

Scully, Mulder, and Rubicon wandered around Xitaclan, walking the length of the overgrown ball court, poking in alcoves and niches, searching for clues, bodies—or even a note explaining that Cassandra and her companions had gone off to get groceries.

Scully said, "Their team consisted of an engineer, two archaeologists, a hieroglyphics expert, and a photographer. No real survival expert in the bunch." She scanned the clotted trees, low palms, the dense vegetation hanging from the branches. The sun lit everything like a spotlight.

"Even if all the helpers ran off, like they did last night, I still can't imagine Cassandra's team trying to make their own way through the jungle. We just completed our own hike to get here," she said. "I wouldn't want to do that without a guide."

"Cassandra was good at survival," Rubicon said. "She had topographical maps and plenty of common sense."

Scully lowered her voice. "I studied the maps myself last night, and I'm not certain our friend Aguilar brought us on the most straightforward path. I think he might have been delaying us for some reason."

"I don't trust him either," Mulder said, "but he seems more like an obnoxious used-car salesman than an outright criminal."

"Remember, this is a rough country, Agent Mulder," Rubicon said. "However, if the Maya helpers had indeed abandoned Cassandra and her friends, it would be only a matter of time before she was forced to take some drastic action. They'd have to find their way back to civilization somehow."

"So Aguilar dropped them off, leaving his Indian helpers here . . . and then the Indians could have abandoned the team," Scully said. "Maybe another ground tremor?"

Rubicon nodded, blinking repeatedly in the bright sunlight. "I hope that's what happened."

"With no more supplies," Scully pointed out, "Cassandra would have had no choice but to fight her way through the jungles."

"But would they all have gone together?" Mulder asked. He ran his fingers along the glyph-carved wall blocks of the ball court. Something small and fast skittered into a shadowy crack. "It would make sense that, say, two of the team members would go to get help while the rest remained here."

"You saw how difficult the jungles were, Mulder," Scully said. "Maybe she thought it was their best bet not to separate."

"It still doesn't sound right," Mulder said.

Rubicon shook his head. His white-blond hair clung to his skull, cemented by perspiration. "For myself, I hope that story is true, because then there's still hope for my little girl."

From not far off in the jungle, they heard a shout of excitement. One of the Indians called over and over. "Let's go," Mulder said, running. "They've found something."

Vladimir Rubicon puffed and wheezed, keeping up with them as they stepped over fallen trees, climbed rocks, splashed through streams. Once Mulder startled a large animal that bounded off into the ferns and shrubs. He couldn't see what it was, but he felt a sudden cold sensation, a lump in his throat. Perhaps he would get a better look at one of those slithering creatures he had half-imagined in the moonlight the night before. Could it be the basis for certain Maya myths, monstrous predators responsible for the numerous disappearances over the years . . . including Cassandra Rubicon's?

Before long, they came upon a small temple barely the size of a tool shed. Though ancient and overgrown, it seemed sturdy enough. Much of the underbrush had been cleared away, the creepers pulled down to expose stone walls, a low-ceilinged interior.

Near the opening, one of the Maya helpers stood looking cowed while Fernando Aguilar snapped at him, his face stormy and livid—but the moment Aguilar saw the approaching Americans, his expression transformed miraculously. He swept off his spotted hat. "Look what we have found, amigos!" he said. "Equipment stored by Señorita Rubicon's team!"

In the temple shadows, a pile of crates huddled under a tarp. Like a matador taunting a bull, Aguilar grabbed the corner of the tarp and yanked it off to reveal the cache of supplies.

"Señorita Rubicon's team must have left these crates here protected from wild animals. Though the other equipment has vanished, these items appear to have been untouched. What a lucky find for us."

"But why would she leave all this here?" Scully said quietly.

"Look, food supplies and the radio transmitter," Aguilar said. "This large box has something else inside it." Aguilar bent down to scrutinize the crate. He gestured for one of the Indians to help him pry open the top.

"Mulder," Scully kept her voice low, "do you know what this means? Cassandra couldn't have gone off in search of supplies. There's enough food here for weeks, and the team could have used the transmitter to call for help any time."

Vladimir Rubicon eagerly bent forward to inspect the large crate, shouldering aside the Indian and using his big-knuckled fingers to pull open the top of the crate while Aguilar stepped back to observe.

Scully watched, surprised to see the contents. "It's an underwater suit and air hoses," she said, puzzled. "Was Cassandra intending to explore the cenote?"

"That makes good archaeological sense," Rubicon said, nodding vigorously. "In those deep wells artifacts are preserved for centuries and centuries. Yes, she would have wanted to go down there, my Cassandra—just like Thompson."

Scully swatted away a stinging fly. "Who was Thompson? I don't recall any member of their team with that name."

Startled from his concentration, Rubicon looked up from the weather-stained crates. "Who? Oh, Thompson— no, I meant Edward Thompson, the last of the great amateur archaeologists here in the Yucatán. He spent years studying the cenote at Chichén Itzá, where he found the single greatest treasure trove of Maya artifacts ever recovered."

Skeptically, Mulder held up the diving suit's limp sleeve of rubberized canvas fabric. "He dove down into a deep sacrificial well like the one out there?" He gestured back toward the main plaza and the tall pyramid.

Rubicon shook his head. "Uh, not at first. He spent years dredging, dropping a cast-iron bucket down to the bottom, scooping up loads of muck, and sifting through it by hand. He recovered bones and cloth and jade, several intact skulls—one of which had been used as a ceremonial censer and still smelled of perfume.

"But after a while, Thompson decided that the clumsy dredge couldn't do as good a job as a diver working hands-on. He had planned for that possibility when he launched his original expedition, buying the equipment, acquiring training. He taught his four Indian helpers how to operate the air pumps, the winches."

Rubicon looked down at the diving suit his daughter had intended to wear, and seemed to suppress a shudder. "When Thompson went under the cenote, the solemn Indians waved goodbye to him, confident they'd never see him again. In his own words, he sank 'like a bag of lead,' thirty feet down into water so dark that even his flashlight couldn't penetrate it. At the bottom he felt around in the mud to find artifacts—coins, jade, sculptures, rubber objects.

"But despite his armored diving suit, Thompson sustained severe ear damage from his dives. The locals looked on him with awe from that point on—he was the only living person ever to have gone into the sacred cenote and survive."

Scully nodded. "And you think your daughter intended to follow in his footsteps, exploring the Xitaclan cenote."

Mulder pawed around the equipment packed into the crates. "Doesn't look like she had a chance to use the suit, though," he said. "The manufacturer's warranty sticker is still on it."

"She was interrupted before she could complete her investigations," Rubicon said.

Mulder saw Fernando Aguilar flash a final angry glance at the Indian, who turned away, his shoulders slumped.

"Yes, but interrupted by what?" Mulder said.

*   *   *

Together, they climbed the steps of the central Pyramid of Kukulkan. Panting in the humid air, they exerted themselves up the steep incline and the narrow and uneven limestone stairs.

"Careful," Mulder said seriously. "It's not very stable."

Rubicon bent to inspect the weathered stairs themselves, pointing out carvings that had been picked clean, the moss removed, the dirt and limestone powder brushed away from the cracks.

"See, Cassandra's team has cleaned the first twelve steps. If I could read these glyphs, we could learn why the Maya built Xitaclan, what made this place such a sacred site." He stood up, pressing a hand against his lower back. "But I'm not an expert in this form. Few people are. Maya glyphs are among the most difficult of all mankind's written languages to decipher. That's why Cassandra brought her own special epigrapher with her team."

"Yes," Scully said, "Christopher Porte."

Rubicon shrugged. "I understand he was quite skilled."

"Let's see what's on the top of the pyramid," Mulder said, and trudged higher up the steep incline.

"Probably an open-air temple," Rubicon answered. "The high priest would stand on the platform and face the rising sun before he made his sacrifices."

At the top, Mulder stopped, placed his hands on his hips, and drew a deep breath as he took in the spectacular view.

The Central American jungle spread out like a flat carpet as far as he could see, trees laden with vines, everything a lush, lush green. Stone temple ruins in the distance poked up through the foliage like giant tombstones.

"The past is strong in this place," Rubicon muttered.

Mulder could imagine the Maya priests feeling godlike, standing so close to heaven under the pounding morning sun. The crowds would have waited in the plaza below, congregating after their labors out in the forest where they slashed and burned to plant crops of maize and beans and peppers. The priest stood here at the top, perhaps with his drugged or bound sacrificial victim, ready to shed blood to honor the gods.

Mulder's runaway imagination was jarred when old Vladimir Rubicon cupped his hands around his mouth and shouted "Cassandra!" into the jungle. His words echoed across the landscape, startling birds from the treetops. "Cassandra!" he bellowed again.

Rubicon looked around, listening, waiting. Mulder and Scully stood next to the archaeologist, holding their breath. The old man had tears in his eyes. "I had to try," he said, shrugging his bony shoulders.

Then, looking embarrassed, Rubicon turned to the tall temple pillars and the flat platform. Mulder saw elaborate stone designs chiseled into the limestone, flecks of paint still visible in the protected crevices and crannies.

The builders of Xitaclan had repeated the feathered serpent motif again and again, creating conflicting impressions of fear and protection, power and subservience. Other drawings showed a tall man, faceless, with some strange body armor or a suit, flames flowing from behind him. A rounded covering on his head that looked unmistakably like a . . .

"Doesn't that figure remind you of something, Scully?" he asked.

She crossed her arms over her chest, then shook her head. "You're not going to connect ancient astronauts with a missing-persons case, are you, Mulder?"

"Just looking at the evidence with my own eyes," he said quietly. "Maybe Cassandra found some information that others wanted to keep hidden."

"That is Kukulkan," Rubicon said, not hearing Mulder as he pointed to other images that showed a strangely shaped ship, coiled designs that may well have been pieces of machinery or equipment. "Very powerful and very wise, he brought knowledge down from the sky. He stole fire from the gods and delivered it to the people."

Mulder looked at Scully, raising his eyebrows. "Just a myth," she said.

Rubicon put his half-glasses on his nose; then, realizing how useless the gesture was, slipped them back off again to let them dangle at his throat. "God of wind, the master of life, Kukulkan brought civilization to the Maya people at the beginning of time. He invented metallurgy. He was the patron of every art."

"A Renaissance kind of guy," Mulder said.

"Kukulkan ruled for many centuries until eventually his enemy Tezcatlipoca drove him out—uh, the guy whose corpse gave off such a smell. Kukulkan had to return to his homeland, so he burned his own houses, which were built of silver and shells, and then set sail to the east on the sea. Kukulkan disappeared, promising he would return to the people one day."

Mulder felt the excitement beating in his heart. "Houses built of silver and shells" could have meant metal and glass; adding all the fire imagery, he pictured a rocket or a spaceship.

"The Maya people were so convinced by their legend," Rubicon continued, shading his eyes to look toward the horizon, "that they stationed sentries to watch the east coast, uh, waiting for Kukulkan. When the Spaniards came in their tall galleons, wearing bright metal breastplates, the Maya were convinced Kukulkan had returned."

"Men in silver suits could easily be confused for spacemen," he said.

"You're welcome to your opinion, Mulder," she said. "I know it's no use trying to talk you out of it. But we've still got a missing archaeology team to find. What do Maya gods and ancient astronauts have to do with our case?"

"Nothing, I'm sure, Scully," Mulder said in a voice that said exactly the opposite. He kept his smile to himself. "Nothing at all."

19

On their way back down the steep stairs on the opposite side of the pyramid, where the steps were more uneven and crumbling, Scully watched as Rubicon pointed out where someone with a clumsy pickaxe and chisel had broken free ornate carvings, alcoves perhaps containing jade artifacts and other valuable objects.

Rubicon, his temper rising, said in disgust, "These artifacts are probably for sale on the black market in Cancún or Mexico City to self-styled pre-Colombian art collectors, or just people who want to own something so no one else may have it. Cassandra may have run into some of these thieves."

"But this area is so isolated," Scully said, following him down the last few steps of the central pyramid. They walked across the flagstoned plaza. "How would the artifacts be distributed? There would have to be some kind of network in place."

"I wouldn't put it past men like him," Rubicon said, gesturing with a sharp elbow toward Fernando Victorio Aguilar, who bustled up to them, tossing aside the remains of another hand-rolled cigarette.

"Did you find anything up there, amigos?" he said, pandering.

A deeply offended anger burned behind Rubicon's blue eyes. "We'll complete our initial inspection of the area today, but if we haven't uncovered any sign of them by tomorrow morning, we should use Cassandra's transmitter and contact the Mexican officials, request immediate assistance. They can send their own inspectors and security forces. National forces, not locals—the locals are probably in on any black-market trade." He scowled. "Many artifacts have already been illegally removed."

Aguilar looked at him, his expression a combination of miffed annoyance and wounded pride. "What you see could have been caused by treasure seekers from long ago, Señor Rubicon. Xitaclan has been unprotected for a long, long time."

Rubicon glared at him. "Mr. Aguilar, anyone with eyes can see the fresh scars. I know these items have been removed very recently, uh, within months, probably weeks."

Aguilar crossed his tanned arms over his chest, pursing his lips. "Then perhaps your daughter's archaeology team removed the most valuable pieces for their own profit, eh? They work for museums back in America, do they not?"

Rubicon leaned closer to Aguilar, thrusting his lower lip out so that his yellow-gray goatee bristled. "My Cassandra and all of her team members would never do such a thing," he said. "They know the value of historical artifacts, especially artifacts that must remain in place for further study."

"I sense that you do not trust me, Señor Rubicon," Aguilar said, tugging on his hat. His voice held a conciliatory tone. "But we must work together, eh? We are isolated here at Xitaclan. We must make the best of it and not become enemies. It could be dangerous if we fail to work as a team."

Scully headed back to their campsite as the discussion between Rubicon and the long-haired Mexican guide became more heated. She removed her pack and dropped it beside the tent. Though it was broad daylight, the entire crew of Maya helpers had once again vanished into the jungles, nowhere to be seen. It made her feel strangely uneasy.

Scully stopped by the nearer of the two tall stelae, elaborately carved with feathered serpents. She examined the eroded carving in the bright daylight, noticing a change in the dull weathered limestone—bright red splattered the carvings, dollops of thick crimson like paint that dripped from the fangs of one of the largest feathered serpents. She leaned forward, curious and revolted at the same time.

Someone had rubbed blood inside the stone mouth of the feathered serpent, as if giving the carving a taste . . . a fresh sacrifice. She followed the trail of blood droplets down the tall pillar to the buckled flagstones at its base.

"Mulder!" she cried.

Her partner came running with an alarmed expression on his face. Rubicon and Aguilar stood frozen, their faces flushed from their argument, looking to see what had interrupted them.

Scully indicated the bright red streaks on the stela . . . and then gestured to the severed human finger that lay in a pool of congealing blood on the flagstone.

Mulder bent down to look at the amputated finger. The expression of disgust flickered for only an instant on his placid face.

Aguilar and Rubicon finally came up and stared down without words at the blood, the severed digit.

"It looks fresh," Scully said. "No more than an hour or so."

Mulder touched the tacky blood. "Just barely starting to dry. It must have happened while we were up on the pyramid. I didn't hear any screams, though. Aguilar, you were down here."

"No, I was out in the jungle." He shook his head in dismay and took off his ocelot-skin hat, as if in reverence for a dead friend. "I was afraid of this, very afraid." He lowered his voice, looking around furtively. He narrowed his eyes, as if concerned the Indians might be watching from the fringes of the jungle, spying on their potential victims. "Yes, very afraid."

Aguilar walked around the stela, as if searching for other evidence. "The Maya religion is very ancient. Their rituals were celebrated for a thousand years before white explorers ever came to our shores, and they became much more violent when they mixed with the Toltec. People don't forget their beliefs so easily, eh?"

"Wait a minute," Scully said. "Are you saying that some of the Maya descendants still practice the old religion? Cutting out hearts and throwing people into sacrificial wells?"

Scully felt a sense of dread as she began to piece together a scenario that even Mulder would believe— how Cassandra Rubicon and her team had become victims in a bloodthirsty sacrificial ritual.

Rubicon said, "Well, some of the people still remember the ancient Toltec chants and observe the festivals, though most have been Christianized . . . or at least civilized. Some few, though, continue to practice the bloodwork and self-mutilation. Especially out here, away from the cities."

"Self-mutilation?" Mulder said. "You mean one of those Indians cut off his own finger?"

Rubicon nodded, touching the pattern of blood on the limestone pillar. "Probably with an obsidian knife."

Scully tried to imagine the religious fervor required to take a splintered stone knife and hack away a finger, sawing through sinew and bone without making so much as a cry of pain.

Rubicon seemed more detached, as if the possibility of his daughter and her companions becoming a blood sacrifice had not yet occurred to him.

"The Maya and Toltec rituals shed a great deal of blood, both their own and that of prisoners and victims. At the holiest of festivals, the high king would take a stingray spine and reach under his loincloth to pierce his own foreskin."

Scully saw Mulder swallow hard. "Ouch."

"Blood is a very powerful force," Aguilar agreed.

"The blood that flowed out dribbled across long strips of mulberry-bark paper, tracing patterns of red droplets. Some of the priests could divine the future from these patterns." Rubicon looked up at the sky. "Afterward, the strips of blood-spattered paper were rolled up and burned so that the sacred smoke could send messages to the gods."

Scully looked grimly at the fresh blood. "If one of those Indians just chopped off his finger with a stone knife," she said, "he requires medical attention. With this kind of crude amputation, the man could easily get gangrene, especially in a tropical climate such as this."

Aguilar found a bent and mangled cigarette in his pocket and tugged it out, sticking it between his lips without lighting it. "You will not find him, Señorita, never," he said. "The man would have run away, far from Xitaclan. He has made his sacrifice to the guardians of Kukulkan—but now that we know his true religion, we will not see him again. The Maya people here have a long memory. They are still deathly afraid of the white man and persecution. They remember one of the first white governors here, a man named Father Diego de Landa. A butcher."

Rubicon grunted in agreement, his face showing an expression of distaste. "He was a Franciscan friar, and under his guidance temples were torn down, shrines smashed. Anyone caught worshipping an idol was whipped, their joints stretched with pulleys, boiling water poured on their skin.

Aguilar nodded eagerly, as if glad to have the old archaeologist back on his side again. "Sí, Father de Landa found Indians who could still read old writings, and he attempted to translate the heiroglyphics. But to him it was all against the Christian Word of God, eh? Cursed. When they showed him a cache of thirty books bound in jaguar skin, many filled with serpent drawings, he decided they contained with falsehoods of the devil. So he burned them all."

Rubicon looked pained just to hear of the loss. "De Landa tortured five thousand Maya, killing nearly two hundred of them before he was summoned back to Spain for his excesses. While he awaited trial, he composed a long treatise detailing everything he had learned."

"And was he convicted for his appalling behavior?" Scully asked.

Aguilar raised his eyebrows and barked a laugh. "No, Señorita! He was sent back to the Yucatán—as a bishop this time!"

Rubicon looked contemplative as he knelt in front of the bloodstained stela. Scully bent over to pick up the severed finger. It still felt faintly warm and rubbery. The thickened blood at the end did not drip off. She saw the ragged stump, where the stone knife had hacked through the flesh and bone.

If some of these people still practiced their violent religion, she wondered what other . . . sacrifices they might have made.

20

X The jungle was the enemy, an obstacle, an object to be defeated—and Major Willis Jakes had no doubt that his hand-picked squadron would succeed in conquering it. That was their mission, and that was what they would do.

The ten members of his covert infiltration squad wore jungle camouflage uniforms and night-vision goggles. After being landed in secret on an uninhabited shore at the northern border of Belize, they had struck off overland through the jungles in a pair of all-terrain vehicles.

The most difficult part had been immediately upon landing, dumped off at the edge of the bay, Bahía Chetumal, crossing a few night-deserted roads and the bridge over the narrow Laguna de Bacalor, and then plunging into the trackless Quintana Roo wilderness.

Negotiating a path through the rain forest, they followed a digitized map, choosing a course that avoided even meagerly inhabited areas as they made a beeline for their destination. Much of the area showed no sign of human settlement, no roads or villages whatsoever . . . just the way the major preferred it.

Jakes's team had to maintain a good pace to put them well past all roads and the populated coastal areas before daybreak. They could not afford to rest but had to proceed, always bearing in mind that they must reach their target—the source of the high-power encrypted signal—sometime during the following night. Under cover of darkness, they hoped to accomplish their mission. Before they could go home, the secret military base must be completely destroyed.

Their narrow-bodied all-terrain vehicles chewed up the offending tangles of foliage, crushing an obvious path through the forest . . . but in a place where no one would ever look. Even if anyone spotted Major Jakes's team, the commandos would be long gone before any organized response could find them. The heavily inflated, armored wheels of the ATV trampled the undergrowth, each axle pivoting on its own gimbal to allow the utmost flexibility in negotiating the terrain.

Half of Jakes's team rode in the vehicles, while the other half strode briskly behind, keeping up the pace across the newly cleared path. Every hour, they would switch, so that the first group of riders walked and the hikers rode. He had learned through experience that this was the most efficient way to bring his team overland under cover, without requiring bureaucratic permission or right of clearance from any foreign government. This covert operation did not officially exist . . . any more than did the secret weapons cache or the undocumented military base deep in the Yucatán jungles.

Major Jakes didn't worry about the implications of such things. His orders were straightforward . . . not simple by any means, but at least clear-cut. He didn't ask questions unless they pertained to the mission, and his team members asked for even fewer details than he did. They knew better.

Intensified by the night-vision goggles in front of his eyes, greenish residual light made the landscape look alien and surreal. Major Jakes knew how to handle it. He and his team had infiltrated and destroyed many

other illegal installations that technically did not exist.
Certainly, they existed no longer.

He rode in the lead all-terrain vehicle. Beside him
his driver, a first lieutenant, moved along at the best
speed he could manage. The driver shone a bright mercury spotlight in front of them, always keeping his eyes
open for insurmountable obstacles. So far, they had
managed to minimize their backtracking and continue
on a very satisfying forward pace.

Get it right the first time, his father had always said—
and young Willis Jakes had learned to follow that credo.
He could think of few things worse than being forced to
repeat a chore, or homework, while his father paced in
the background, a stern taskmaster and absolutely unfor-
giving.

"The world is never forgiving," he had told his son.
"Best you learn that early in life." Jakes had spent hours
upon hours standing motionless against a wall, contemplating his grades or his test scores. He had learned how
to focus utterly on a goal . . . how to get it right the first
time.

The spotlight gleamed across the leaves of the jungle,
which swayed in unfelt breezes as if the forest itself were
alive. Suddenly Jakes saw two piercingly bright coins, the
eyes of a predator, above head level in the trees.

The first lieutenant swept the spotlight up to catch
the movement, and a sleek spotted cat bounded away
from one branch to another. Jakes knew that his other
nine soldiers had automatically flinched for their
weapons, prepared to shoot the large cat. But the jaguar
showed no stomach for fighting and fled into the darkness.

They rode in silence, rocking and bucking, the vehicle
lurching over fallen trees and rocks, yet maintaining its
balance. Major Jakes and the other riders struggled to
keep hold of their seats. His ribs ached, and his stomach
gurgled. He didn't find the rough ride more comfortable
than walking, but it did allow some muscles to rest while
taxing others.

On one mission in southern Bosnia, he had added a new member to his team, a radio operator who seemed to consider it part of his job as a communications specialist to *talk* all the time. Jakes and his team preferred the silence, focusing their efforts on attuning all reflexes and all senses to maximum performance—but the new communications specialist wanted to chat about his family, about his high school, about books he had read, about the weather.

Major Jakes knew the young man wouldn't work out from the beginning. He had already decided to request a replacement, but the new radio operator had been shot by sniper fire while retreating from a microwave-relay substation the commando team had just destroyed.

The mission itself had never been mentioned in any newspaper or on any TV network. As far as the boy's parents knew, he had died in a freak training accident in Alabama, during specialized exercises. Luckily, the boy's parents had been members of the "Stars and Stripes, God, and Apple Pie" party and had never even considered asking for an investigation or bringing a wrongful-death lawsuit that would have required even more complicated coverups. . . .

Now, journeying into the jungles, the other members rode in silence, as usual, contemplating the Xitaclan mission, going over the details step by step. They were *professionals*, and Jakes knew he could count on them.

Behind him, the explosives expert grunted and sighed as he pressed his hands together in an endless ritual of isometric exercises to keep himself in shape. Major Jakes did not question his actions, because the man had always performed impeccably.

Jakes checked his watch, then called for a brief halt. "Time to switch crews," he said. "But first let's triangulate on the signal and verify its position."

In the front of the second all-terrain vehicle, the new communications officer flipped up a flatscreen grid. He extended antennas from the sides of the ATV and adjusted frequencies until he picked up the pulsing message that even the Pentagon's best decryption experts found incomprehensible.

The signal pulsed loud and clear, like a subsonic jackhammer broadcast in all directions far and wide. Major Jakes couldn't comprehend who might be its intended listener, or who had sent it. It sounded like a foghorn, a warning ... perhaps even an SOS. But what could that mean? So far, no one had bothered to reply to it.

"We are on course, Major," the communications specialist said. "The signal is loud and strong, and its position has not changed. According to my estimate on this topo map, we've already passed fifteen kilometers beyond Mexico Highway 307."

"Good," Major Jakes said, "we're ahead of schedule then. That should give us a leg up on dawn." He climbed down and stretched his legs, brushing his camouflage pants. "All aboard, Crew Two."

The second shift came aboard while he, the first lieutenant, and the other three men went to follow the two vehicles. The new drivers started up immediately and forged ahead.

Major Jakes trudged along, securing his rifle across his shoulder, holding it ready to be used in an instant. No hesitation. No contemplation. He and his team were the Good Guys, and they had been given orders to take out the Bad Guys. No sweat, no regrets.

He didn't know if the stakes were high enough that his actions might save the world ... but someday that could well happen. Major Jakes treated every mission as if it could be The One.

He thought of all the James Bond movies he had seen, the banal secret agent adventures that were so preposterous and yet so uninteresting compared to his own missions. Each one of those movies featured a megalomaniacal mad genius bent on world domination; each one included a bizarre, high-tech fortress isolated in the wilderness.

As Jakes and his team tunneled deeper into the Yucatán forest, homing in on the ominous signal, he pondered what sort of crazed genius might have selected the vast Central American jungles to hide his stronghold. Why would anyone choose to erect a super-secret base in an ancient Maya ruin?

No matter. His team would destroy Xitaclan—and any people they found there—then they would return home. Major Jakes did not think beyond that.

They marched mile after mile, deeper into the jungles. With every step the source of the mysterious signal grew louder.

21

Xitaclan ruins
Tuesday, 7:04 A.M.

After another sweaty night filled with biting insects and unexplainable noises, Scully woke up and lay on her bedroll, trying to decide whether to rest for a few more minutes, or to get up and face the day.

In the light that filtered through her tent, Scully inspected the day's assortment of itching red insect bites, swellings, and skin rashes. From her small kit, she took out a tube of cream and rubbed a dab on the worst spots, then crawled to the flap and thrust her head into the hazy morning light.

The camp was quiet and brooding, as if holding its breath. Inside its ring of stones, the campfire had burned down to cold, gray-white ash. She stood up, hearing Mulder rustle inside his tent, but she stopped short when she turned to Vladimir Rubicon's tent.

It had collapsed in the night, fallen in on itself . . . as if some giant beast had stomped it flat.

Uneasy, she looked around, shading her eyes from the morning's slanted glare. The hazy mist added a soft focus to everything, feathering the air. She saw no sign of the old archaeologist, nor of Fernando Victorio Aguilar, nor any of their Indian helpers.

She called out, "Hello, Dr. Rubicon?" She waited for an answer, then shouted his name again.

Mulder climbed out of his tent, stretching.

"Dr. Rubicon seems to be gone," Scully said. "Look, something's happened to his tent. Did you hear anything last night?"

Mulder immediately grew concerned. "Maybe he's just off looking for his daughter. Getting a head start."

Scully cupped her hands around her mouth and shouted again. "Dr. Rubicon!"

Out in the jungle birds squawked, angry at the disturbance. Scully and Mulder heard crackling branches at the edge of the trees. They both turned uneasily, waiting to see what might emerge from the swaying ferns.

Fernando Aguilar led a group of his Indian helpers. They all grinned, immensely pleased with themselves. Between them they carried a dead jaguar trussed on a branch pole, as if they had walked out of an old cartoon about big game hunters.

"See what we have caught!" Aguilar said. "This beast was prowling around the campsite last night, but our friends shot it with their arrows. Jaguar pelts are very valuable." Aguilar raised his eyebrows. "It's a good thing he wasn't hungry enough to come looking for us, eh?"

"Well, maybe he was," Mulder said. "We can't find Dr. Rubicon." He indicated the collapsed tent.

"Are you certain he isn't just out exploring?" Aguilar said. "I have been with my friends here since sunup."

"Dr. Rubicon could be looking around some of the other structures we missed yesterday," Scully admitted, "but he doesn't answer my calls."

"Then we must look for him, Señorita," Aguilar said. "But I'm sure he is all right. We already killed the jaguar, eh?"

The locals held up their pole triumphantly. The spotted cat lolled, bloody from dozens of small arrow wounds.

Aguilar kept his attention focused on the dead jaguar. "We'll be busy dressing and skinning this cat," he said. "You go ahead and search for Dr. Rubicon."

"Let's go, Mulder," Scully said.

Mulder nodded seriously. "Can't blame the good doctor for not wanting to waste a moment. Let's split up," he said. "Do a broad, rapid sweep until we find him. I'll go inside the big pyramid. I know Dr. Rubicon wanted to poke around in there."

"Agreed. I'll climb to the top temple and have a look around again. Maybe I can spot him from up there."

Behind them, in front of the pair of feathered serpent stelae—Scully wondered if the jaguar hunters had chosen that spot for some religious purpose—the locals took out black obsidian knives, while Aguilar removed a wicked-looking hunting blade. Together, they bent over and set to work flaying the dead cat.

Scully climbed the steep hieroglyphic staircase at the side of the pyramid. Her arms and legs ached from the physical activity of the last few days, but she ascended the crumbling narrow steps one at a time, leaning forward and using her hands for support, as if scaling a cliff. She tried to imagine how the heavily robed priests could have been graceful as they ascended to the upper temple to perform their ancient rituals.

People would have gathered around the base of the plaza chanting, beating on tortoise-shell drums with deer antlers, wearing colorful finery decked with feathers of tropical birds, carved jade ornaments. When she reached the temple pillars at the top of the ziggurat, Scully saw where royal spectators could watch and perhaps share in the bloodletting. Due to the steepness of the pyramid, the details of the sacrifices would not have been visible to the general audience below—only the blood, the raised hands, the murder. . . .

She shook her head to clear the vision, remembering what Dr. Rubicon had muttered as he stared in awe around the Xitaclan site. *The past is strong in this place.*

Scully shaded her eyes and looked around. "Dr. Rubicon!" she shouted. Her voice rang out like an ancient priest's chant, summoning the gods. She looked at the bas-reliefs around her, the stylized images of the god

Kukulkan, designs and incomprehensible diagrams that Mulder insisted were blueprints of ancient spacecraft.

"Dr. Rubicon!" she repeated, still scanning the surrounding jungle. Below in the courtyard she saw a splash of red as the Indians and Aguilar skinned the jaguar. Three of the wiry men carried the raw and dripping carcass into the jungle. She wondered if they intended to eat the meat.

With a shudder Scully thought of the mysterious Indian who, in his superstitious fervor, had hacked off a finger with one of his obsidian knives—and another image came to the forefront of her mind unbidden: some of these natives in a jungle thicket hacking out the raw red heart of the spotted cat and sharing it among themselves, eating the bloody flesh of their great jungle spirit.

She shook her head. She felt very alone and exposed, vulnerable atop the tall pyramid.

Giving up on finding any sign of the lone old man snooping in the jungles, Scully turned, looking closer to the great pyramid. She squinted, unwilling to call out again, remembering the old archaeologist's own shout for his daughter as he waited and watched for her in vain. Cassandra Rubicon hadn't responded to the call either.

Scully was about to give up when she went to the edge and looked down, away from the plaza. Then she caught her breath.

Mulder poked his head inside the dank opening of the pyramid, peering into the shadows. He noted prybar marks where Cassandra Rubicon and her helpers had broken open the ancient edifice. No doubt they had been careful, but smashing through sealed stone blocks required a certain amount of brute force.

He switched on his flashlight, and the brilliant beam stabbed into the unknown like a javelin, penetrating the mysterious blackness in the labyrinth built by Maya slaves. The flashlight comforted him, heavy in his hand. He was glad he had changed the batteries not long ago.

Though the tall pyramid had lasted for well over a thousand years, the interior did not appear sturdy enough to reassure Mulder—especially after the tremors their first night at Xitaclan. The hand-chiseled limestone blocks had begun to crumble at the edges, surfaces flaked by ravenous lichens and mosses.

His footsteps echoed on the stone floor. He shone the flashlight down, looking at the dust and powder to see scuffed footprints—Mulder couldn't tell if the shoeprints matched any member of Cassandra's team, or black-market grave robbers, or if they had been left by the old archaeologist just that morning.

"Hello, Dr. Rubicon—are you in there?" Mulder said, flaring his flashlight in different directions. His words reflected back at him with a resonating quality, a bell-like sharpness.

Mulder proceeded deeper into the pyramid, casting a glance over his shoulder to see the dwindling daylight from the opening. He wished he had brought bread crumbs to leave a trail . . . or at least sunflower seeds.

Water dripped from somewhere. Out of the corner of his eye he thought he saw movement—but when he flashed his light in that direction and saw the sharp shadows jumping, he knew it had only been an optical illusion. The darkness and the leaden air felt oppressive.

Thankful he wasn't claustrophobic, he rubbed the back of his hand along the tip of his nose. The temperature had dropped, as if some force gradually drank all the heat from the air. It had been at least a dozen centuries since the interior of this temple had been open to the sunshine. Playing his flashlight ahead, he saw that the ceiling had been supported by wooden beams, rough-hewn tree trunks recently placed there, no doubt by Cassandra's assistants. She must have been desperate to explore inside, he thought, excavating deeper and deeper into the pyramid, trying to unlock its secrets.

"Hey, Dr. Rubicon," he said again, in a normal voice this time, afraid of the machine-gun echoes.

He looked down at his feet, at the dusty floor,

untraveled—but then he saw a pair of footprints made by smaller shoes, definitely not old Dr. Rubicon's, apparently a woman's. Excitement beat in his heart. Cassandra had been here!

He proceeded cautiously now, intrigued on several different levels. His spatial perception suggested that he was approaching the heart of the pyramid. He was winding deeper, perhaps even underground.

The inner walls looked different now, unlike the corridors he had just passed through, which were made of simple blocks hewn from limestone. Those on his left were dark and unusually slick and smooth, as if they had been partially melted. This wall composition implied something new and unusual—of a different nature than the rest of the ancient structure.

Touching the slick glassy surface, he walked on. Up ahead, fallen rubble blocked off the corridor, a partially collapsed ceiling that sealed the passage leading directly into the pyramid's center. Mulder stopped short, thinking he had taken a wrong turn. Neither Vladimir nor Cassandra Rubicon could have proceeded any farther than this—but then he saw an opening dug through the fallen rock, a narrow window that only a very slender or very desperate person might wriggle through.

He crept to the edge, feeling as if he were intruding upon something. The temple around him swallowed all sound and heat. Mulder's light stabbed into the shadowy opening.

He raised himself up on the pile of rubble, pushing the flashlight ahead of him to look in. "Cassandra Rubicon?" he called, feeling foolish. "Are you in there?"

He was amazed at what he saw in the hidden chamber. His light played across smooth walls, reflected metal, curved objects made of glass or crystal. The eeriness and completely unexpected condition of the inner chamber made him pause with a thrill of discovery.

What had Cassandra thought when she first spotted this surprising change in architecture?

As visions of Kukulkan danced in his head, Mulder

tried to peer deeper, but his flashlight began to flicker. He rattled it to keep the batteries in contact, the beam steady.

He would return to this spot and explore, as soon as they found Dr. Rubicon, Mulder thought. Maybe the old archaeologist could provide an explanation. It would take some work, though, to clear away an opening large enough for someone to get inside without tearing his clothes or losing some skin.

Mulder heard a distant voice, and froze. The words bounced through the winding passages of the temple. He didn't have time to marvel at the acoustics as he recognized the faint sounds of Scully calling his name.

Her voice carried an urgency that made him snap into action, sliding back down from the rockfall and racing along the passages, taking the turns from memory. He shone his flashlight ahead of him—the batteries seemed to be working fine, now that he had moved away from the heart of the pyramid.

She called again and again. He heard the strain in her voice, and he raced faster. "Mulder, I found him! Mulder!" Her words rang between the stone walls, and finally he saw the light ahead, Scully standing at the opening, a humanoid silhouette surrounded by glare.

He burst out into the daylight, panting, his heart pounding.

She looked devastated. "Over here," she said.

He was breathing too hard to ask her questions, but simply followed. She hurried around the base of the pyramid, through the narrow jungle path. They reached the fallen-brick platform where sacrifices had once been performed at the edge of the deep circular well.

Mulder stopped short and looked down at the murky, unfathomably deep water. Scully stood next to him, swallowing hard, saying nothing.

There, like a doll that had been twisted and broken and then cast aside, floated the body of Vladimir Rubicon, facedown in the sacrificial cenote.

22

Xitaclan ruins
Tuesday, 11:14 A.M.

They anchored ropes to sturdy trees near the rim of the cenote, then dropped the cables down into the water. Everyone stood brooding, like spectators at the scene of a car accident, stunned by the discovery of the old man's body.

Fernando Aguilar offered the assistance of the Indian workers, suggesting that some of the wiry and muscular locals could easily scramble down the rope and retrieve Vladimir Rubicon. But Mulder refused. This was something he had to do himself.

Without a word, Scully helped to lash a rope harness under his arms and around his shoulders; she tugged the knots, checking that they were secure. Gripping the rope, Mulder eased himself over the rim and started down the rough side of the limestone sinkhole. Surrounding ledges made the wall itself lumpy and rugged, as if it had been chewed out of the rock with a giant drill bit. Mulder drifted away from the ledges and dangled as the Indians lowered him.

On the rim above, Fernando Aguilar stood close to Scully, bellowing instructions, berating the Indians when they did not move exactly as he said, though the helpers seemed to know what they were doing and paid no attention to Aguilar's specific commands.

Upon hearing the news of the archaeologist's death, the long-haired guide and expediter had reacted with shock and horror. "The old man must have wandered out in the middle of the night," Aguilar said. "The edge is abrupt here—he must have fallen in—and it is a long drop. I am sorry for his misfortune."

Mulder and Scully had looked knowingly at each other, but neither chose to challenge their guide's interpretation, at least not openly . . . at least not yet.

Mulder reached the level of the placid water. He could smell the dankness, the sour algae and a taint of trapped vapors from the abortive volcanic outburst the first night they had arrived at Xitaclan. His feet dangled below, just touching the water.

Immediately beneath him floated Vladimir Rubicon, his drenched shirt clinging to his bony back, his shoulder blades protruding. The old man's blond-gray head was twisted at an odd angle, his neck obviously broken—but had it been broken by the fall itself, or from a direct physical assault? Rubicon's arms and legs dangled unseen in the deep dark water.

Mulder gritted his teeth and held his breath as the Indians dropped him the last few feet. He plunged into the water, getting completely soaked. The rope harness held up most of his weight, and he managed to swim. He stroked with his hands and feet, pulling himself over to Rubicon's drifting body. The second rope tugged at him as he stretched it.

"Be careful, Mulder," Scully called, and he wondered what she might be warning him about.

"That's foremost on my mind," he said. The water felt thick, almost gelatinous, warm with the jungle heat, and yet tingling against his skin. He hoped the sacrificial pool wasn't infested with leeches, or some worse form of tropical life.

He looked down to where the water swallowed up

his feet and his lower body. He could see nothing. Mulder couldn't tell what might lurk in the depths of the cenote beyond the range of sunlight. He thought of old Lovecraftian stories where ancient monsters from beyond time and space—feathered serpents, perhaps?—swam in the dark ooze, waiting to devour unwary innocents.

He thought he felt a ripple below his feet, and he jerked his leg away. Rubicon's body bobbed in the water, jiggling from some unseen disturbance. Mulder swallowed hard, looking down, but still he saw nothing.

"Just my imagination," he muttered to himself, knowing he did have a very good imagination.

He disengaged the second rope from around his chest and tugged for more slack. Above, the Indians obliged. Aguilar waved at him in encouragement.

Mulder draped the loose rope over his shoulder, wet and slick. Touching the old man's waterlogged shirt, he pulled Rubicon's limp body toward him in the water, then worked the end of the rope around the bony chest. He felt as if he were embracing the archaeologist.

"Goodbye, Vladimir Rubicon," he said, securing the knot. "Now at least your search can stop." He tugged on the rope, then shouted up, "Okay, pull him out!" His voice bounced around the wall of the sinkhole.

The ropes tightened as the Indians worked and heaved up above. Even Aguilar pitched in. The ropes strained, tugging Rubicon's body free of the water as if the cenote only reluctantly gave up its new prize— leaving Mulder alone in the water. He hoped that whatever gods still lived in Xitaclan didn't want to make it an even trade, Rubicon's body for his.

The old archaeologist rose up like a soggy scarecrow. Water trickled off his arms and legs. His blunt, big-knuckled fingers hung clenched like claws, and his head lolled to one side. His goatee was scraggly, wet, and clumped with green algae from the surface of the deep well.

Mulder swallowed and waited, treading water in the cenote as the wet corpse was hauled up to the rim of the well like a load of loose construction material. The helpers seemed decidedly uneasy to be so near the dead man.

Mulder watched them swing the body over the lip of the limestone well, then drag it onto the dry ground. Scully helped, leaving Mulder alone for a moment.

The water around him seemed cold, like cadaverous hands feeling his arms and legs, tugging on his wet clothes. Mulder decided not to wait any longer and swam to the steep limestone inner wall, beginning to ascend the corkscrew ledges without any assistance at all.

He had made it halfway up before Aguilar and the Indians got around to taking up the slack on the rope and helping him the rest of the way to the top.

Dripping wet and cold even in the Central American heat, Mulder finally looked back down from the rim of the cenote, staring into the dark water. The sacrificial well seemed undisturbed, placid, infinitely deep . . . and still hungry.

Back in the plaza by the remains of their camp, Mulder raised his voice, trying to get through to Fernando Aguilar and losing patience. "No more excuses, Aguilar! I want to get that radio transmitter up and running now. We know where it is, so stop stalling. Dr. Rubicon intended to send a message this morning, and now it's even more urgent."

Aguilar finally conceded and smiled at him, backing away. "Of course, Señor Mulder, that is a very good idea. In light of this tragedy, we cannot handle the situation alone, eh? It is good that we give up our search for Señorita Rubicon and her team. Yes, I will go get the transmitter."

Looking relieved to get away from Mulder, Aguilar sped off to the old cache of the UC–San Diego team's equipment, which had been untouched since its discovery the day before.

Mulder didn't tell him, though, that he had no intention of abandoning his efforts to find Cassandra.

Scully had laid out the body of Dr. Rubicon on the flagstones and began checking him over, trying to glean scraps of information from the condition of the cadaver. "I'm not going to need an autopsy bay to determine what killed him, Mulder," she said.

She ran her hands over the old man's neck, feeling his large Adam's apple, then she unbuttoned his shirt to check his clammy chest, his rubbery arms.

The others had fled, not wanting to be around the corpse while she worked with it. For the moment, Mulder didn't mind the solitude. The jungle isolation and their untrustworthy companions were making him more and more uneasy.

Scully pushed down on Rubicon's chest, feeling his rib cage, cocking her head to listen as she expelled air from his dead lungs. She looked up at Mulder, her eyes wide and concerned. "Well, he didn't drown—that much is for certain."

Mulder looked hard at her. She felt delicately around Rubicon's neck. "Several of his vertebrae are broken."

She rolled him over, exposing a livid spot at the base of his neck, turned purplish from the skin's immersion in the cold water. "I'm also convinced this injury wasn't caused by a simple fall," she said. "Dr. Rubicon didn't trip over the edge and drop into the water. I think Aguilar wants us to believe he died by accident—but the evidence shows Rubicon was struck hard from behind. Something crushed his neck. My guess is that Dr. Rubicon was dead before he was thrown into the cenote."

"Aguilar didn't want him to make his transmission this morning," Mulder pointed out. "Maybe that argument yesterday was more serious than I thought. What's he hiding?"

Scully said, "Don't forget that Aguilar led Cassandra Rubicon's team to this site in the first place—and now they're all missing. I think we have to presume them dead."

"Do you believe he intends to kill us?" Mulder realized that was an absolutely serious question, no paranoid fantasy at all. "He holds all the advantages here."

"We've still got our handguns, if it comes to that."
Her shoulders slumped. "Look, Aguilar knows we're federal agents. He knows how the United States comes charging in if something happens to their own agents—remember when those DEA undercover officers were murdered here in Mexico? I don't think he'd be foolish enough to bring that upon himself. He can still write off Rubicon's death as an accident, unless we prove otherwise—but he couldn't explain away all of our deaths as accidental."

Mulder looked furtively around the plaza, seeing Aguilar and his ever-present Indian companions finally marching back out of the jungle. They carried a crate of equipment with them. The expression on Aguilar's face did not give Mulder a warm fuzzy feeling.

"Aguilar might realize the consequences," Mulder said, "but what if it's not him after all? What if these locals themselves are making sacrifices, like our friend Lefty who cut off his finger yesterday?"

Scully looked grim. "In that case, I can believe they wouldn't be overly concerned about U.S. government intervention."

Fernando Aguilar hurried up to them while the Indians hung back, afraid of Rubicon's body spread-eagled on the flagstones. "Señor Mulder," he said, "I have bad news. The transmitter is broken."

Mulder said, "How could it be broken? We just took it out of the box yesterday."

Aguilar shrugged, taking off his spotted hat. "The weather, the rain, the conditions here . . ." He held out the transmitter, and Mulder noticed that the back plate was loose, bent out of its groove. The inner workings were muddy and corroded.

"Water has gotten in, or insects," Aguilar said. "Who can tell, eh? The transmitter has been in that old temple, unattended ever since the first team got to Xitaclan. We are unable to contact outside help."

"That's a tragedy," Mulder said, then muttered, "and also quite convenient."

Scully shot him a look, and he knew that the two of them would have to play their cards carefully. If he stretched his imagination to the limits of credibility, he could believe in the accidental destruction of the transmitter, or he could believe in the accidental death of Rubicon, or in the accidental disappearance of Cassandra and the other archaeologists.

But he couldn't take it all together.

Scully said with forced brightness, "We'll just have to make the best of it, then, won't we, Mulder?"

He knew that she, too, felt trapped in the wilderness, with no contact from the outside . . . and the only people around them a potentially murderous crew who had no qualms about eliminating any inconveniences they might encounter.

23

Scully felt the weight of the rubberized canvas diving suit on her shoulders, a heavy alien skin that muffled her movements and insulated her body. Here out on dry land, stumbling across the weathered promenade toward the sacrificial well, the suit felt incredibly unwieldy and clumsy. The weights at her waist clanked together. She hoped that once she descended into the water, the suit would become an advantage instead of a hindrance.

Mulder stood back and looked at her, his hands on his hips, eyebrows raised. "That's quite a fashion statement, Scully."

She tugged at the thick fabric folds, adjusting the diving suit as she stood on the edge of the cenote. She felt an eerie sense of displacement. The suit had been purchased for Cassandra Rubicon to use during her own searches for ancient artifacts and the answers to Maya mysteries.

Now Scully was the only one who could fit into the suit—and her personal search was for something much more sinister, something much more recent.

After finding the body of Vladimir Rubicon, her dread had grown. She had little doubt that the five members of the UC–San Diego research team floated below the surface of the sacrificial well, waterlogged, decaying. If she did indeed find the archaeologist's daughter, beaten like her father, her only consolation was that Dr. Rubicon himself would not be around to witness the grim conclusion to their investigation.

Mulder held the heavy insulated helmet in his hands. "And now to complete the ensemble," he said, "your lovely hat."

Even fresh out of the crate, it seemed an old suit, bargain basement. Scully hoped the equipment had been checked out and proven functional. Like many research expeditions, the UC–San Diego team had operated on a tight budget, forced to cut corners wherever they could. According to paperwork tacked inside the crate, translated by Fernando Aguilar, the suit had been donated by the Mexican government as part of its joint financing of the Xitaclan expedition.

As Scully lowered the heavy helmet over her reddish-gold hair, Mulder's expression became serious. "Are you ready for this, Scully?"

"It's part of the job, Mulder," she said. "This is our case, and somebody has to go down and look." She lowered her voice. "Just keep your weapon handy. You'll be alone up here on the rim, and I'll be alone down there. Not a strategically advantageous situation."

Mulder had kept his 9-mm Sig Sauer close at his side ever since discovering the old archaeologist's "accidental death"—but the Indians far outnumbered them, and they had shown no qualms about getting hurt, if they intended to make another blood sacrifice.

Even if Mulder and Scully encountered no violence, they remained at the mercy of Fernando Aguilar to get them back out of this jungle.

Not a strategically advantageous situation, she thought again.

Scully secured the heavy diving helmet, locking it to the collar attachment rings. Inside, her breath echoed like a breeze through a cave. She swallowed heavily.

Mulder helped her check the air connections on the back of her suit, long rubber-wrapped tubes like garden hoses that dangled from her back. A small generator would pump and circulate air into her helmet, though it looked barely large enough to power a portable hair dryer.

Aguilar and the Indians stood around the equipment, watching her with a curiosity mixed with anxiety. Scully glanced at them uneasily, but saw no one with missing fingers or a bandaged hand.

"I do not see what you expect to accomplish down there, Señorita," Aguilar said again, his arms crossed over his khaki vest. "We are in a terrible situation here and should leave as soon as possible."

Aguilar gestured to the Indians, speaking quietly, though Scully doubted any of them could speak English. "My associates are very distressed about the prospect of disturbing the sacred cenote. It is cursed from the victims sacrificed there. They say the ancient gods have taken their revenge on the old man—and if we continue to disturb them, the gods will attack us as well."

"Just like they attacked the members of the archaeology team?" Mulder suggested.

Aguilar tightened his ocelot-skin hat, letting his dark ponytail dangle behind him. "Perhaps there is a reason why Xitaclan remained deserted for so many centuries, Señor Mulder."

"I'm going down," Scully said firmly, her voice sounding hollow through the open faceplate. "We have an obligation to investigate if it helps us find our people. The cenote is the most obvious place we haven't searched, especially in light of finding Dr. Rubicon." She checked the weights at her waist, the utility flashlight hanging from her belt. "While I respect their religious beliefs, your 'associates' need to respect international law, Mr. Aguilar."

Scully sealed the faceplate and then gestured for Mulder to switch on the air generator. A whining, puttering sound throbbed into the jungle like noise from miniature construction machinery. She breathed deeply, smelled the stale air, sour from sealants and old rubber. When she felt a faint breeze stir around her face, she knew the air had begun to flow.

She gestured for them to help her descend into the cenote, hoping that the generator and the suit would last long enough for her to look around under the water. The Indians gazed at her solemnly, as if bidding her a final farewell.

Gripping the same ropes Mulder had used to walk/climb down the rugged limestone walls, Scully made her way one laborious step at a time. Her tedious descent took her many minutes, and the suit seemed as heavy as a truck on her back—but when she reached the edge of the deceptively placid pool, she found herself reluctant to plunge in.

She did not dwell on her irrational fears, but let loose of the wall. Scully plunged into the water, sinking like Thompson's proverbial bag of lead due to the weights around her waist.

The murk swallowed her up like syrup, a primordial ooze that embraced her. Water engulfed her enclosed helmet. The fabric of the suit pressed against her arms and legs, squeezing her intimately as she dropped deeper and deeper. The depths and the opaque water smothered the light, blinding her for a moment.

A fizz of bubbles curled around the seals in her rubber-lined suit. Scully breathed again, double-checking, verifying that no water seemed to be leaking in and that her vital air supply continued pumping through the hoses. Gradually, her confidence grew.

Under the tug of gravity, she continued to sink toward the bottom . . . if the cenote had a bottom.

As her eyes adjusted, the water around her became murky and greenish, like wan sunlight filtered through thick smoked-glass panes. She moved her hands and legs experimentally, floundering in the water. Disoriented, she felt only that she continued to go deeper. Deeper.

The pressure around her became heavier, and her

ears sensed the strain, the water like a vise squeezing her helmet. She thought again of Dr. Rubicon's story of how Thompson had sustained permanent ear damage from a faulty suit during his descent into the Chichén Itzá cenote.

She forced those thoughts away and tried to look around, turning her head in the confining helmet. She continued to drop, meter after meter. She couldn't imagine how deep this well was. Surely, she had already gone below the thirty-foot depth of the Chichén Itzá well.

The circle of light above had dwindled to only a faint, faint reflection of the bright Mexican sky. Her breathing echoed around her ears like distant surf, and she could barely feel the exchange of air through the hoses.

She heaved another breath and could smell the stink of the old tubes, the residual chemicals like the whiff of a long-dead cadaver. The suit seemed terribly hot and stuffy, the helmet claustrophobic.

Her vision swam for a moment, and she became dizzy trying to inhale another breath, then she calmed herself. Her problem had been only imaginary; she had begun to hyperventilate.

Scully noticed a faint lambent glow deep below her, much farther than she wanted to descend—a blue-white light that seemed to seep from the bottom of the sacrificial well, a glowing mist that oozed from the porous limestone itself.

As her eyes adjusted, Scully saw there could be no mistake—the haze of illumination pulsed and throbbed as if sending some sort of signal, a flashed SOS beacon, but at much slower intervals.

The faint light below seemed cold and unearthly. Her skin crawled even as she chastised herself for being foolishly spooked. It was the type of irrational nervousness brought about by telling horror stories around a campfire. Mulder would have loved it.

Her partner might have suggested the light was from a cluster of ghosts, remnants of Maya sacrificial victims. Scully's scientific mind postulated a colony of phosphorescent algae or anaerobic microorganisms living off the limestone far below, shedding faint, heatless light into their surroundings. Vengeful ghosts or extraterrestrials—she knew that couldn't be true.

She realized her descent had slowed, her belt-weights reaching equilibrium with the natural buoyancy of her body and the suit, counteracting her ability to sink. She hung in the water like a suspended anchor, feeling the pressure of the depths around her, but imagining herself to be weightless.

Scully fumbled at her wide belt, reaching for the utility flashlight. She unclipped it, fastened the chain around her wrist for safety, and gripped its handle for comfort.

Swallowing away her uneasiness, Scully switched on the dazzling beam, which stabbed through the murk like a snowplow through a blizzard. Kicking her booted feet, she turned in the thick sluggish water, looking around.

And came face to face with a corpse.

A bloated body hung in the water not three feet from her, arms spread, eye sockets open, flesh tattered and leprous after being gnawed by small fishes. The mouth hung wide, and tiny minnows darted out from between his jaws.

Scully gasped. A huge outburst of bubbles squeezed from seams in her suit as she jerked. In reflex, her hand released its grip on the heavy utility light, and the beam plunged downward, pointing deep below.

She scrambled desperately for the light, suddenly realizing her mistake. The flashlight dangled and stopped, bobbing up and down—then she remembered she had tethered it to her wrist.

Her heart pounded. Scully grabbed the flashlight and pointed the beam back up, studying the corpse that had terrified her.

It was a man, his dark hair drifting about in clumps. Rocks hung from cords tied to his waist. He had been killed and thrown into the cenote. Recently.

She felt the hot air booming in her helmet now, though an incredible cold seeped through the canvas fabric of her suit from the water around her.

Scully swung her flashlight like a lighthouse beam, sweeping through the undisturbed depths of the cenote. She did not linger on the corpse in front of her, but searched through the depths.

The flashlight beam played across other stick-like silhouettes floating like smashed, waterlogged insects, sunk beneath the water.

She had discovered the missing team of American archaeologists.

24

The flagstone plaza was littered with bodies.

Since the Indians had refused to help retrieve the bloated corpses from the cenote, it had taken Scully and Mulder hours to hoist the dead figures up to the top of the sinkhole, one at a time.

While still deep in the stygian well, Scully had used her utility knife to saw through the cords holding the stones that weighted the corpses, and the waterlogged cadavers had slowly drifted up to the surface.

Standing on the rim, watching anxiously for his partner, Mulder had been shocked to see one swollen form drift up to the top of the cenote, then another and another, while Scully remained deep below, breathing through her air hoses. Finally, she too came back to daylight, opening the faceplate of her helmet and drawing huge breaths of the humid air before proceeding with the most unpleasant part of the task.

As they had dragged the dripping, stinking bodies up and out of the water, sprawling them on dry ground, Fernando Victorio Aguilar had stood by, looking extremely agitated and queasy. Mulder had kept his FBI standard-issue handgun in plain sight. Finally, the guide had grudgingly assisted him with the ropes, helping to haul Scully back up the limestone wall.

Panting, her nerves jangled, she had shucked out of the cumbersome suit, standing in her sweat-dampened shorts and blouse, then stared down at the most difficult part of the work. Four bodies, and plenty of questions.

Aguilar had stammered, staring down at the gray-green, shriveled skin on all the cadavers lying on the packed ground next to the brick sacrificial platform. The distorted, half-decomposed features of the research team stared back up at him with empty, accusing eye sockets. His Adam's apple bobbed up and down, and he rubbed his cheeks as if he needed a shave.

"Just help us get them to the plaza," Scully had said. "They can't walk by themselves."

When they had finally taken the soggy, stinking bodies around the tall pyramid and to the open plaza near their camp, Aguilar continued to look furtively around, swallowing repeatedly as if to prevent himself from vomiting. Finally, he cleared his throat and excused himself. "I'm afraid I am going to be sick if I remain here any longer," he said, stumbling backward. "That foul stench . . ."

The entire crew of Indians had already fled into the jungle with so much wailing and shrieking Scully doubted they would ever return. She wondered if the Indians had a village nearby, or if they had just found a place to huddle under the overspreading trees . . . where they could tell each other superstitious stories and cut off their own fingers.

"Go see if you can find our cheerleading squad, Aguilar," Mulder said to the retreating guide. "We'll need those helpers to get out of here. Now that we've found our missing people, we can go."

"Yes, Señor," Aguilar said. "I will be back as soon as I can, and, uh . . ." He shuffled his feet. "Congratulations on finding your people . . . though you have my sorrow it had to turn out like this, eh? Just like the old man." He scuttled off, disappearing into a fern-lined path, his dark ponytail bobbing.

Mulder fidgeted in the late afternoon light, gazing at the silent temples and overgrown ruins, listening to the brooding sounds in the jungle. He kept an eye out for anything suspicious, while Scully devoted her attention to the four wet corpses that lay beside Vladimir Rubicon's. Next to the bloated new bodies, the old archaeologist seemed like a contented retiree who had died peacefully in his sleep.

"Since we have such a limited pool of possibilities," Scully said, "it'll be fairly easy to identify the four bodies," she said, her voice droning, businesslike because she had no choice.

She had taken the dossiers from her pack inside the tent and looked at the sheets of paper, the photographs: smiling pictures of ambitious young grad students eager to make names for themselves in an obscure field. The team had gone off on an innocent adventure to the Yucatán, expecting that their future would hold guest spots on talk shows or slide presentations in academic venues around the country.

Instead they had found only death.

Scully glanced at the photos, the identifying information. She studied the hair color, the height, the general bone structure. After advanced bloating from prolonged submersion and the onset of decay, their handsome facial features were unrecognizable.

"This dark-haired one is Kelly Rowan," Scully said. "He was the tallest of the group, the secondary leader, easy to identify."

Mulder knelt down beside her. "This should have been one of his most glorious accomplishments," he said, looking down at the young man's destroyed features. "Dr. Rubicon said he was a talented scholar with a great potential for archaeology, a good partner for Cassandra."

Scully did not dwell on the subject. In times like this, when performing autopsies and identifying corpses, she found it best to lock away the part of her mind that considered these figures ... these *objects* ... to be actual people. For now she had to be professional, despite the primitive conditions.

"The second man is John Forbin," Scully said, moving on to the next corpse. "He was the youngest of the lot—you can see it on him. In his first year of graduate school. An architect with a specialty in large, ancient structures."

Mulder shook his head. "He must have felt like a kid in a candy store here, all these untouched temples to study."

Scully pressed on with the identification tasks. "This young woman is obviously Cait Barron, the photographer and artist. She liked to paint watercolors more than she liked to take photographs. Her hair color and body weight are all wrong for her to be Cassandra."

Mulder nodded. Scully drew a deep breath, forcing herself to shut out the smell. She frequently rubbed camphor ointment under her nostrils to mask the stench during an autopsy, but here in the jungle she had to rough it.

"And that leaves this one to be Christopher Porte, the expert on Maya hieroglyphics," she said. "What did you call it, an epigrapher?"

Mulder nodded. "Not too many people have that knowledge, and now the field has one less." He cocked his ear, as if he had heard something, pausing. . . .

A sudden noise made him spin around quickly, his hand on his pistol—but it turned out to be only a group of squabbling birds in the overhanging vines. Looking sheepish, he turned back to Scully.

"So what did happen to Cassandra Rubicon? Are you sure you didn't find her body down there under the water? It was dark, and cold—"

"I searched, Mulder. All these others were clustered together, weighted and hanging at the same depth. Believe me, I spent a lot more time than I wanted to beneath the surface with this group of corpses." She nodded to the bodies. "But there just wasn't anyone else. Unless something happened to place her in a different spot, Cassandra's body wasn't down there."

"So we've solved one mystery, and now we're left with another that could be just as difficult."

Scully felt hot and sweaty and dirty. The cloying putrescence of the waterlogged corpses clung to everything, a sweet nauseating odor that clawed its way through her nose and mouth to lodge permanently in her lungs. She desperately wanted a shower or a hot bath, anything to feel clean again. A swim in the cenote just wouldn't do it.

But she still hadn't finished her task. Afterward, she might treat herself to a quick sponge bath.

"Let's see if we can determine anything about the cause of death from the condition of the bodies," Scully said. She used her knife to cut away the clothes, exposing the torsos of each of the victims.

"It's been too long to determine if they'd merely drowned," she said, "because the air would have outgassed from their bodies, and their lungs would have filled up with water anyway."

She moved John Forbin's head from side to side, seeing the neck move, but not too flexibly. "Unlike Dr. Rubicon," she said, "the neck hasn't been broken."

She rolled Cait Barron over and looked at the grayish-white skin on her back. Two circular puckered holes marked the base of the young woman's lower back.

"Bullet wounds," Scully said, raising her eyebrows. "I'll bet they were all shot before being thrown in." She shook her head, lost in thought.

"But where was Cassandra during all this?" Mulder asked, pacing on the flagstones. "She's still missing."

"Yes, we can keep our hopes up," Scully said. She examined each of the bodies. All four had been shot . . . most of them low in the back, in a paralyzing but not fatal blow. The similar placement of the wounds could not be accidental. The victims had been thrown into the sacrificial well while still alive.

"We have some very bad people here, Mulder," Scully said.

Mulder frowned. "After seeing the severed finger and

the blood sacrifice, and watching how superstitious these locals are, it seems that the violent old religion is really still prevalent. The Indians could have been the ones who performed these sacrifices, murdering convenient strangers.

"I read that the old tribes would take prisoners to slaughter in front of the gods, cutting out their enemies' hearts rather than killing their own people." He turned to look up at the central Pyramid of Kukulkan looming in the center of the plaza.

"Their hearts weren't cut out, Mulder. These people were shot."

Mulder shrugged. "Tossing victims into the sacred cenote was another perfectly legitimate way to appease the gods. If the Indians paralyzed the archaeology team before hurling them in, the sacrifices would still have been living and breathing—appropriate offerings."

Scully stood up, feeling her knees ache. She wiped her hands on her already stained slacks. "Mulder, remember that these people were shot with guns, not attacked with primitive obsidian knives. It doesn't seem their style."

"Maybe they're modernizing their religion."

Mulder actually took out his pistol this time and held it as he continued to scan the jungle warily. "This is their backyard, Scully, and there's a lot of them. Why do I feel very much like another convenient sacrifice . . . say, like a turkey feels around Thanksgiving time?"

Scully moved next to him, closer than she needed to. They looked out at the wilderness, the only human beings in sight. Even with Mulder next to her, she felt very, very alone.

25

Full darkness had fallen, leaving them in the company of only the late-rising moon and their laughably small campfire. The looming darkness of the surrounding jungle threatened to swallow them up. Mulder felt very small and very vulnerable in the vastness of the wilderness.

Staring into the fire, Scully said, "Remember when I told you that Mexico sounded better than an Arctic research station or a chicken-processing plant in Arkansas?"

"Yes."

"I think I've changed my mind."

In light of the unspoken threat from the Maya sacrificial cult, or treacherous Aguilar, or whoever else was responsible for the numerous murders, the two agents had decided to take turns at watch throughout the night. But neither Mulder nor Scully felt the least bit interested in sleep.

Mulder sat on the flagstones watching the campfire, looking up at the moon, and listening to the songs of jungle insects. The smoke from damp, moss-covered wood curled around his nose, thick and pungent, a relief after the underlying stench of decay that arose from the corpses. He cradled his 9-mm pistol in his lap, fully attentive, alert.

Though night had fallen hours before, Scully had crawled out of her tent to sit up beside him. "We could heat some water," she suggested, "have coffee or tea. Seems appropriate for a night around the campfire."

Mulder turned to smile at her. "Did we bring any hot cocoa mix, the kind with the little marshmallows?"

"I think Aguilar took that with him."

Mulder stared out into the surrounding trees, seeing the silver dapple of moonlight. The Indians had not returned, nor—disturbingly—had Aguilar. Mulder wasn't sure if that was a good thing, or if he wanted the others to come back and lead him and Scully back to civilization.

Meanwhile, their only companions in the camp were the lumpy forms of the five corpses spread out not far from the tents, blanketed by a stained tarp Mulder had recovered from the team's supply cache. Mulder kept glancing over at the shapes, unable to dispel images of the bloated, waterlogged forms of the four archaeology team members and the bony body of Vladimir Rubicon, whose open blue eyes had looked surprised even in death.

He looked over at Scully. They were both grimy and dirt-streaked—they hadn't showered for days. Their hair hung in unkempt tangles from the sweat and humidity. He was glad to be there with her, rather than anyone else in the world.

"Scully," he said, his voice quiet and serious, "with the . . . unorthodox explanations I often find when studying the evidence, I know you're always skeptical—but every time you're at least fair to me. You respect my opinion, even when you don't agree with it." He looked at his hands. "I don't know if I've ever told you, but I really appreciate that."

She looked at him and smiled. "You've told me, Mulder. Maybe not in words . . . but you've told me."

He swallowed, then brought up the subject he had been avoiding. "I know you're probably not going to believe this either, blaming it on a trick of the moonlight or my own grogginess from lack of sleep—but two nights ago I heard noises out in the jungle. I poked my head out to investigate, and I saw something moving, a large creature that wasn't like anything I've ever seen before. Well, that's not completely true ... I've seen it many times before but not in real life."

"Mulder, what are you talking about?" she said.

Out in the jungle they heard other sounds, rustling noises, something large coming closer. Mulder perked up his ears and felt his blood run cold.

"I think I saw ... one of those feathered serpents. Just like that statue." He indicated the coiled snake engraved in the limestone column of the stela in the plaza. "It was larger than a crocodile, and it moved with such grace. Ah, Scully, you should have seen it. It reminded me of a dragon."

"Mulder, that feathered serpent is a mythological creature," she said, automatically falling back into her role as skeptic. "What you saw must have been inspired by looking at Maya carvings for days and all the research you've been doing into pre-Colombian legends. You probably spotted a cayman—those are large reptiles found in these jungles. When you saw it move, your imagination could have added other details you wanted to see."

"That's possible, Scully," he admitted, shifting the pistol in his lap from one hand to the other. He heard more branches cracking, additional movement in the jungle, creeping closer to them.

He spoke more rapidly. "On the other hand, look at the sheer number of feathered serpent images throughout the Maya artifacts, at all different sites ... here at Xitaclan in particular. It's such an odd thing. A snake with feathers? What could have inspired such a myth if the Indians of the Yucatán hadn't seen such a creature with their own eyes? It could even be an explanation for the prevalent myths worldwide of dragons and reptilian worms."

His words picked up speed as he followed his imagination. "Does it seem likely to you that dozens of cultures around the world would create an image so precisely similar? Think of the drawings you've seen of Chinese dragons. They weren't called feathered serpents, but they had the same configuration. Long feathery scales and a sinuous body."

Out in the jungle the crashing, lumbering sounds became louder and louder. Some creature unmistakably was making its way toward Xitaclan as if drawn to a magnet. As the noise grew, it sounded as if many large creatures were converging on the plaza itself. Mulder raised his pistol.

"Listen to that, Scully. I hope we don't get a chance to meet one of my imaginary feathered serpents face-to-face," he said.

The sounds continued to increase. Trees bent, cracked, and fell over; ferns swayed. Scully cocked her ear and turned her head toward Mulder. They huddled around the campfire, both of them with their weapons in hand, ready to make a last stand, if necessary.

But Scully suddenly became more curious than frightened. "Wait—Mulder, that's a mechanical noise," she said.

As soon as she spoke, Mulder realized that the growling, grinding sound he heard was indeed an engine noise, the crunching of tires, and the humming of generators.

Then, with a blinding roar, stars exploded in the sky, brilliant white glares like aerial combat. Fireworks shot into the air and burst like a white chrysanthemum.

"Those are phosphorous flares," Mulder said. "Military issue."

Under the glare of the scalding white light, two lumbering all-terrain vehicles smashed through the fallen underbrush and rolled up onto the flagstones of the Xitaclan plaza. Behind the ATVs, dark figures wearing camouflage outfits scrambled out of the jungle. They crept low, holding their rifles, snapping abbreviated instructions to each other as they rushed into position like army ants swarming to a new nest.

"What's going on here?" Scully said, looking both alarmed and perplexed at her partner.

"I guess it's not a good idea for us to run for it."

Scully instantly assessed the weaponry, the soldiers, the vehicles. The hulking all-terrain vehicles rolled to a stop, crunching the weathered flagstones beneath them, smashing upthrust tree roots. The camouflaged commandos ran about, intent on their mission—and Mulder realized with surprise that the terse phrases they snapped back and forth at each other were in English, not Spanish.

On first sight he had imagined a Central American guerrilla army, but though he saw no markings on their uniforms or on their vehicles, he knew he had found a different answer.

"Those are Americans," he said. "U.S. military. Some sort of commando operation."

Mulder and Scully sat frozen next to their little campfire, hands raised, pistols in nonaggressive positions. The commando squad ran up and surrounded the two, pointing rifles at them.

"I knew I should have paid that parking ticket," Mulder muttered.

While two of the soldiers aimed rifle barrels directly at their chests, another man crept forward and cautiously removed Mulder and Scully's weapons, holding them at arm's length, as if the small 9-mm pistols were poisonous spiders.

The phosphorous flares had gradually faded out. Several of the camouflaged commandos rigged up brilliant arc lights, flooding the plaza with a harsh glare.

A slender, dark-skinned man marched up to Mulder and Scully, clearly in command of the operation. He had high cheekbones, an aquiline nose, generous lips, and a pointed chin. His eyes were narrow and as dark as obsidian. On his shoulders he wore the maple-leaf-cluster insignia of a major.

"Habla Español?" the major demanded. *"Que pasa?"*

Scully leaned forward. "We speak English," she

said. "We are Americans, special agents of the Federal Bureau of Investigation."

The commandos stopped and looked at each other. The major stood rigid. "What are you doing here?" he said. "On foreign soil?"

"We could ask you the same question," Mulder said.

"My partner and I are here on a case involving missing U.S. citizens." Scully reached into her pocket. The soldiers tensed, but she moved slowly enough. "I'm going for my ID," she said and carefully withdrew her badge and photo identification card.

Mulder looked at her, amazed that even here in the jungle she still kept her ID in her shirt pocket.

"We are legal attachés, LEGATS, to the U.S. Consulate," she said. "Our assignment here in Quintana Roo is to search for a missing archaeological team."

"Major Jakes, over here!" shouted two soldiers who had been exploring the open plaza area. They held back the tarp that had been covering the five bodies beside the feathered serpent stela. "Casualties, sir." The major turned to look, saw the corpses.

Mulder shrugged. "Well, actually we've already found most of the missing team," he said.

Major Jakes gazed around the ruins and the plaza. Seeing no one other than the two agents, he raised his voice to issue orders to his soldiers. "Continue securing the site. This isn't what we expected to find, but we still have our orders. We must complete the mission, destroy this command outpost, and be gone before morning."

"While you're at it, do you suppose you could give us a lift out of here?" Mulder said. "If you have room in the back seat of one of those ATVs, I mean?"

"If the parameters of the mission allow it," Jakes said, his voice entirely deadpan. He bent over to study Scully's ID. "My men are not here in any official capacity, and we are under orders to respond with full denial."

"We've heard that before," Mulder said.

"We can operate under those conditions," Scully

answered more firmly, "if that is the requirement for getting us out of here. What is your mission, Major?"

"To destroy this military site," he said matter-of-factly. "Eliminate the source of a strange encrypted transmission."

"*This* is a military site?" Mulder said in astonishment. He spread his hands to indicate the crumbling pyramid, the weathered stelae, the fallen temples. "These are ancient Maya ruins, abandoned for a thousand years. You can see that with your own eyes. My partner and I have been here searching for days, and we haven't found the slightest evidence of high technology or stored weapons. This place has no military significance whatsoever."

Then, as if specifically to contradict him, a rain of automatic-weapon fire showered from the shadows of the jungle, pelting the commando team.

26

As the sharp, high-pitched shots rang out with a sound like a chainsaw, Scully ducked reflexively.

Mulder tackled her, knocking her down beside the meager shelter of their low tents. Her face pressed against the cold flagstones, Scully could see winking flashes of fire as hidden snipers continued the attack.

Major Jakes and his commando squad exploded into motion, their own response as fast as a swarm of angry wasps. "Get to cover, everyone!" Jakes shouted. "Fire at will!"

"Of course, I could be wrong about this place having no military significance," Mulder said, breathing hard, close to Scully's ear. "Are you hurt?"

"No," she said, panting. "Thanks, Mulder."

Though Scully could not determine where the shots came from, the American commandos responded with an impressive display of firepower, the quantity of bullets sufficient to make up for their lack of a precise target.

One of the soldiers next to her spun around as if from an invisible force, and he sprawled on the broken flagstones. The young first lieutenant gasped and choked as bright arterial blood spilled from both the entry and exit wound in his rib cage. Scully could see at a glance that the young man had received a mortal injury.

Return gunfire rang out from the jungle snipers. A bright puff of splintered stone blossomed on the lime-stone stela nearest their tent, making a gouge across the feathered serpent carving still smeared with rusty brown splotches from the previous day's blood sacrifice.

The soldiers sprinted back toward the two armored all-terrain vehicles. One man ducked behind the lime-stone stela, another flattened himself behind the low, tarpaulin-covered corpses on the flagstones.

"Who's firing at us?" Scully demanded when she had caught her breath.

The American commando squad continued blasting the trees, but they had only a slim hope of actually strik-ing one of the shadowy enemies. Someone unseen screamed in pain, then renewed gunfire drowned out all other sounds. A lucky shot from the jungle shattered one of the portable arc lights the commandos had erected.

A deep voice bellowed out of the jungle, using no loudspeaker, but with enough strength to penetrate the chaos. His crisp Mexican accent sliced through the night. "American invaders!" the man shouted. "You are ille-gally in the sovereign state of Quintana Roo. Your defi-ance of our laws and our borders is against all international treaties."

As they both remained low to the ground, trying to remain minimal targets, Scully looked over at Mulder. She recognized the voice. "That's the police chief, Carlos Barreio!" Bullets sang low over their heads. "But why is the chief of state police firing at us in the middle of the night? In the middle of the jungle? This isn't a law-enforcement raid."

Mulder raised his eyebrows. "It seems Chief Barreio has gone out for some extracurricular activities."

One of Major Jakes's soldiers launched another garish phosphorous flare into the sky, where it burned white-hot, splashing a glare down upon the field that caused more confusion than illumination.

"Identify yourself!" Major Jakes shouted, crouching beside Mulder and Scully in the illusionary shelter of the tent. "We have superior firepower."

More shots spat from the trees, tearing holes through the fabric of the tent. Jakes ducked sideways, collapsing on top of Mulder and Scully. A furrow of blood appeared at his shoulder—merely a flesh wound, nothing serious. Major Jakes didn't even seem to notice.

"This is an act of war," Barreio shouted back. "You invaders have brought contraband arms into our land." The gunfire dwindled as the guerrillas' leader spoke, with only a few sharp sounds peppering a flare-lit night. "We have no choice but to protect our culture. We cannot allow military intruders from the United States to walk off with our national treasures."

"But we're not here to steal artifacts," Major Jakes muttered to himself, shaking his head. "We're just here to blow up the pyramid."

Mulder rose to an elbow and looked over at the major. "Well then, if it's all just one big misunderstanding, maybe we can shake hands with him and talk about this?"

Major Jakes didn't appear to hear. "It all makes sense now," he said. "These are freedom fighters, members of the violent revolutionary front in the Yucatán—*Liberación Quintana Roo*. They want to make their own little country and secede from the Mexican nation, regardless of what the rest of the Yucatán population wants. They don't have many weapons, nor do they have any moral compunctions."

Mulder looked at him coldly. "Unlike you and your men."

Major Jakes returned the gaze, his expression blank, completely without anger. "Correct, Agent Mulder."

"Throw down your weapons and surrender!" Barreio continued to bellow. "You will be arrested, charged as illegal aliens, and punished accordingly . . . unless your country chooses to extradite you."

Major Jakes's nostrils flared. Since this was not an official mission, Scully knew the government would deny its existence and write off the commando squad. Jakes and his men would be abandoned to whatever kangaroo court or dim torture chambers the guerrilla group chose.

"My men will never surrender," Major Jakes shouted back, and more gunfire rang out. "Not to cowardly snipers, and not to terrorists."

"I always wanted to be in a real Mexican standoff," Mulder said.

Scully knew that the covert American commando group might be able to outgun and outfight the *Liberación Quintana Roo* rebels in a standing battle—but they could not escape or retreat with so many snipers hidden in the jungles. They were trapped at Xitaclan.

The phosphorous flare fizzled and faded out, and the second arc light shattered, plunging the site back into a darkness broken only by occasional gunfire and afterimages on Scully's eyes.

"You two will stay next to me," Major Jakes said. "I realize you are both noncombatants—though I'm not sure there's a satisfactory way to resolve this."

"Then could we have our weapons back, sir?" Mulder asked. "Since it's already come down to a fight."

"No, Agent Mulder. I don't believe that would be in your best interests." Major Jakes turned his night-vision goggles toward the forest.

As she lay on the flagstones, wincing every time bullets whined over her head, Scully felt the ground tremble, building to a vigorous vibration, as if even more heavy machinery were rolling toward them—then she realized that this tremor originated from deeper within the earth. Another rumbling came, a quaking, as volcanic pressure built up beneath the limestone crust.

"Scully, hang on," Mulder said. He grabbed her arm, though Major Jakes and his men did not understand what was happening.

The ground bucked and shook as seismic forces

writhed beneath them. The great pyramid of Xitaclan rattled and trembled. Blocks of loosened stone tumbled down the steep steps. From the jungle, some of the snipers wailed in terror, while Jakes's commandos scrambled about in equal confusion.

The more distant of the plaza's two feathered serpent stelae groaned, then toppled over onto the flagstones. The ancient obelisk crumbled into broken rubble. The trees danced and waved.

Steam blasted from small openings in the plaza flagstones. Little fumaroles split through the ground, releasing tremendous pressure.

"Come on, Scully, let's get out of here!" Mulder shouted, tugging at her arm. "We can run—use this as a diversion, get to shelter." He stood and staggered away, the ground leaping like a carnival ride beneath his feet.

Scully rose to join him, but Major Jakes stood next to her, blocking the way. "Not so fast, you two. You're staying here."

Angry shouts rang out from the forest, and Scully could hear trees toppling, uprooted by the tremors. She tried to stare down Major Jakes as he held his weapon at her, and she knew from the expression in his eyes that she couldn't flee. Mulder had already crossed half of the plaza, ducking and weaving, trying to get to the cover of one of the low temple ruins. Mulder turned back to her, an anguished expression on his face. He paused as if he meant to come running back, to surrender to Jakes in order to stay beside her.

"Just go, Mulder!" she said. "Get out of here!"

He took that to heart and put on more speed, dashing toward the cover of the pyramid's lower platform. Gunfire splattered against the uneven flagstones near his heels, bullets ricocheting into the night—she couldn't tell if the shots had come from the guerrillas in the jungle or from Major Jakes's commandos.

The ground lurched with one titanic jolt, and Scully heard a sound like muscles tearing, as if the ground below were giving birth. A giant pillar of steam exploded from behind the Pyramid of Kukulkan, water boiling away and draining into the ground.

She realized the steam explosion came from the cenote—a crack in the earth had split the bottom of the intensely deep well, dumping water into a volcanic cauldron.

Scully caught only a glimpse of her partner's silhouette, but she knew with a dismay that made her chest ache that Mulder was running straight toward it, as if drawn.

27

By the time Mulder reached meager cover, the ground had stopped swaying and hiccoughing beneath his feet. A few snipers took potshots at him, but most of them seemed concerned more with their own safety. Before the gunfire could pick up again, he took advantage of the stunned motionlessness around the ruins and ran on, taking shelter at the edge of the immense pyramid.

He felt dismayed at leaving Scully behind, a prisoner of—or perhaps "under the protection of"—Major Jakes and his commando squad. But she had told him to run, told him to get away. Her last words piercing through the volcanic tremors had cut him free, as if a leash holding him back had suddenly snapped. If he could solve the mystery, find the answers that Barreio's guerrillas and the American soldiers both wanted, perhaps he could use it to gain Scully's freedom.

Now he plunged in a single direction, for better or worse. He knew that he, one man—unarmed, since Jakes had relieved him of even his handgun—could do little against two opposing military forces. Mulder hoped to approach the problem from a different direction, finding an unexpected solution from left field.

He needed to discover the secret of the great pyramid of Xitaclan. What had Cassandra Rubicon found there?

The abortive eruption and tremors had failed to produce gushing lava and ash, but as Mulder staggered toward the abrupt edge of the sacrificial sinkhole, he came to a quick stop—and stared down, awestruck.

Somewhere deep in the basement of the Earth the ground had cracked, splitting open the bottom of the sacrificial well. The limestone sinkhole had dumped its contents into a smoldering pit of volcanic heat—all the cold, quiet water of the cenote, the still depths that had cradled the sunken bodies of Cassandra Rubicon's team as well as the broken old archaeologist himself. As he ran, Mulder had watched the mushroom cloud of stinking steam pour into the sky as if from a boiler explosion. . . .

Now the sinkhole lay empty, dripping and crackling, like a dry, wide-open mouth. Its limestone walls remained slick and lumpy. Steam still curled up with a sour biting stench of volcanic gases.

Mulder looked down into the gasping cenote, a pit into hell like the legendary entrance into Hades from Greek mythology. Deep below, he saw a faint glow. The haze of illumination was unlike firelight, unlike the smoldering glare of volcanic heat. This seemed more of a cold glow, a shimmer that throbbed and pulsed like a beacon shouting silently into the bottomless shaft.

Scully had told him she'd seen a similar unsettling glow during her diving expedition, like distant heat lightning, far below the depth where she had discovered the bodies of the research team. Phosphorescent algae growing far from the touch of sunlight, she had speculated. As Mulder stared at the faint haze, watching the flickering light, he could not accept his partner's scientific explanation. This rising and falling glitter seemed too orderly, too regular, a pattern . . . some kind of a signal.

He thought of the major's claim that the Xitaclan ruins were the source of some mysterious encrypted signal, a transmission whose code the U.S. military presumably could not break. . . . But what if the transmission was not encrypted or encoded in any way, but simply in a language that Major Jakes could not understand, that no human had ever learned?

Vladimir Rubicon had gently chided Mulder for his imaginative interpretation of the carvings atop the temple . . . for his explanation that the wise god Kukulkan, who had come in a silver ship trailing fire, might have been an ancient astronaut, an extraterrestrial come to Earth at the dawn of human civilization. But now, observing the eerie glow deep down in the drained cenote, Mulder felt certain this must be some kind of SOS beacon.

Mulder saw the tangled ropes still lashed to the gnarled trees, dangling along the side of the now-empty sacrificial well. He stared down at the steep curving limestone walls. With the knobs and handholds and sloping ledges, plus the support of the old ropes, he could make the descent. Probably.

The glow called to him. He had to go down there. No question about it.

He grasped the ropes, wet and warm and slick in his palm. They must have been cooked like vegetables in the noxious vapors that had boiled up out of the sacrificial well—but the cables appeared undamaged. They would hold his weight . . . he hoped.

He tugged, securing the knots firmly above, and lowered himself backward over the edge, digging the heels of his shoes into the damp limestone. As he expected, he found sufficient lumps and footholds to assist his descent—but the drop seemed impossibly far down.

Straining his arm muscles, Mulder picked up speed as he gained confidence, making his way from ledge to ledge, working himself downward. He grasped the rough rope, but frequently used it only as a crutch and not for actual support.

Mulder's head began to spin from the foul odors hissing up from below like the fetid breath of a dragon.

He couldn't imagine how deep the sinkhole actually went. Luckily, the beckoning glow did not arise from the absolute depths, but only partially down.

Razor-sharp cracks of gunfire rang out across the air again. Mulder froze, plastering himself in the darkness under an overhang as the blasts reverberated in the hollow chamber of the cenote, but he realized that no one had shot at him intentionally. The fighting had started again, now that the hidden assailants had recovered from their fear and confusion after the violent tremors.

"Guess I better pick up the pace," he muttered. He wasn't going to let anything as trivial as a minor Central American revolution distract him from learning what he needed to know.

Mulder dropped down to another ledge, and the color of the limestone changed from faded white to a darker, browner shade, stained with slimy residue. He was now below what had been the surface of the water.

Another shot rang out far above, and he heard thin voices in Spanish or the back-of-the-throat Maya derivative the local Indians had spoken. He wondered if Fernando Aguilar and his native helpers had returned, bumbling into the conflict . . . or perhaps Aguilar was somehow in league with Barreio and his *Liberación Quintana Roo* movement.

He and Scully now had another set of murder suspects. Evidently, Barreio's group of violent rebels might have chosen to assassinate a team of American archaeologists defiling their national treasures. The price of revolution.

But . . . if Mulder's suspicions about the fantastic origin of this ancient Maya city proved to be true, then the relics of Xitaclan belonged to no nation on Earth.

It had always bothered him—why had the Maya people abandoned this lush, isolated site, and so many of their grand cities? Why had they built Xitaclan here at all, far from trade routes or rivers or roads? What had fostered the birth of their entire great empire? Why did the Maya develop such an interest in astronomical knowledge, calendrical cycles, planetary orbits?

The Maya had been obsessed with time and the stars, the passage of the Earth around the sun. They had kept meticulous track of days and months, like a child crossing off dates on his calendar in the month before a birthday.

He had a feeling all the answers lay below, in the light.

Underneath the water's former surface, the cenote's ledges and outcroppings were thicker, knobbier, unweathered. He climbed down, his heart beating faster, his curiosity burning.

Then he ran out of rope.

Mulder looked at the frayed end, the long dangling strands that clung to the cenote wall, all the way to the rim above. He had no choice but to continue downward, unaided.

The glow grew brighter around him now, colder. He sweated from the thick volcanic heat, the leftover steam, the sauna of vapors around him in the empty cenote pit. But the light grew whitish-blue and cold, pulsing through the surrounding rock. The walls seemed barely able to contain the energy seeping out.

Finally, working his way the rest of the distance, his fingers clenching slippery handholds and knobby outcroppings of limestone, Mulder arrived panting at a wide ledge, an arched opening . . . exposing a smooth rectangle of metal.

More gunfire rang out in the night, but Mulder didn't hear it.

The alloy frame was encrusted and corroded, but remarkably clean after centuries of submersion in the cold cenote waters. The shape and appearance of the portal was unmistakable, and Mulder reached out to touch it, his fingers trembling.

The exposed opening was clearly some kind of door.

The door to a ship.

28

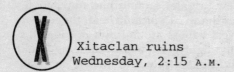

Xitaclan ruins
Wednesday, 2:15 A.M.

The ancient metallic hatch opened with a drawn-out hissing breath of equalizing air pressure—a sound, Mulder suspected, similar to what a feathered serpent might make just before it attacked. . . .

Despite his desperate curiosity, Mulder turned away and held his breath, afraid of what toxins he might inhale inside the newly opened chamber. In other investigations he had been overcome after catching a whiff of the noxious blood from decomposing alien figures. Whatever lay beneath the Xitaclan ruins had been entombed for centuries, and he had no way of knowing just what might lie inside this long-abandoned . . . craft?

His eyes stung from the fumes still rising from volcanic cracks in the unseen floor of the cenote. He hoped the ground didn't spasm again anytime soon.

But hearing the faint popcorn sound of gunfire above even louder than the dripping echoes trickling down the curved limestone walls, Mulder knew he could not spare any time or energy to worry about his own safety. He had to get his answers, and then get back to Scully.

For that, he needed to go inside.

He planted his foot one step through the doorway, feeling the solidity of the floor. The entrance corridor was smooth-walled and womb-like, the walls a polished metallic substance that absorbed the light and reflected it back. Mulder could not see any source to the glare. It was a blinding harshness, clearly designed, he thought, for eyes adapted to the light of a different sun.

The Maya had never been skilled metalsmiths, had no smelting capabilities to create the materials he saw around him. He proceeded farther down the corridor, as if drawn. The walls hummed with a high-pitched throbbing sensation, like alien music. He felt it deeply within his bones, his teeth, the back of his skull. Mulder wanted to tell someone, share his amazement. But that had to wait until he escaped again.

He recalled a far more mundane scenario out at the jogging track near FBI Headquarters, when he had finished a long, exhilarating run, the second time he had encountered the man he came to call "Deep Throat." When Mulder had questioned him about alien visitations, hard evidence of conspiracies locked away in secret government vaults, Deep Throat had given his usual answers that weren't answers.

"They're here, aren't they?" Mulder had said, sweating from his run, demanding to know.

With his calm, unassuming smile and his knowing voice, Deep Throat had raised his eyebrows. "Mr. Mulder, they've been here for a long, long time."

But could it have been as long as thousands of years?

Now Mulder stepped deeper down the armored corridor, exploring the remains of what must be an ancient derelict, the ship of an alien visitor who had landed—perhaps crashed—in the Yucatán Peninsula centuries and centuries before, here at the birthplace of the Maya civilization.

"Talk about illegal aliens," Mulder muttered.

The winding passages opened up, revealing dark, half-collapsed chambers, what had been other metal-walled rooms. Where corroded alloy plates had tumbled to the floor, the holes had been repaired with pieces of carved stone. Little of the original ship itself remained, barely a metal framework patched up with limestone blocks.

Mulder imagined Maya priests entering the "sacred" pyramid long after the alien visitors had vanished, still attempting to be caretakers but not knowing how. Generations and generations of awestruck visitors would have worn the floor smooth.

Perhaps the missing equipment and girders had been cannibalized from the main structure to be used in other Maya temples . . . or perhaps they had been stripped and destroyed by treasure seekers . . . or cast away by religious zealots such as Father Diego de Landa.

A sense of wonder engulfed him, coursed through his veins as he continued to explore. Never before had he seen such overwhelming evidence, such incredible remains of an extraterrestrial construction.

The corridors in the derelict ship reflected the same blueprint that Mulder had encountered while moving through the labyrinth of the pyramid above in his search for Vladimir Rubicon the day before. Up there, Mulder had explored the dark tunnels until stopped by the strange sealed passage. Perhaps, he thought, it was an upper entrance to the entombed ship.

Mulder wondered if the craft itself had crashed, plowing a crater in the middle of the jungle. When the local, uncivilized people had come to investigate, Kukulkan, the "wise god from the stars," had taught them immense knowledge, fostering the birth of a great civilization.

He ran his fingers along the gaps in the metallic walls, touching the polished limestone. More than anything, he wished Vladimir Rubicon could have lived long enough to see this.

Over the millennia the Maya—or later treasure seekers—had stripped the derelict to the bone, leaving only this skeleton of the original ship. But it was enough. Mulder knew this proof could not be denied.

If only he could bring Scully down here, where she could see.

With a pang he hoped she was still all right, that Major Jakes had at least protected her against a resurgence of the guerrillas, as a hostage if nothing else.

If only he and Scully could get out of here alive. She had told him once before, during their frantic escape from the radio telescope at Arecibo, Puerto Rico, "Evidence is worthless if you're dead."

He came to an ascending, spiraling ramp, and followed the bright, pulsing glow steeply upward. He had no idea how deep underground he still was.

His amazement doubled when he reached the next level. He had arrived at the chamber from which the glowing beacon emanated. He had to shield his eyes from the light, which burned so brightly that his skull hurt. *This must be the control bridge,* he thought. He slowly scanned the entire room.

The entire chamber remained virtually intact, its oddly complex protrusions—machinery?—apparently functional. Mulder instantly realized that this place must have held enormous religious significance for the Maya.

Suddenly Mulder saw something that made him freeze, his stomach tightening. One of the chambers was filled with a strange translucent substance, an ethereal gel that held a shadow, an outline—a silhouetted humanoid figure, poised motionless in the far doorway, arms outstretched, legs partially apart. The silhouette looked slender, skeletal, distorted by the engulfing murk.

Drawn like a moth to a flame, Mulder staggered across the sloping deck of the bridge to reach the narrow chamber—and he saw then that the silhouetted figure surrounded by the gelatinous substance was that of a young woman with long hair and human features.

Mulder hesitated. The rational part of his mind knew it couldn't be his sister. It couldn't be her.

As he stood before the outline, blinking and squinting in the bright light all around him, he studied the woman who hung frozen in place, trapped like an insect in amber. . . .

As he strained to make out the details, Mulder saw that her face seemed surprised, her mouth partly opened, her eyes wide, as if she had been suddenly captured there like a photographic image. The gelatin grew clearer, as if stirred by unseen currents of energy. He noted her green-brown eyes, her petite figure that looked as if it could well have fit inside the diving suit Scully had used. Flowing cinnamon-colored hair, a spray of fresh red scratches on one cheek.

Of all the wonders that Mulder had seen and found inside the derelict ship, he was most surprised by this one.

After their days of searching, he had finally found Cassandra Rubicon.

29

Major Jakes ordered Scully to get down, and she had no choice but to obey.

He bellowed orders for his forces to launch their all-out counterstrike. Random sniper fire from the jungle shot out one more hastily erected arc light, but dazzling phosphorous flares lit the sky to compensate, creating a strobelight effect that accentuated the explosions and gunfire.

From the weapons supplies inside one of the armored all-terrain vehicles, two soldiers set up a small rocket battery and then a grenade launcher. Scully covered her ears as the commandos began to wreak Armageddon on the dense jungle.

Startled gunfire rang out from the scattered *Liberación Quintana Roo* freedom fighters. But as trees erupted into gouts of fire and detonations thundered through the underbrush, Scully heard more wild outcries, panicked shouts, and screams of pain.

A salvo of automatic-weapon fire chattered back out of the trees. Two of Major Jakes's commandos were hurled to the ground, torn apart by heavy caliber bullets. One moaned, one didn't.

"Stay under cover!" Major Jakes shouted, with a firm hand pressing Scully down beside the pathetic shelter of the low tents.

The surrounding jungle began to burn. Another commando took the place of the fallen soldier at the rocket launcher and shot four tiny missiles toward the heart of the hidden gunfire. The detonations sounded louder than the recent volcanic tremors.

The sniper fire trailed off again. Over the crackle of flames in the smothering underbrush, Scully could hear receding shouts under cover of the mahogany trees and creeper-entangled jungle. The flares in the sky cast a parade of shadows.

One of the grime-smeared, breathless young commandos came running up, squatting as he scurried for cover. From the soft, rounded features of his face, Scully couldn't imagine that the soldier was more than twenty, but his eyes were flinty and hard, aged well beyond his years.

"The enemy seems to be falling back, sir," the young soldier said. "Temporarily, at least."

Major Jakes nodded. "Superior firepower is always enough to intimidate upstart forces. I want you to run and get a damage assessment."

"I can give you a preliminary, sir," the soldier said. "At least four men down, three fatally, one . . . well, it still looks pretty bad, Major."

Jakes looked deeply stunned, as if the wind had been knocked out of him, then he drew a deep breath, the nostrils of his aquiline nose flaring wide. "Six left," he said.

Another soldier came up, bleeding from the right side of his rib cage; he didn't allow the injury to slow him down. "The guerrilla force has disappeared into the trees, sir," he said. "We suspect they're regrouping for another assault."

"They know they can't outgun us," Jakes said. "But they can wait us out."

"Do you request that we go out on a hunting expedition, Major?" the soldier asked, distractedly squeezing his side to stanch the blood flow.

Major Jakes shook his head. "Any word on their leader? The man issuing demands?"

"Preliminary only, sir," the soldier said. He pulled his hand away from the wound on his side, flexing his sticky fingers. Scully could see a gouge of ripped flesh, cauterized from the heat of a passing bullet. The soldier looked at the wet sparkle of blood on his palm, then nonchalantly wiped his hand on the leg of his camouflaged pants as if getting rid of a squashed bug.

"The leader has also run for cover, we believe. Unfortunately, we must presume he is not injured. He was last seen making a break for the main citadel in the ruins, there." The soldier gestured toward the Pyramid of Kukulkan. "Perhaps that's some sort of rebel stronghold or additional weapons stockpile. Clearly our primary target."

"This is an archaeological site, not a military target," Scully said, forcing herself to her knees and pushing away from Jakes. It infuriated her to see the death and injuries, the wanton destruction caused by both Barreio's freedom fighters and Major Jakes's commandos. "It's just an ancient Mayan ruin, can't you see? Nothing more!"

"All evidence to the contrary." Major Jakes looked at her, his face stony. "If Xitaclan is merely a site of historical interest, then why is this gang of rebels defending it with lethal force?" He turned to the injured soldier, who stood waiting for further orders. "Proceed with the objectives of the mission. I want two mortar launchers set up and ready to go within ten minutes."

"Yes, sir," the man said, then ran off, ducking low and weaving for cover across the battered plaza despite the lack of gunfire.

"By what right do you come in here and attack a sovereign country and destroy a site of priceless archaeological value?" Scully demanded. "These ruins are thousands of years old, never before studied by science or historians. You have no proof that this is some weapons stockpile or revolutionary base."

Major Jakes withdrew her confiscated badge and ID wallet from the generous pocket of his camouflaged pants, scrutinized her identification again, and handed the wallet back to her. "Very well, Special Agent Scully of the Federal Bureau of Investigation," he said. "Let me show you my evidence. Since you are already inside the security restrictions of this mission, you're bound by the legalities and classification of what you've seen."

"I have a security clearance, and I know how to keep my mouth shut," Scully said. "But I don't have any answers. Yet."

"Come with me, please," he said, "over to the lead vehicle." Without waiting for her, he ducked and ran toward the ATVs. Scully scrambled after him, imitating his evasive pattern as she remembered the training she had undergone at Quantico. She found it amazing how the presence of danger sharpened her memory.

But this operation was different from a simple suspect shoot-out: Xitaclan had become the site of an all-out war. Luckily, though, the offensive sniper fire did not ring out again, and the two of them reached the large-wheeled vehicle without incident.

From a sealed compartment, Major Jakes removed a thin dossier packet: pictures and files printed out on flimsy, water-soluble paper. With strong hands, he pulled out two curling black-and-white satellite photographs. They were blurred, as if they had been faxed several times.

"This photograph shows what remains of the stronghold of a major Central American drug lord, Xavier Salida," Jakes said. "Heavily guarded and well provisioned with weapons. We've known about his illegal activities for some time. The Drug Enforcement Agency has worked with the local Mexican police in an attempt to set him up—but Salida was untouchable. Too many corrupt politicians in his pocket. That's always the problem with the drug lords out here."

"If you worked with local police like Carlos Barreio, I can see why," Scully said sourly. She bent closer to study the satellite photograph. "So why am I looking at a crater? Did your team take him out because you couldn't extradite him legally? Is this what you intend to do here at Xitaclan? Leave a big crater?"

"No," Jakes said, not the least bit offended. Even the close firefight seemed not to rattle him. The small injury to his shoulder had stopped bleeding. "We had nothing to do with this event.

"The crater radius and the condition of the surface, as well as concurrent seismic evidence and a faint atmospheric flash detected by one of our side-looking horizon satellites, allows us to draw only one conclusion: without question, this is the result of a tactical nuclear strike."

"You mean somebody lobbed an atomic bomb at a Mexican drug lord?" Scully said in disbelief.

"That's what the evidence conclusively proves, Agent Scully. Nothing else could have released this much heat and energy in a single burst."

"But how?" Scully asked. "Where would a rival drug lord get his hands on a warhead?"

Jakes nodded to himself, pursing his lips. "Here's a scenario: A certain number of displaced nuclear armaments may have been diverted during the breakup of the former Soviet Union. It's possible some of these lost assets may have fallen into the hands of terrorists. These slimeballs do a better job of eliminating each other than we do of apprehending them."

Scully stared at the curled photo again. "With a nuke? Isn't that going a bit overboard?"

Major Jakes sidestepped the question. "We also know that the revolutionary group *Liberación Quintana Roo*—the gentlemen shooting at us this evening—have been gathering up weapons for their hopeless fight against the central Mexican government. We are greatly concerned that one or more of these missing tactical nuclear weapons may have fallen into their hands. We believe the guerrilla group would hold few compunctions against using it in a major populated area."

Scully nodded, concerned to see the actual reasoning behind the drastic actions Major Jakes and his commandos had undertaken. She pressed her lips together as her thoughts whirled, wondering if the murders of the archaeology team had something to do with gun-running activities or weapons sales to drug lords. Could the illegal revolutionary group have been using Xitaclan as a secret base, undiscovered, until a nosy team of American scientists came in to poke around?

But that didn't help Mulder, who had run off in the direction of the pyramid two hours ago. She hoped he hadn't been taken prisoner by the revolutionaries, or shot.

"That still doesn't tell me why Xitaclan," Scully said. "Why here? These isolated ruins have been untouched for centuries. There are no roads, no facilities, no power—obviously it's not a high-security compound. There's nothing here. Why an all-out strike in the middle of nowhere?"

Jakes reached over into the control panel of the all-terrain vehicle. He switched on the flatscreen grid, which glowed gray and silvery blue before the images resolved into a topographical line drawing of a close-up of their location, centering down from the overall Yucatán Peninsula. Jakes punched several commands, and the map zoomed to a smaller and smaller scale. A pulsing light throbbed from a location on the map like a sonar signal or a heartbeat.

"This transmission emanates from here, Agent Scully. Prior to the strike on Xavier Salida's fortress, the signal appeared on our military receivers. It seems to be encoded. We cannot determine its origin or its purpose, but we believe the signal is linked to these activities. Therefore my team has been given orders to penetrate whatever defenses might surround this isolated jungle base—and to destroy the transmitter."

Scully watched the pulsing signal, the hypnotic pattern of flashing light on the screen. "How do you know that's a military transmission?" she said. "If it's in a code you don't understand, you have no reason to believe it could be a threat. That's quite a leap of logic."

Major Jakes remained staring at the screen, his dark

eyes intent. "Our intelligence has classified it as a military threat."

"What intelligence?" Scully said, gripping the side of the vehicle. "What do they know beyond what you're telling me?"

"It's not my place to question them, Agent Scully," Major Jakes said. "I need only to know the target and the objective. My commando squad is tasked with carrying out those orders, not in debating them. From experience, we know that's best for all concerned."

The first injured soldier staggered up to the all-terrain vehicle, panting. Scully noted that the narrow gash in his side had split open again, spilling fresh blood into his uniform. "All set up, sir. Ready to rock and roll, as soon as you give the order."

"Very well—the order is given." Jakes straightened, crossing his arms over his chest. He did not turn to face Scully. "Let's take that pyramid down."

Scully looked toward the silhouetted ziggurat in the flickering flames from jungle fires, wondering if Mulder had found shelter.

"Let 'er rip!" a young voice shouted.

Scully watched in horror as the commandos began to launch explosive mortars into the ruins.

30

When Mulder finally recovered from the shock of finding Cassandra Rubicon, caught in the derelict ship like a fly in a spiderweb, he stepped back. He drew several deep breaths, calming himself, remembering to focus, to study all the details, acquire all the information, before he did anything rash. Assess the situation . . .

He stepped as close to the suspended figure as he could without touching the strange, gelatinous barrier, then he paused to consider what he should do. He couldn't risk damaging anything here . . . and he had no intention of becoming trapped, as the young woman had been.

But this was incredible!

Forcing himself to turn away, he spun around, scanning the amazing room, looking for more clues. With a start, he saw that other small, dim chambers similar to the one that imprisoned Cassandra dotted the walls around him—dim alcoves like empty coffins in a mausoleum . . . empty except for one, which held someone—something—else.

Resisting his unsettling curiosity about the archaeologist's daughter, Mulder moved to the single other occupied chamber in the control-room wall, dreading what he might find there.

"Let's see what's behind door number two," he said.

The figure lay crumpled, a mound of wadded rags and desiccated flesh, as if he had been struck down where he stood. The mummified, hardened remains were distorted like a lump of mahogany driftwood, stripped of all moisture, barely more than tatters of iron-hard tissue that held crumbling bones together.

At first glance Mulder couldn't tell if the mummy was actually human. He recalled similar dried corpses he had encountered while investigating other cases—in a high-schooler's grave in Oregon, in a buried boxcar in New Mexico—desiccated remains, possibly of extraterrestrial origin, possibly not.

With a sense of amazement tinged with desperate hope, he wondered whether this forlorn figure could have been one of the original occupants of the derelict craft. Perhaps even Kukulkan himself?

Scully would never accept that conclusion until she could do an autopsy herself. But when taken together with the other evidence—the buried ship and its artifacts, the Maya carvings of spacemen and feathered serpents—this long-dead inhabitant would be compelling enough even to the most hardened skeptic. Even to Scully.

He turned back to the murky, bizarre chamber that held Cassandra Rubicon, and the differences between the two . . . specimens . . . struck him. Whereas Cassandra hung perfectly preserved in a coffin of petrified light, as if time had somehow stopped for her, the other occupant looked as if time had rolled over him with a steam roller and left him like roadkill in the dust. This dried-out corpse had suffered some kind of mishap. Mulder wondered what had gone wrong.

He resisted going inside the mummy's alcove. Not yet. The walls of the main chamber blistered with the pulsing light that sent a vibrating tingle through his head.

A message only recently sent out to a distant people who must have stopped listening a thousand years before.

Tearing himself away from the mummified corpse and the trapped figure of Cassandra, Mulder studied the limestone walls, where metal had fallen away in the main chamber. He saw chiseled images similar to those on the temple at the apex of the pyramid. But these images were less stylized and more realistic.

As far as he could tell, the scenes depicted a tall silhouetted form, a godlike figure, an alien surrounded by Indians who seemed to worship him . . . or fear him. The godlike image—Kukulkan?—stood accompanied by several monstrous feathered serpents.

Mulder felt a shiver crawl down his back. These were well-rendered images of the creature he had seen in the moonlit shadows two nights earlier. Slithering, glossy . . . unearthly.

He followed the succession of carvings that paraded across the walls, impressions of the Maya people building temples, erecting cities in the jungle, treating the ancient astronaut with great reverence. In each scene the visitor had his back turned, his head lifted up, his unseen face toward the sky . . . as if waiting for someone to come. A rescuer perhaps?

But for whatever reason, Mulder thought, "Kukulkan" had intentionally come back inside the derelict ship, placing himself into one of these chambers to stay . . . to die.

Unless there had been an accident.

Mulder approached the young woman's frozen alcove again, straining to see if she had moved—blinked her eyes, drawn a breath . . . but nothing had changed.

Through the "amber," Cassandra did not look lifeless, though. The flush of blood still colored her face, a sparkle of tiny injuries on one cheek as if she had been sprayed with splinters. Her hair seemed sweat-dampened, her skin dusty as if she had worked her way through the partially crumbled catacombs in the pyramid above. She looked exhausted, overheated . . . frightened.

But not dead. Mulder had seen enough corpses to know.

Assuming that this place was indeed a buried spaceship, he wondered if this could perhaps be some sort of suspended animation chamber, a stasis booth where time would stop for extraterrestrial explorers making an incomparably long journey across the void of space. He had seen the same idea in plenty of science fiction movies . . . maybe the aliens had thought of it for themselves.

He searched the walls beside Cassandra's glowing doorway, but found no controls, no status indicator, no colored buttons that might show him how to thaw the frozen substance.

So, instead, he reached out to touch the cold, dim gel himself, imagining that perhaps he could just take Cassandra Rubicon's hand and raise her up out of her glass coffin, like the prince awakening Sleeping Beauty in the forest.

He hesitated before he let his fingertips brush the tangible substance, afraid that it might somehow suck him in as well, like alien quicksand—two specimens for the price of one. But he had to know. He had to risk everything. Mulder pushed his hand through before his doubts could grow stronger.

When he touched the cold gelatinous wall, it . . . *burst,* popping like a soap bubble. Puddles of slick, volatile liquid splashed across the floorplates.

Coughing and gasping for breath, Cassandra Rubicon lurched at him, already running, as if she had paused in the middle of a panicked flight. Dripping wet and horrified, she crashed into Mulder and screamed. He reached out to defend himself as she drove him to the floor, pounding him weakly with her fists.

"No!" she croaked. "Leave us alone!" She grabbed the heavy flashlight that hung from her waist and swung it at Mulder as if it were a large metal club.

He reached up to defend himself. Using his best hand-to-hand combat training, he grabbed her wrist, used his other arm to snatch the flashlight away, and pinned her hands in the air. "Easy! I'm with the FBI, Federal Agent. I'm here to save you."

She trembled and held herself motionless, but coiled, vibrating like a tightly wound spring. "There was someone shooting . . . and a bright light." She looked around, her muddy green eyes unfocused. She smeared thin slime away from her face, shuddering and dazed. She seemed to drift in and out of coherence, as if her brain had not yet entirely unfrozen.

Mulder sat up guardedly, still keeping his eye on her. He knew he must look a frightful mess—battered, muddied from the climb down the slippery walls of the cenote, sweaty from days of trekking through the jungle. But coated with the volatile ooze, the young woman looked far worse.

He brushed at his shirt. "I take it you're Cassandra Rubicon?" he said. When she nodded, he continued. "You and your team have been missing for over two weeks."

"Impossible," she said, then coughed again, wiping her hands on her pants in disgust. "We just got here a few days ago." She sniffed her wet shirt. "What is this stuff?"

Mulder shook his head. "Your father contacted us a week ago Tuesday. My partner and I came with him to search for you here at Xitaclan." He hesitated, but she needed to know. Better to give her all the shock at once—though he couldn't bring himself to tell her about her father just yet. "I'm afraid we found the other four members of your team dead—shot, and then sunk in the cenote."

Cassandra blinked and looked around, clearing her throat. Her voice was rich and resonant, filled with more anger than fear. "Those men, men with guns," she said. "Bastards. What did they want? Who were they?"

"I think they're part of a violent revolutionary group. They've been keeping us company outside tonight."

Cassandra looked down at her fingers, blinking but seemingly not seeing. These events had happened for her only moments before. "So how . . . how did I get away?" She clamped her teeth together and hissed, "Bastards."

"We found the other four, but you were still missing," Mulder continued. "I've just discovered you here by accident. You were trapped in . . . and I set you free from . . . whatever it was you had gotten yourself into."

Cassandra wiped at her eyes and stared at the metal walls around her. But her vision did not seem to focus. "This stuff burns my eyes . . . can't see very well."

Mulder used his sleeve to dry her face. She continued talking. "I ran into the pyramid to get away . . . got lost . . . stumbled in here. Then I don't know what happened. Light gushed all around me, drowning me, burning and cold." She sat down on the floor next to him, deeply puzzled. "Did I hurt you?"

Mulder shook his head. "Good thing you don't know karate," he said, rubbing his bruised arm.

Then he suddenly realized that the throbbing SOS signal had ceased as soon as he had released her from the alcove. The diaphanous light throughout the main chamber began to fade. The signal had stopped, and now the derelict ship seemed to be . . . waiting, settling back to sleep.

Tears streamed out of Cassandra's reddened, irritated eyes.

Mulder wiped her face again and decided it would be too much to tell Cassandra he believed they were inside a derelict ship, an extraterrestrial spacecraft buried beneath the pyramid of Xitaclan. Or that he thought she had stumbled upon a lifeboat. She must have activated its automatic system which placed her in suspended animation.

Mulder stood up and helped her to her feet. Cassandra stretched, flexing her arms experimentally. The cold, wet gel began to dry into a thin coating on her clothes and skin. She swayed dizzily for a moment, then drew a deep breath.

Mulder looked around, but the pulsing signal had not resumed. He wondered again if her actions had triggered a distress call, a homing beacon. Perhaps the original inhabitant had tried the same thing, but hadn't succeeded because his lifeboat had been damaged somehow.

Mulder decided it was time to get moving. "Thanks to your explorations, we know there's a passage through to the pyramid level. Good thing, too," he said. "I don't look forward to climbing the cenote wall again."

"I still can't see very well." Cassandra followed close beside him as they picked their way away from the main chamber, then she asked in a hesitant voice, "My father . . . did he come with you?"

Mulder swallowed, his heart leaden. The passages around them grew darker. "Yes, he came with us. We tried to have him wait for us back in the States, but he wouldn't hear of it. He wanted to help you himself," he said. "But Dr. Rubicon . . . he was another casualty of the people who tried to kill you. I'm sorry."

Cassandra stopped in midstep and swayed, leaning into the rough wall where metal plates had loosened and fallen to the floor. She looked as if Mulder had just punched her in the stomach.

She said nothing but slid down to sit, shuddering, where the wall met the floor. She drew her knees against her chest. She stared at her dirty hands.

Mulder looked down at her, understanding. He quickly ran a hand through his hair, then touched her lightly on the shoulder. She needed to be alone.

"I'll go on ahead and find the way out," he said. "You take the time you need."

Cassandra nodded, intensely weary. With a last glance back at her, Mulder set out, trudging up the slope. His heart pounded, heavy with grief for her, filled with amazement for the things he had already seen, yet with an equivalent amount of dread for what he might encounter up above—the battleground, the snipers, the explosions. He hoped Scully had managed to keep herself alive and safe.

The passageway became dimmer, the walls made of vitrified stone. The deck plates transformed into a lime-stone path under his shoes. He realized he had emerged into the pyramid levels again. Up ahead, he recognized the same area he had seen when he went looking for

Vladimir Rubicon, though now he stood on the opposite side of the fallen barrier. Elation surged through him—home free!

Then he turned the corner and came face to face with Carlos Barreio. The police chief's flashlight beam shone through the dimness, pinning Mulder like a moth in a specimen box. Barreio held out a nickel-plated revolver, pointing it at Mulder.

"Agent Mulder," he said. His lips formed a humorless smile. "I thought I might find you inside the pyramid. Unfortunately, I cannot allow you to leave here alive."

31

Reflexively, Mulder took a step backward, but found no escape.

Barreio's police revolver pointed directly at him, unwavering. Mulder could not see the man's finger on the trigger. He would never know when it began to squeeze, when the gunshot would ring out.

Once again, Mulder wished fervently that Major Jakes had left him with his own weapon.

"Let me make a wild leap of logic," Mulder said, taking another gradual step back, "and guess that you were the one responsible for killing the archaeology team members." He carefully began backing down the corridor.

Barreio, with the gleam of the hunt in his shadowed eyes, stalked after him, gun forward. He answered only with an enigmatic smile, his large mustache folded in the cleft of his cheeks.

Mulder pressed, "So you let the archaeologists uncover new treasures for you—priceless pre-Colombian relics that brought fabulous prices on the black market."

Barreio shrugged his broad shoulders. "*Liberación Quintana Roo* needed the money."

Mulder took another step backward, the flashlight beam dazzling his eyes. Barreio seemed amused at his attempt to escape.

"And I suppose Fernando Victorio Aguilar would find customers for you?" Mulder said. "He's in this too, isn't he?"

"He only made himself rich." Barreio growled. "It is distressing to see a man with no drive or purpose other than his own greed."

"Yeah, I can see how you're much more admirable," Mulder said.

The slope was steep. He continued backing down, kept talking. Barreio followed, confident, watching his victim proceed deeper and deeper into the trap. "But why kill the archaeologists?" Mulder continued. "You just called attention to yourself. They were Americans on a visit sanctioned by the central Mexican government."

Barreio shrugged again. "The government knows nothing of the problems of Quintana Roo. We have our own land, our own history. We should be our own country like Honduras, like El Salvador, like Belize."

"Don't you have a brochure or something I could read?" Mulder said. "Instead of giving me the whole speech?"

"We had intended to take the Americans as hostages. That is all. Political hostages."

Mulder raised an eyebrow. "I suppose they were shot trying to escape? And then you had no choice but to throw them into the cenote?"

"Some of our revolutionaries still believe in sacrifices to the old gods," Barreio said, shoving the revolver closer. He shone the flashlight directly into Mulder's eyes. Mulder blinked and held up his hands to ward off the bright beam, stepping back toward a corner. "We all have to make sacrifices," Barreio observed.

Mulder backed around the corner, unable to believe that Barreio kept stringing him along, kept playing him.

The police chief followed him, closing the distance for the last time. Barreio grinned, flashing white teeth in the dimness. Mulder knew his time had run out.

As the burly man rounded the corner, Cassandra Rubicon stepped out of the shadows, holding one of the metallic plates that had fallen off of the walls. She hefted it over her head and brought it crashing down against the side of Barreio's skull. His policeman's cap toppled to one side; his body toppled to the other.

Still barely able to see, Cassandra dropped the plate with a loud clang, amazed at what she had done. Carlos Barreio grunted in pain and shock, reeling, stumbling into the wall. He was not dead—not even unconscious, just stunned for a moment.

Mulder did not want to risk grabbing for Barreio's revolver. He snatched Cassandra's arm as she blinked her eyes. He yanked her after him. "Come on, we've got to run!" he said. "That was one of the men who shot at you." She jogged after him, hustling back down toward the control bridge.

"That man killed Cait and John, Christopher and Kelly?" she said, her voice icy.

"Yes, I'm afraid he did," Mulder said.

"Then I should have hit him harder," Cassandra answered.

Mulder helped her as they both ran down the slippery slope. Moments later, with a bellow of rage, Carlos Barreio came charging after them. He fired his revolver twice, and the bullets plowed gouges along the walls, ricocheting into the darkness.

Gasping for breath, Cassandra said, "Men shooting guns. This was what led me down here in the first place. I still can't see . . . my eyes—they burn!"

They ran back into the tunnel, whose walls still sizzled with a faint light that grew dimmer by the minute. The corroded, half-collapsed metal-and-crystal outcroppings gave a drastically anachronistic counterpoint to the Maya glyphs carved on the exposed limestone in the walls: symbols that ancient priests had added in hopes of restoring the damaged or pilfered artifacts removed from the derelict.

Mulder led her along, guiding her as she tried to clear

her vision and find her way. He guided her behind one of the glistening metallic mounds. "Stay down here," he whispered.

"Do you actually have a plan?" Cassandra said. "Or are we just running?"

"Running seemed like a good idea at the time." Mulder swallowed and came to a stop in the confusing but awesome control chamber.

Then Carlos Barreio staggered onto the bridge, weaving unsteadily on his feet. His eyes seemed unfocused, and he blinked repeatedly, as if to stop his ears from ringing. Blood poured from a gash in his scalp, wetting his dark hair, dribbling around his ear and down his cheek. He had left his policeman's cap back in the outer tunnel where it had fallen.

Leaving Cassandra huddled behind the shelter, fighting to regain her vision, Mulder backed away in another direction. Carlos Barreio caught the movement. He swung his revolver and fired spasmodically, but his aim was off. Several bullets ricocheted off the metal wallplates. One struck inside the dark lifeboat chamber holding the mummified remains of what Mulder believed to be Kukulkan.

"Where are you?" Barreio croaked, wiping blood out of his eyes, smearing it on his cheeks. He roared with pain as he inadvertently touched the wound on his head. "What is this place?" The burly man seemed barely able to focus on his amazingly unexpected surroundings. Mulder wondered if Cassandra had given him a concussion.

Barreio staggered forward and swiveled the revolver around, shooting blindly. The bullets struck the central mound of metal shapes and crystals, sending up sparks and blue-green fire that rippled out in icy cold flames.

Hoping to distract the police chief somehow, Mulder grabbed a small, broken lump of crystal from the rough floor and hurled it, hoping to strike Barreio in the head—but he missed. Barreio caught the swift motion past his face and whirled, hearing the chunk strike the wall inside the narrow alcove—the chamber that had held Cassandra suspended. The police chief charged toward the sound like a five-hundred-yard-dash runner, waving his pistol.

Barreio fired once and strode into the lifeboat chamber.

Suddenly a flood of light poured over the police chief like a waterfall of lightning.

Instinctively, Mulder shielded his eyes.

Barreio thrust his hands out, trembling, his jaws clenched, his eyes opened wide. Dazzling, ethereal gel suddenly congealed around him, as if solidifying from the air itself. His nostrils flared—then he froze exactly in place, pinned by the lifeboat's automatic stasis systems. The amber hardened.

Barreio hung motionless, like an exhibit in a museum, one breath half indrawn, his eyes still hot, though dazed, the blood petrified along his cheek.

Mulder heard the dull throbbing begin again inside his head as the derelict's signal thrummed once more from within the wrecked ship—the SOS, the reactivated homing beacon.

But whom it meant to summon, Mulder could not guess.

Cassandra picked herself up from the floor, panting. She brushed herself off, looking satisfied. She shook her head to clear her thoughts. Creeping forward, she stood just in front of the glowing light wall, squinting slightly, trying to focus her eyes.

Mulder took his place beside her, staring in, feeling his heart pound.

The young woman shook her head and directed a cool smile at Barreio. "At least I'm on the right side of the wall this time," she murmured. "I like it better this way."

32

When the thunder started from above, Mulder turned up to see the control chamber's ceiling vibrating, trembling. As a second pounding thump reverberated through the walls, he feared another volcanic quake might be striking Xitaclan—and this time he was trapped inside a crumbling underground derelict that did not look as if it could withstand such severe stresses.

With another loud, discrete boom, he hunched down. Dust pattered from above.

"Those sound like explosions," Cassandra said, crouched beside him.

"Yes," Mulder agreed. "It's bombs exploding. I think Major Jakes's military tactics have heated up just a little bit—and I don't know if this old ruin is going to take much more pounding. I'm not too keen on the idea of being buried alive, are you?"

Cassandra's face turned pale and she shook her head. "My goal in life is not to become a specimen for some future archaeologist."

"Let's try this again," Mulder said, leading her toward the upper exit. "We'll make our way to the pyramid levels.

If Barreio could make his way down here, the passage must be open."

"At least for now," Cassandra said.

Together, they scrambled up the steep ramp, leaving the murderous police chief trapped in his coffin of light. If everything turned out all right, Mulder could always come back and arrest Barreio later.

Cassandra led the way upward, her hair flying all about her face. Mulder shone his flashlight ahead as the passages became dimmer, where the skeletal remains of the derelict gave way to limestone and hand-carved blocks.

Eager to escape, Cassandra pulled ahead of him as they reached the partially blocked passage where the stones had tumbled across the corridor. The barrel-chested Barreio had opened a wide enough passage for both of them to crawl through.

Cassandra scrambled up and into the dusty opening, wriggling her way ahead. Mulder gave her feet a push, and the muscular young archaeologist disappeared into the shadows. She twisted around and returned, reaching across for his hand to help him up. With surprising strength, she dragged him across the broken stone and into the cramped opening. He pushed his way past a shard of rock and tumbled beside Cassandra, into the upper corridors of the Xitaclan pyramid.

Mulder looked around and brushed himself off.

More thunderous booms sounded from above and outside, closer now. Mulder shone his flashlight beam to see a snowfall of dust pattering down through the ceiling stones. One of the support beams began to groan from the strain.

"We'd better hurry before it gets even cozier around here," Cassandra said. Running along the winding tunnel, they followed the line of vitrified blocks of the inner temple that covered the entombed derelict like a shrine.

"Just a minute!" Cassandra reached into her back pocket and pulled out a crumpled piece of graph paper on which she had sketched her explorations through the pyramid's lower levels. "Let's check our route. You'll have to read it—I still can't focus well enough."

"I got to this point myself two days ago," Mulder said, remembering how Scully had called him upon finding Vladimir Rubicon's body in the cenote. "I didn't get any farther though," he said. "I was . . . interrupted."

Cassandra did not pick up on the grimness in his voice. She licked her lips and said, "Well, in my mind it's only been an hour or so. I believe it's this way." She turned down a different passageway leading upward.

Another explosion struck much closer. The pyramid floor and the thick stone walls rocked. The hand-hewn limestone blocks rattled together like chattering teeth.

"That sounded awfully loud," Cassandra said. "The good news is, we must be close to the opening."

"Let's hope so," Mulder said, then he heard another thump and whoosh of air, moments before another equally loud detonation. "Hey, those are mortars. Somebody's launching mortars." Then he swallowed hard as he remembered Major Jakes and his covert search-and-destroy mission. "I think they're aiming to take down the pyramid."

"Nothing like respect for antiquities," Cassandra said.

They turned the corner and just up ahead saw the opening that led out into the wide plaza. Outside, the night was lit by fires in the jungle and dwindling white flares from burning phosphorus.

"I'm not sure it's a good idea to run out into the middle of that," Mulder said. "Keep your head down."

Just then he saw the flash, heard the whistle, and instinctively grabbed Cassandra. He dove with her against the wall. One of the mortars hurtled into the stairstepped facade just above the doorway, detonating with a monstrous roar of fire and smoke and blasted debris. The shockwave made his ears pop.

An avalanche of rubble, rocks, and chiseled limestone blocks collapsed to block the entrance. The low ceiling of the claustrophobic corridor split open and fell in as Mulder dragged Cassandra deeper into the tunnels, both of them blinded by the flash and the sudden darkness.

He breathed a searing mixture of hot gases and pulverized limestone dust, choking and coughing. They staggered back the way they had come. "This is getting ridiculous," Cassandra wheezed. "We'll never make it out of this pyramid."

"Back to the drawing board," Mulder said. "Let's try the passage I used to enter this place. Third time's the charm."

Down, down, deep underground, Mulder followed the image in his excellent memory, though he cheated a little by spotting his own footprints scuffed in the dust of the long-abandoned corridors.

"This passage leads out to the cenote," Mulder said. "Once there, we'll have to climb up, hand over hand."

"The cenote?" Cassandra said. "We must be below the level of the water. Are we supposed to swim, or what? At least I can wash the rest of this slime off."

Mulder looked at her, surprised. "Oh, I forgot to tell you—the sacrificial well is just a big empty hole in the ground now, thanks to the last tremors."

"Tremors? What tremors?" Cassandra asked.

"You've been sleeping for a long time."

They arrived at the ancient door hatch, the metal bulkhead that Mulder had reached by climbing down the cenote walls. Standing in the mysterious entrance to the derelict, Cassandra stared out at the dripping corkscrew walls of knobbed limestone. The empty well remained wet, still stinking of sulfurous volcanic gases.

"I've heard complaints about how pristine archaeological sites are destroyed as soon as outsiders arrive at the scene," Cassandra said. "But this goes beyond my worst nightmares."

Up above, flashes from continued mortar fire and smoldering forest blazes lit the sky.

"Steady." Mulder reached out to take her hand as

they both stepped out onto the algae-encrusted limestone ledge. "We're on our own for the first half of the climb," he said, "but from that point we can use the ropes we hung down."

"Ropes? What did you need ropes for?" Cassandra asked.

Mulder swallowed. "Well, my partner, Agent Scully, used your own diving suit to go underwater to explore. That's where she found the bodies of your team members . . . and I used the ropes to retrieve your father. We found him floating here in the sacrificial well."

Cassandra's lips whitened as she pressed them together. Then she nodded. "I'm glad you got him out before all the water drained into the ground . . . though I couldn't imagine a more appropriate burial for a hardened relic digger like himself."

Mulder reached up for the first handhold and climbed cautiously, finding the ascent somewhat less terrifying than the downward climb. This way he could look up and see his goal, rather than slipping and working his way down to the unknown depths of a bottomless pit.

Wiry like a wildcat, Cassandra found tiny outcroppings that even Mulder didn't dare try. They picked their way around the circumference, ascending at an angle, completely encircling the sacrificial well until they reached the right height to grasp the ragged ends of the dangling ropes.

From deep below, volcanic vapors continued to gurgle and belch and gasp. Mulder knew that the eruption had not yet peaked, but had merely paused to gain its second wind.

His shoe slipped, and he dropped, grabbing for a hold. Cassandra reached out, her hand as fast as a rattlesnake strike, as she grasped Mulder's wrist. His other hand maintained its grip on the rope. "Thanks," he said.

"Any time," she answered. "Just make sure you do the same for me."

Once he regained his footing, they climbed the last few meters up to the edge of the cenote, the flat limestone rim where drugged sacrificial victims had once been hurled down into the deep well that would swallow them up for thousands of years.

Silently deciding to keep themselves low, Mulder and Cassandra raised their heads up, peeping over the edge to where they could see the Pyramid of Kukulkan silhouetted in the firelight.

Half of its side had sloughed down. Mortar explosions had gouged great craters into the carefully crafted hieroglyphic stairs. Mulder saw other people running in the plaza, dim forms scurrying for cover.

Both of the carved feathered serpent stelae had toppled over, and only one of the tents remained upright. Mulder could see cautious figures scrambling about in camouflaged uniforms; one wore a different outfit. Scully.

Before he could haul himself over the ledge, though, a renewed outcry came from the jungle, shouts in the guttural Maya language. A loud crackle of gunfire came in a staccato burst as the regrouped guerrillas charged out of the cover of the trees. The revolutionaries fired at the surviving members of the military team, who responded in kind.

Gunshots grew into a deafening hail of sound in the sky. Two more phosphorous flares soared into the night, overwhelming the light of the moon.

Mulder held on, and watched, thinking of the relative peace inside the derelict spacecraft.

33

Xitaclan ruins
Wednesday, 3:26 A.M.

Scully covered her ears as the mortar launcher fired another projectile toward the half-demolished ziggurat. She cringed, and the other soldiers ducked away, also covering their ears.

The mortar struck the base of the great pyramid, dead on target. With the explosion, fire and smoke and shrapnel blossomed outward, hurling chunks of broken rock in all directions. After the impact, cracks appeared along the steep ceremonial stairsteps—steps she had climbed only days before to get a panoramic view of the surrounding jungle.

The pounding had continued for nearly an hour, but the ancient structure withstood the most vigorous barrage from Major Jakes.

So far.

Scully had repeatedly argued with Jakes, insisting that he cease the destruction, that he and his troops stop pummeling the archaeological treasure. But foremost in her mind was an engulfing dread about where Mulder might be. She didn't know where he had run—but no matter what, she knew Mulder would be in the thick of things.

"How long are you going to keep this up?" she screamed, her voice muffled in her ringing ears. "There may be people inside that pyramid!"

"Regrettable casualties," the major answered.

"Don't you care?" she said, grabbing his sleeve like a persistent child . . . and feeling as helpless. "Can't you see what you're doing?"

Jakes turned his emotionless gaze down, staring at her. The weird light splashed colors across his dark skin. "No, Agent Scully—I don't care. I am not allowed to care. That's too dangerous."

"Is that what you tell yourself, just to keep ignoring your ill-advised actions? Can't you think about the consequences?"

He didn't move. "My mind is my tool, capable of accomplishing seemingly impossible missions—but only because I never allow myself to deviate from orders. Too much thinking creates confusion, double-talk, doubts.

"I have been through hell numerous times, Agent Scully. The maps called it Bosnia, or Iraq, or Somalia—but it was hell." Now his eyes flared with embers of emotion. "And if I ever let my conscience get too heavy, then I would either be insane or dead by now."

Scully swallowed, and the major turned back to face his remaining men.

After repeated direct hits from the mortars, the ancient pyramid looked ready to collapse. Heavy blocks jarred loose from where they had rested for centuries, tumbled down, smashing the intricate carvings and glyphs. The pillars of the apex temple platform had all fallen over, the feathered serpent statues blasted to dust. An avalanche began along the eastern face of the ziggurat, roaring down the steep stairs and adding to the nighttime din.

"We've almost got it," Major Jakes said. "A few more direct hits, then our mission will be accomplished. Gather the casualties. We can fall back."

"No! We can't leave Mulder!" Scully shouted. "We have to find him. He's an American citizen, Major Jakes. Your actions have put him into the middle of an illegal military action—and I hold you personally responsible for his safety."

Jakes looked at her again with his placid dark eyes. "Agent Scully, I am not even here. My team is not here. Our mission does not exist. We are not officially responsible for you or anyone else."

Then a bullet took him high in the left shoulder, spinning him around and hurling him into Scully, knocking them both to the ground. He grunted, but did not cry out in pain.

"The snipers are coming back," one of the commandos yelled.

The other soldiers scrambled away from the mortar launcher as a renewed shower of gunfire came from the jungle. The guerrillas howled their challenges.

The commandos took shelter, ducking beside the all-terrain vehicles and the mortar launcher. They leveled their automatic weapons and shot at will, targeting on the bright spitfire that came from the shadows, the surging forces of the *Liberación Quintana Roo* guerrillas who charged out of the trees.

Major Jakes heaved himself off of Scully with a barely restrained hiss of pain. He stood up and squeezed his shoulder. Blood welled up in his uniform. He looked down at her, and she saw the splatters of blood staining her own jacket.

"I apologize for bleeding on you," he said, then offered her a hand up.

The commando closest to the mortar launcher fell backward without an outcry, his head suddenly splashed with bright red.

"Another down," Major Jakes said. He looked at his own bleeding shoulder. "My team is dwindling with every moment."

"Then we've got to get out of here," Scully said, clamping her teeth tightly together. "Find Mulder and go."

"The mission is not yet accomplished," Major Jakes said.

The guerrillas, bolder now, came out of the trees, firing. Major Jakes's commandos shot back, though their defense seemed to be crumbling. One of the soldiers launched a grenade into a knot of *Liberación Quintana Roo* fighters. It exploded right in their midst. Broken bodies flew, arms and legs akimbo, hurled into trees that also burst into flames from the backwash of the exploding grenade.

The viciousness of the response caused the guerrillas' surge to falter. Major Jakes grabbed Scully's arm. "Come on, I want to get you back to your tent. You'll take shelter there, so I can concentrate on our defenses."

"I'm not going back to my tent," Scully said. "I need to be out here, looking for my partner."

"No, you don't," Jakes retorted. "You'll follow my orders. Period."

"That tent isn't going to offer me any protection whatsoever."

"It'll offer enough," Jakes said. "The attackers won't be able to see you. You won't be a specific target. That's the best I can do."

"I didn't ask you to—"

"Yes, you did," Major Jakes said. "You said I was personally responsible for your safety. Therefore I want you away, where I don't have to worry about you—and where I don't have to listen to your constant insubordination."

With his good arm he wrestled her into the flap opening of the tent. She struggled and turned around, shouting at the top of her lungs, "Mulder!"

"He can't help you, wherever he is," Major Jakes said. "I'm trying to protect you, ma'am."

She glared at him. "I need for him to know where I am."

"Just get inside the tent, ma'am."

She bristled. "Don't call me ma'am."

"Don't force me to be rude."

Defeated and helpless in the middle of a war zone, Scully crawled into the dim confines of the tent, huddling among the blankets. Major Jakes dropped the tent flaps back down.

Scully felt as if she were inside a cloth tomb. The sounds outside were muffled. Moonlight filtered through the heavy canvas, intermixed with staccato bursts of light from flares, gunfire, another mortar launch, and distant explosions.

She listened to the deafening, chaotic sounds of the assault and knelt on her blanket. She rapidly lifted up her pillow, checking that no scorpions had snuggled under the rolled-up cloth.

More gunfire rang out. Scully heard a gasp from Major Jakes and a thump. Outside she saw silhouettes, shadowy figures—then a bullet tore through the tent, missing her head by inches. Another small circular hole ripped through the fabric, singed around the edges.

She ducked down, flattening herself to the ground, and listened as the fighting continued outside.

34

Mulder helped Cassandra over the limestone lip of the sacrificial well, then stretched out, relieved just to be on solid ground again. Exhausted, he tried to decide which direction to run that would have the least likelihood of getting both of them killed.

Mulder felt sick in the pit of his stomach as he watched the destruction of the pyramid continue. The artifacts buried in the derelict ship would answer the questions archaeologists had wondered about for nearly a century. But every blast pummeled and crushed the evidence of extraterrestrial influence on the Maya culture. Now the answers were reduced to rubble and debris.

He and Cassandra sprinted for cover every chance they could, stealing around the perimeter of the ziggurat. He intended to reach the base camp in the plaza. Despite its dangerous openness, the plaza was the most likely place for him to find Scully. That was his first order of business . . . that and preventing them from getting killed.

Another mortar sailed high and dropped like a wrecking ball onto the top platform where ancient priests had performed their bloody sacrifices. The pillars that supported the delicate Temple of the Feathered Serpent had already crumbled and collapsed, slumping down into a mound of debris.

Rubbing her eyes, Cassandra watched in dismay, her face seething with anger. "First my team, then my father—and now this . . . this desecration." She snarled and then stood tall, balling her fist and shouting into the night. "You can't do this!"

As if to defy her, another explosive detonated. The shockwave blasted debris from one of the stairstep terraces directly above them, causing a rain of broken blocks.

"Look out!" Mulder said and dove toward Cassandra, but the shattered rubble dropped down on her like the proverbial ton of bricks. A jagged chunk of stone emblazoned with a partial Maya glyph clipped her across the top of the head. With a thin gasp of pain, she collapsed, bleeding from her scalp, a scarlet stain oozing into her mussed cinnamon hair.

Mulder bent over her, cradling the young woman's head in his lap as a few remaining chunks of shrapnel pattered around him. Miraculously, he himself suffered only a large bruise on one shoulder blade and a nasty cut in his right leg.

The side of the great pyramid seemed to sag as rubble and stone blocks sloughed toward the base.

"Cassandra," Mulder said, pushing his face close to hers. "Cassandra, can you hear me?" Her skin had a grayish color, and sweat broke out on her forehead.

The young woman groaned and sat up, blinking and stunned. She shook her head and then winced. "Bullseye," she croaked, pressing a hand against her temple. "Ouch."

Mulder gingerly felt around on her scalp, probing the seriousness of the gash. Though she bled profusely, it seemed to be a shallow wound. His main concern was that she had suffered a concussion or fractured skull.

"We can't stay here, Cassandra," he said. "We've got

to find some kind of shelter, or we'll have a lot more to worry about in a few minutes."

He looked around, trying to focus in the uncertain strobe-light of flares against the enveloping darkness. "If we can find my partner Scully, she'll be able to give you emergency medical attention."

He scanned the plaza, watched the scurrying figures, the smattering of gunfire like deadly fireflies blossoming into the night. Ahead, in the open plaza, he saw a tall figure hustling a woman's petite form—obviously Scully—toward the tent. The two seemed to be arguing, and then the man pushed her inside, dropped the flap, and stood up to stand guard beside the tent.

Was the man protecting her ... or holding her prisoner? Mulder couldn't tell if he was one of the American commandos or one of Carlos Barreio's guerrilla freedom fighters.

"Come with me, Cassandra," Mulder said, draping her arm over his shoulder and helping her to her feet. She groaned, and her eyes blinked, unfocused, her pupils dilated in their muddy-green irises. The blood continued to flow down her face.

"Hey, I can walk," she said, but her voice came out with a quaver, like a child trying to impress her father with her bravado. Mulder loosened his hold, but Cassandra began to slide toward the ground like over-cooked pasta.

"Maybe I'll just help you out after all," he said, placing his arm around her for support. The two of them stagger-walked toward the plaza. Mulder kept his eyes toward the indistinct figure standing next to Scully's tent.

Continued gunfire prevented even an imagined moment of peace. A chain of popping sounds cut through the scattered background noise. The commandos scattered again, but the guardian figure beside Scully's tent did not move fast enough. Mulder watched as the rain of automatic-weapon fire nearly ripped him in half. Several bullets tugged at the peak of the tent like thick darning needles, and Mulder prayed Scully had kept herself low.

"We have to get over there," he said, with greater urgency. Cassandra stumbled as he walked with her, hunched over to present a smaller target. He expected to be shot at any moment.

He and Cassandra reached the more distant of the two feathered serpent stelae at the edge of the plaza. Both carved pillars had toppled over, smashing the already disturbed flagstones. Some of the rubble had fallen across the tarpaulin-covered corpses he and Scully had fished out of the cenote—but the victims didn't seem to mind.

Mercifully, Cassandra seemed too dazed to recognize her team members, or even to know what the shrouded forms might be. He helped her to crouch beside the fallen limestone monolith, taking shelter.

Then, to Mulder's surprise, the din stopped. The combat field grew still and oppressive . . . as if a blanket of silence had descended upon Xitaclan. Mulder stopped moving, letting Cassandra lean back against the fallen pillar. He craned his neck to look around. As he waited, the silence seemed to grow louder. Something strange began to happen.

He felt his skin crawl, and the hairs on the back of his neck tingled with static electricity. Mulder huddled next to Cassandra behind the stela. Some force in the air compelled his gaze upward.

He watched the light come down from the sky.

The glow came from inside and out of a huge vessel poised in the night. He saw it for only an instant—but his imagination supplied the remaining details. It was an immense construction, a dazzling chiaroscuro of angles and curves forming a geometrical shape that no architect had ever conceived. A blaze of light glowed around it like a halo, keeping all details indistinct.

A ship.

He knew it had to be a ship. When Cassandra Rubicon had accidentally fallen into the lifeboat chamber, she must have triggered a pulsing message, a distress signal transmitted across the starlanes . . . a beacon shining along an infinite distance.

Until finally the rescue craft had arrived.

Mulder recalled the blurred images of Kukulkan on the walls of the buried control chamber: the towering extraterrestrial visitor staring hopefully up at the stars. But the rescue craft had come more than a thousand years too late for him.

"Cassandra, look at that!" he said, glancing down and shaking her shoulders. "Look at it!"

She groaned and blinked her eyes. "It's too bright," she said.

Mulder looked up again. The moment the luminous craft reached the partially demolished pyramid, long spikes of searing light burned from the ship's belly . . . glowing, pulling an invisible thread. Mulder gasped and shielded his eyes from the dazzling glare.

Beneath him, the ground trembled, strained, ripping like a thin sheet of iron tugged by a powerful magnet. Temple blocks flew off the top of the ziggurat. The rubble blasted away on all sides. Debris pounded down around them like meteors.

He tried to look again, but the blazing light blinded him, and he had to cover his eyes. Mulder heard the strange craft continue its excavations, oblivious to the covert U.S. squad, to the Central American guerrillas, to the FBI agents. The powerful beam knocked the entire broad-based pyramid down, razing it one stairstep layer at a time, like a child toppling a house made of building blocks.

Mulder understood everything now, knew his speculations must have been correct. Kukulkan had never been rescued because his lifeboat chamber had failed, entombing him—but Cassandra's accident had once again summoned help from the stars.

And now the rescue ship had come to excavate the derelict.

The ground bucked and heaved as the dazzling craft devastated the remainder of the pyramid, leaving only ruins. Shouts and panic rang out from the jungle and from the surviving U.S. commando fighters.

Cassandra groaned again. "Please don't break it," she said.

"Not much I can do to stop it," Mulder answered, trying to make out details through the cracks between his fingers. The light grew brighter, hotter, in the belly of the hovering ship. More glaring beams lanced out. Mulder watched, drinking in the details, still awestruck.

Finally, the inner pyramid lay bare—the original structure that enshrined the derelict ship. Sudden darkness fell again, disorienting Mulder as the rescue craft floated silently over. He supposed it was probing, scanning . . . and then the brilliant beams ripped out again, titanic forces stripping away layers of the ground to excavate the skeletal remains of Kukulkan's ancient ship.

The earth cracked and shook—until finally, with a great rending tear, the piercing light from the hovering ship ripped free the remains of the crashed craft. Mulder was hurled to the ground as metallic girders and curved hull plates protruded through the base of what had been the great Xitaclan pyramid. Risking blindness from staring at a light as bright as the sun, Mulder tried to watch as the rescue ship heaved Kukulkan's derelict entirely out of the ground, like a Maya blood priest ripping out the heart of a sacrificial victim.

Dirt and stone showered all around them. Mulder ducked, confused by the garish shadows that had become razor sharp in the backwash.

Defying gravity, the crushed remains of the derelict rose into the air. The glowing rescue ship gained altitude with astonishing speed, tugging the skeletal girders along with it. Debris pattered around them, a blizzard of rubble that sprayed the entire site.

Mulder gazed into the sky, his mouth dry, watching all hope for finding artifacts and incontrovertible evidence rising into the sky . . . forever out of his reach. The rescue craft had come like a soldier crossing enemy lines to bring back the dead. Mulder had no idea where the craft might go, what descendants of Kukulkan might mourn his mummified remains.

Eyes stinging with tears, he stared as the brightness compressed itself and shrank into a blinding star that streaked off into the night, leaving him only with colorful afterimages on his eyes.

With a shock, Mulder realized that the Mexican police chief Carlos Barreio remained trapped in one of the lifeboat chambers. Perhaps Barreio would survive the passage. Or perhaps he had already been killed during the unearthing of the derelict. Either way, the extraterrestrial craft took the revolutionary leader along with it.

Mulder knew this was one abduction he would not mourn, one alien kidnapping he would never bother to investigate. He looked at the gaping, smoking crater where the pyramid had been. "Good riddance," he said.

35

X Feeling helpless and trapped, Scully huddled in the imaginary shelter of the tent while she listened to the tumult outside, destructive sounds like the end of the world . . . or at least a Maya version of the last days of Pompeii.

She heard explosions and crashing stones, but they did not seem to be coming from continued mortar fire. The commandos had dashed for cover, and the launcher had fallen silent. Several more bullet impacts had ripped holes like tiny skylights in the top of her tent. Scully heard nothing more from Major Jakes or his surviving men.

She tried to decide how long to wait before she made a break for it. She hated being sequestered in here, like some princess locked away in a castle tower. Jakes had thrown her inside this smothering enclosure just because she was a woman, or a civilian—but she had no better chance of survival cowering in a tent than if she actually dashed out across the plaza, to the ruins, to the jungle, in search of Mulder.

"Enough waiting," she said. "I'm getting out of here."

Scully yanked open the tent flap and crawled out,

keeping low, expecting one of the soldiers to shove her back inside at any moment. A harried Major Jakes might even bash her in the head with the butt of his rifle, she thought, just to keep her under submission "for her own protection."

But no one noticed her. She crouched beside the tent, ready to dive for cover. But no shots rang out to strike the flagstones at her feet.

She stood up on shaking legs to look around, blinking in the uncertain light of the burning jungle. Xitaclan seemed to be quivering in shock.

Scully found Major Jakes where he had fallen. Heavy-caliber bullets had ripped his chest apart. He lay sprawled in his own blood, staining the flagstones like another sacrifice to the ancient Maya gods. Even in death, his face remained expressionless, as if it were all part of his beloved mission.

A frantic soldier ran toward her, dodging fallen stone blocks and uprooted trees, his uniform torn and stained. His rifle dangled from his shoulder, out of ammunition. The clips on his utility belt hung empty, as if he had already used every one of the grenades and throwing knives he had carried.

"We're under attack from the sky," the soldier said. "I've never seen an assault like this—but we can't resist! They've already destroyed the pyramid." His face dripped with perspiration, his eyes opened wide and white.

Then he looked down to see the bloody corpse of Major Jakes. "Oh, damn," the soldier moaned, glancing quickly at Scully in embarrassment. "Excuse the language, ma'am."

"Don't call me ma'am," she muttered, recalling what she had said to Major Jakes, but she didn't expect the young soldier to understand.

"Okay, it's fallback time!" the soldier shouted to his unseen companions. He looked at her, his eyes haunted. "Ma'am, you'd best make your own way out of the jungle as soon as possible before that ship comes back. You can request asylum from any authorities you may encounter. Our team, on the other hand, does not have that option. If we're captured, we're dead. Only three of us left now."

Without another word, the soldier dashed back across the plaza, holding his empty rifle in front of him, sprinting for the cover of the trees. Scully turned around to stare at where the tall Xitaclan pyramid had once stood—but now she saw only a gaping crater.

"My God," she said, awed, feeling an uncontrollable urge to cross herself. The rubble lay piled up, massive blocks thrown hundreds of meters as if tossed by some titanic force. She glanced down at the major's motionless form. "It looks like you accomplished your mission, Major Jakes."

Deep in her heart, though, she suspected that no amount of mortar fire or grenade blasts could have leveled the centuries-old structure so utterly. She thought of what the soldier had said—an attack from the sky. Some other military force, an air force? A bombing raid?

Another tactical nuclear weapon, an atomic artillery shell?

"Scully!" The shout sounded like music in her ears, and she whirled around upon hearing Mulder's voice. "Scully, over here!"

She saw her partner, bedraggled and exhausted, supporting another woman who staggered next to him. The two of them worked their way across the plaza.

"Mulder, you're safe!" She ran toward him.

"Let's not come to any premature conclusions," he said. His face was flushed, his eyes glazed with shock— or amazement. "Scully, did you see it? Did you see it?" He gestured frantically over to the crater where the pyramid had once stood.

Scully shook her head. "I was stuck inside the tent, so I didn't see much of anything," she said. "Major Jakes is dead. So are most of his men. We've been told to move out as soon as we can. We're all by ourselves, Mulder."

Finally, as if getting a second wind, more sporadic

gunfire popped through the trees, and Scully felt very vulnerable. Major Jakes's three surviving commandos had already fled, piling onto one of the all-terrain vehicles. They roared off into the jungle without waiting for stragglers.

"She's hurt, Scully," Mulder said, indicating the reddish-haired woman he supported. "She was hit on the head by a piece of shrapnel from one of those mortar explosions . . . but at least she's alive."

Scully looked at the woman's head wound, saw that the blood was already clotting, matting her hair in place over it. "Mulder, is this Cassandra? Where did you find her?"

"It's a long story, Scully—and I'll tell you right now you're not going to believe it. But she's here, living proof."

Before Mulder could explain further, the ground began to writhe yet again. The flagstones shimmied from side to side, as if some legendary titan buried beneath the earth's crust were trying to break his way out using a jackhammer.

"I don't think it's kidding this time," Scully shouted.

A section of the flagstones blasted skyward as a geyser fountained up. The entire plaza shifted sideways as underground plates moved. The stress became so great that a fissure ripped the courtyard in two, tumbling the wall of the long-abandoned ball court off to the side of the pyramid ruins.

"The ground here is unstable enough." Mulder shook his head as if to knock the dazedness from his brain. "With all the explosions, I think Xitaclan is about to become a thing of the past."

Gouts of sulfurous ash spewed from the pyramid crater, an upside-down waterfall of lava and smoke. The limestone rocks cracked, igniting like candle wax. The ground split open, collapsing the sides of the drained and hissing cenote.

"Remember that new Parícutin volcano from 1948?" Mulder said. "My guess is that this place is going to erupt and keep erupting until we've got another national land-mark on our hands." He helped the dazed Cassandra to her feet again. "If it's all the same to you, Scully, I'd rather not have my name on a little memorial plaque near the Visitor's Center. Let's get out of here."

The gunfire had ceased, the guerrillas having scrambled back into the destroyed jungle, their victory complete now that virtually everything standing at Xitaclan had been destroyed.

Scully pointed to the remaining all-terrain vehicle. "We can take that ATV, get better speed through the jungle . . . though I have no idea where we're going."

"How about away from here?" Mulder said. "Do you know how to drive this thing?"

Scully looked at him. "We're intelligent people, Mulder. We should be able to figure it out." But as she said it, she wasn't terribly convinced herself.

"Don't be so sure," he said. "It's military technology."

As she and Mulder helped the injured Cassandra Rubicon, they staggered toward the remaining vehicle under the lava firelight and the conflagration of the jungle.

36

X Orange gouts of lava shot up into the sky behind them as Mulder fought to control the all-terrain vehicle.

"You have to hurry, Mulder," Scully said, her face flushed, her expression urgent.

Scully had settled Cassandra Rubicon into one of the vehicle's seats and looked at the injured young archaeologist while glancing over her shoulder at the flames, the cracking ground, and the shooting fire and steam.

"I'm used to driving Ford rental cars," Mulder said. "This is a bit more challenging."

The ATV's engine had started up with a cough and a roar. Mulder worked the pedals, the gear shift—and they lurched off with all the ease and comfort of a plane crash. They followed the trampled path hacked through the jungle by the commando team earlier that night. The vehicle's thick tires swiveled and rolled over the dense underbrush, smashing down ferns and fallen branches.

Scully did her best to prop up Cassandra Rubicon's groggy form. She used a torn strip of cloth to probe her head injury, studying the seriousness of the gash. "What is this substance coating her?" she asked.

The young woman winced and tried to squirm away from Scully's ministrations. "I'm all right," Cassandra croaked, and with a sigh slumped back to half-consciousness.

Mulder plowed deeper into the jungle, but their pace remained maddeningly slow as he dodged tree trunks and boulders and crashed through thin streams and shallow trenches.

Flames from the fresh crack in the earth backlit the jungle. Spewing magma boiled up from the open wound where the immense alien rescue craft had excavated Kukulkan's long-buried derelict. Greasy gray smoke roiled where the grenade launchers had blasted parts of the forest.

With the loud rumbling behind them and the continued hissing of the eruption in progress, Mulder could hear few subtle background noises, but he thought he spotted running figures scrambling through the underbrush. Some of the shadows might have been guerrilla soldiers fleeing, others might have been the surviving members of Major Jakes's commandos trying to make their way back to a safe rendezvous point.

"This woman needs medical attention," Scully said, "but she'll be all right for the time being. Nothing serious, just a little banged up ... but everything I see here are fresh wounds—not weeks old." She looked over at Mulder, her blue eyes filled with curiosity, her eyebrows raised. "So where has she been all this time?"

"She was trapped down in the pyramid, Scully."

Scully frowned skeptically. "She doesn't look like a woman who's been in hiding for days and days. I see no signs of malnourishment or physical stress."

He looked at her with a deep intensity, feeling the passion of his convictions bring a flush to his cheeks. "I'll tell you everything once we get out of this alive."

Scully cradled Cassandra's lolling head so that it did not bang against the side of the ATV. Far behind them another huge explosion ripped through the night, spraying more ash and lava into the sky, spitting fire in all directions. Mulder flinched, then tried to coax greater speed out of the groaning all-terrain vehicle.

The front left side of the ATV smashed into the bent bole of a tree, and Mulder overcompensated by swerving to the right, then zigzagging back to return them to their course. In the darkness and the chaos he had already lost the beaten track. Maybe, he thought, he could stop at a gas station for directions.

He squinted ahead and swerved again, struggling to find a reasonable course through the overgrown jungle. "I hope we're not lost out here in the wilderness for the rest of our lives. I've got season tickets to the Redskins games."

He looked down at the high-tech apparatus and control panels that equipped the vehicle. "Check in the glove compartment, Scully. See if you can find a Triple-A map."

Scully reached over and scanned some of the screens. "Major Jakes showed me a dossier file—satellite images of an enormous crater left behind when a local drug lord was supposedly attacked by a tactical nuclear device. You'd probably consider it the result of some sort of alien technology gone awry . . . but let's not get into that. The major had precise maps, topographical contours, detailed studies of the jungle." She shuffled around before letting out a defeated sigh. "But all of that was in the other ATV, of course."

On an impulse she switched on a flat grid in the dashboard unit, which displayed a digital compass and a glowing LCD map of the Yucatán. "Well, here we go," she said. "I couldn't find the cigarette lighter or the radio, but this should do the trick."

Mulder heaved a sigh of relief.

Suddenly a slim and wiry figure charged out of the underbrush, striding in front of the ATV's path. He looked sweaty and exhausted, his khaki vest torn, his ocelot-skin hat lost somewhere in the jungle. But his dark eyes narrowed with a fanatical gleam as he held a wicked-looking automatic assault rifle, no doubt taken from one of Major Jakes's fleeing men.

"I will shoot you now, or I will shoot you later," Fernando Victorio Aguilar said, thrusting the rifle toward them. "But either way you will stop. Now."

37

Wrenching the controls, Mulder pulled the all-terrain vehicle to a halt. Aguilar's leveled rifle provided quite an incentive.

With the denseness of the foliage, the tight-packed trees, and tangling ferns and creepers, he didn't have enough momentum or enough confidence in his driving ability with the clunky military vehicle to roar forward and trample the long-haired guide. If he missed the man on his first attempt, Aguilar could easily dodge them and shoot at point-blank range. He wouldn't risk Scully or Cassandra that way.

From her seat, Cassandra groaned and brought herself close enough to consciousness that she blinked at Aguilar. "Him," she said. "Bastard! Abandoned us . . ." Then she slumped back, as if that effort had cost her all the energy reserves she had managed to rebuild.

Aguilar looked at her in shock, then jabbed his rifle at them. "Where did you find the archaeologist's daughter, eh? Barreio's men searched for days, but they kept getting lost in the pyramid."

"She found a very good hiding place," Mulder said.

"In fact, Señor Barreio found the same spot—but I don't expect we'll ever see him again."

"Too bad. He was a political fool, anyway." Aguilar held up the rifle, pointing it directly between Mulder's eyes. He could feel the black hole of the barrel boring through his forehead, as if the long-haired guide were performing some sort of virtual trepanning operation.

"What do you want, Aguilar?" Scully said.

The man swung the rifle to point it at her. Mulder saw that his ponytail had come undone and his dark hair hung in greasy, ropy strands to his shoulders. Aguilar smiled at Scully. "For the moment I'd like hostages—and this vehicle, Señorita." He rubbed his cheeks with one hand as if the faint stubble bothered him. All of his supposed plans had crumbled around him, but Aguilar still seemed amused by the entire situation.

"It's too late to say that nobody will get hurt if you do exactly as I say ... but, believe me, *Liberación Quintana Roo* meant to do this in a bloodless fashion. All I wanted was the artifacts, all they wanted were the political hostages. We could have gotten away without any casualties whatsoever, but alas, circumstances did not permit that. Thanks to your American soldiers, and your own stubbornness, eh?"

Mulder heard a crackle of branches overhead and glanced up at the trees. Aguilar saw the sudden movement and jerked his rifle back at Mulder. "Don't move a muscle," he said.

Mulder didn't move, though he could still hear a rustling, creeping sound through the twigs high above. Other ferns began to stir behind Aguilar, but the guide kept his attention on the vehicle.

"We were obtaining artifacts from lost Maya sites," Aguilar said. "*Our* Maya sites. It was like stealing, but no one got hurt, no one lost anything. *Bueno!* The jungle had buried these treasures for centuries, and now we were making money from them, eh?

"Barreio squandered his profits on political fantasies of independence and all the headaches that carried with it, while I put the profits to good use, making myself comfortable—for once in my life. I grew up on the streets of Mérida, Agent Mulder," he said with a snarl. "My mother was a prostitute. From the time I was eight years old I lived alone, rummaging in garbage bins, stealing from tourists, huddling under a box when it rained.

"But thanks to Xitaclan I have made myself a reasonably wealthy man—and no one was hurt by it—until too many people poked their noses where they didn't belong!" He tossed his head. "The locals knew enough to leave these ruins alone. The American archaeology team should have known as much . . . and so should you."

"You've already promised to kill us," Scully said. "Now are you trying to gain our sympathy?"

Aguilar shrugged. The deadly end of his rifle bobbed up and down. "We all desire to be understood," he said, with a smile. "It's human nature, eh?"

Then the branches overhead snapped and broke. To Mulder's utter amazement, a giant, sinuous shape dropped down like a gleaming tentacle, a coiled mass of muscle.

Aguilar looked up and screamed, swinging the rifle—far too slowly, far too late.

There was a gleam of translucent fangs as long as stilettos, as sharp as needles. A wide, hungry mouth flared. Feathery scales spread out in a crown around bony headplates, looking like beaten scales of precious metal. The monster moved, quick as lightning.

Aguilar fell to the ground under the weight of the creature. The vicious reptile wrapped around him, squeezing its serpentine body like a braid of steel cables.

"My God," Scully whispered.

Aguilar screamed in pain as well as terror. His rifle fell away into the underbrush. He clawed and pounded at the armored, flexible body of the feathered serpent. Blood sprayed from his mouth, a fountain of red as the feathered serpent squeezed.

The man shrieked as his bones cracked like dry wood. Then the huge serpent monster moved off into the underbrush, dragging its crushed victim along until the foliage-entangled deadfalls shielded the carnage from view.

Aguilar screamed twice more, then the noise was cut off with a high gurgling pop. They could hear nothing more than rustling sounds . . . breaking bones and tearing meat.

Scully sat next to Mulder, transfixed, her face pasty white, her eyes wide, her lips pale and bloodless. "Mulder . . . I—"

Cassandra coughed groggily and croaked, "Kukulkan."

Something fast and fluid rushed through the tangled underbrush on the other side of the all-terrain vehicle, moving too swiftly for Mulder to track. It slid through the creepers and ferns, then burst up with a spray of fallen leaves and moss-covered twigs. Looking at them.

Another feathered serpent—even larger than the first—reared up in front of them like a cobra before a snake charmer, baring its long fangs with a bubbling hiss, only feet away.

"Mulder, what is that thing?" Scully asked, her breath slow and thin.

"I'd suggest we don't move for the moment," he said through clenched teeth.

The sinuous creature weaved back and forth in front of them, huge and intimidating, larger than any crocodile ever born. Its feathery scales thrust out like spines. Its breath came in a sharp, unending hiss, like steam forcing itself out of a boiler.

"What does it want?"

The iridescent, oily serpent moved with a blur like an optical illusion, as if its entire body were made out of quicksilver, as if it had been bred for a different gravity, a different set of environmental conditions.

Mulder couldn't move. He simply stared at the beast, hoping none of his actions would intimidate it.

As the monster fixed its attention on them, it stared with eyes of burning pearls, grunting with an unfathomable intelligence driven by a brain of incomprehensible alienness.

Mulder remembered the carvings, the stelae, the images of Kukulkan deep within the ship. These serpentine creatures had been the ancient extraterrestrial's pets or companions or helpers . . . or something else entirely.

Though Kukulkan himself had died many centuries ago, his mummified corpse nothing more than petrified tatters of flesh clinging to naked bone, descendants of the original feathered serpents had remained behind. Stranded. Over the centuries they must have made their home in the Central American jungles, surviving hidden in the densest rain forests.

The creature in front of them stared, bowing closer. The moment froze in time.

"Mulder, what should we do?" Scully asked.

Mulder met the creature's burning, opalescent gaze. They stared at each other for a moment, a flash of understanding passing across a gulf vastly wider than any simple species barrier.

Mulder realized he was holding his breath.

Scully sat wide-eyed next to him, her knuckles white, her fingers clenched against the seat. Cassandra Rubicon groaned, staring at the creature with glassy eyes.

Finally, the tension inexplicably evaporated, and the feathered serpent backed away, slithering into the underbrush. It vanished as quickly as it had come, leaving only broken and rustling branches behind.

The forest fell silent again.

"I don't think we'll have any more trouble with them," Mulder whispered.

"I hope you're right, Mulder," Scully said, then swallowed hard. "But let's get out of here before one of those things changes its mind."

38

With a clean shave and clean clothes, and after a good night's sleep, Mulder felt like a visiting relative as he entered Jackson Memorial Hospital in Miami, where Cassandra Rubicon had been taken to recover from her injuries.

Now that he had returned to civilization, the dense jungle wilderness seemed another world away, with its bugs and scorpions and snakes and miserable rainy conditions . . . though it had been only two days ago. The ordeal had still not faded from his mind.

With the aid of the ATV's computerized map, he and Scully had managed to work their way east toward one of the paved roads in the state of Quintana Roo. Then, like a survivalist senior citizen driving a "Don't bother me or else!" RV, Mulder barreled along the roads, terrifying shepherds and pedestrians, dark-haired Indians wearing colorfully embroidered Maya clothes.

Using a small first-aid kit she found in the all-terrain vehicle, Scully had taken care of the worst of Cassandra's injuries, giving her painkillers and applying disinfectants. She could do nothing more until they found an actual hospital.

Finally, a Mexican police cruiser had stopped them, the officer demanding to know what they were doing there in a U.S. military vehicle. Scully had politely requested to be taken to the nearest American embassy.

During the grueling drive through the unmarked forest, they had found MRE rations in the storage compartment—"Meals Ready-to-Eat"—as well as bottled water. Cassandra had been unable to talk or eat, and she seemed so dazed by her ordeal that Mulder had doubted she would remember anything to back up his theory about the alien space craft rescue, any more than he expected to find witnesses from the commando operation. Scully and Mulder ate some rations, however, and by the time of their arrest they felt relatively comfortable again and ready to go back home.

Cassandra had been treated in a Mexican emergency medical care center while Mulder made the appropriate phone calls and Scully filled out the extensive paperwork. Upon arriving in Miami, Cassandra had been taken to Jackson Memorial for observation and recovery. The young woman was so weary after her ordeal that she viewed the forced hospital stay as a relief instead of a burden.

Walking down the linoleum-tiled hall, Mulder wondered if the archaeologist's daughter would recognize him, now that he had cleaned up and changed clothes. She had never seen him in his suit-and-tie FBI uniform.

He punched an elevator button and rode up to see her. The heavy doors closed on him, sealing him alone in the small elevator—and he experienced an unexpected dread as he thought of Carlos Barreio trapped in the lifeboat chamber onboard the derelict ship, dragged into the air with the salvaged wreck . . . and from there to the stars.

Fortunately, the hospital elevator didn't prove nearly so threatening.

Cassandra Rubicon lay propped on the bed surrounded by bleached white sheets, her head bandaged like a Civil War veteran's. She stared at the television mounted high on the wall, wearing a look of combined boredom and amusement as she absorbed a women's afternoon talk show. The topic of the heated discussion was "Women who claim to be married to aliens from outer space."

"I should have remembered to set my VCR," Mulder said. "I wanted to catch this one."

Cassandra saw him standing at the door to her room, and her face brightened. "There are some things I don't miss out in the jungle," she said. She picked up the TV remote control and stabbed the POWER button; the picture on the tube winked out with a faint cry of dismay.

"Feeling better?" he asked, coming to stand beside her bed.

"Much," she said. "And your own appearance is much improved."

He glanced down at the uninteresting and uneaten meal on a tray at her bedside. "You should eat your Jell-O—after all, you've had a pretty rough time."

She forced a smile for him. The heavy bandages covered much of her mussed cinnamon-brown hair. "Well, archaeology isn't for wimps, Mr. Mulder."

"Please, just call me Mulder," he said. "I can't help but think that Mister Mulder was my father's name."

At Mulder's mention of his own father, the young woman's face tightened again.

"I have to ask you this, Cassandra," he said, growing more serious, "because everything we saw has been destroyed without a trace. Did your team happen to smuggle out any notes, any photographs, any hard evidence from the Xitaclan site?"

She shook her head, then winced as a flicker of pain crossed her face. "No, there's nothing. My entire team died down there: John and Cait, Christopher and Kelly—all dead, struck down at the beginning of their careers. My own father was murdered because of me, because of Xitaclan." She swallowed, then looked back at the television herself, as if wishing she could be distracted by the talk show again, anything but the discussion she was now having with Mulder. "No, Mulder. It's all gone now, including our records. The only thing I have left is my memories—and even those aren't too clear."

Mulder stood next to her, momentarily turning his attention to the blank television set, trying to find the right words.

Cassandra seemed withdrawn, as if searching for an inner reservoir of strength. When she spoke, it surprised him. "There are still a thousand unexcavated sites in the Yucatán, Mulder. Maybe when I get back on my feet I'll put together a new expedition. Who knows what else we might find?"

Mulder allowed himself a small smile. "Who knows?"

39

X With her little dog curled up asleep on the sofa, Scully flicked on the computer and sat down at her desk, taking a deep breath.

So different from wandering lost in the wet and bug-laden jungles of Central America, she thought. And quite an improvement.

Now that she had returned home, she had to get into the right frame of mind to work on her official report about Xitaclan, juggling the loose ends in her mind until she finally succeeded in tying them together. There were other cases, other investigations . . . other X-Files. She had to close this one and move on.

In a few hours of peace and solitude in her own apartment, Scully could finish up the backlog of paperwork that had piled up during their trip to Mexico. It felt good to be back in civilization.

She crossed her legs in her chair and rested a lined legal notepad on her knee to jot down notes, sketching out her thoughts before committing her report to the computer. She scribbled several headings, writing her ideas under broadly defined categories.

Their specific assignment—to search for the missing

archaeology team members—had been completed. Scully felt grateful to be able to mark an official case CLOSED, technically at least. Assistant Director Skinner would appreciate that.

On the legal pad, she listed the names of the four murdered team members, adding details of how she had discovered their bodies submerged in the cenote, how she and Mulder had recovered them from the water. She described the apparent cause of death—murder by gunshot wounds, broken vertebrae, and/or drowning. She concluded that Cait Barron, Christopher Porte, Kelly Rowan, and John Forbin had all been killed by members of the guerrilla organization *Liberación Quintana Roo.*

She didn't know what to write under "Cassandra Rubicon." She had been found alive and unharmed—though how, Scully did not understand. She still had no satisfactory explanation for the young woman's disappearance, the lost two weeks in her life. Had she been out wandering in the jungle or hiding down in the ruins of Xitaclan while the rest of her team members lay dead in the sacrificial well? Scully could not include Mulder's talk about buried spacecraft and suspended animation chambers.

As a side note, she scribbled a sentence about how, in the wake of the Xitaclan disaster and the debacle of the U.S. military covert operation, the Mexican government had finally come in with a sufficient force to crack down on the guerrilla activities. Soldiers had confiscated the remaining illegal arms and arrested the surviving revolutionaries who could be found hiding in jungle villages.

The violent *Liberación Quintana Roo* movement had been crushed. Their nominal leader, the turncoat police chief Carlos Barreio, remained at large. Mulder maintained his own explanation for what had happened to the man. Despite Scully's coaxing, her partner had not been forthcoming with sufficient details that she felt comfortable about including Mulder's speculations in her report. They didn't have a specific bearing on the case.

As for the tactical nuclear weapon that had supposedly obliterated Xavier Salida's fortress—their investigations had uncovered no evidence of additional black-market armaments, other diverted nuclear devices that had fallen into the hands of Central American criminals. A continued search, though, would have to be conducted by other federal agencies, such as the CIA or the State Department.

Under "Vladimir Rubicon," Scully summarized the scenario of how the old man had been killed: struck on the head by Fernando Victorio Aguilar because the old archaeologist had threatened to broadcast his report and call in additional government-sanctioned help—all of which would have interfered with Aguilar's artifact thievery.

Hesitating, she made a notation that their guide Aguilar, Rubicon's murderer, had been killed by "a wild animal" in the jungle.

Then she swallowed and procrastinated, doodling with her pencil before getting up to make herself a cup of instant coffee, heating the water in her microwave.

The monstrous feathered serpents were the hardest part for Scully to explain. Their presence posed the greatest difficulties for her rational report. She did not know how to account for the creatures, but she had seen them with her own eyes. She could not ignore their existence.

Earlier, Mulder had described his glimpses of the unearthly serpent creatures in the moonlight, and she had thought he had just been imagining things. But she herself had watched the towering, coiling beast with its long iridescent scales and curved fangs.

Finally, steeling herself, Scully sat at her desk again and picked up the pencil. Without further thought, she wrote down her own explanation, the best she could come up with.

The feathered serpents must be members of a large, previously uncataloged species of reptile, perhaps nearly extinct, but with enough representatives surviving into historical times to account for the numerous legendary images on Maya structures and artifacts. In retrospect, she realized Mulder had been right—the feathered serpent image appeared on so many glyphs and stelae that it seemed likely the ancient Maya had seen some of the creatures in life. Mulder had even suggested that the carnivorous feathered serpents could be responsible for the numerous accounts of missing people in the area around Xitaclan.

She commented on the density of the Central American rain forests, how many thousands of new species were identified every year. She conjectured that it was not completely beyond the realm of possibility that a large reptilian carnivore—especially one with such apparent intelligence—could have remained heretofore undetected by scientific expeditions and zoological study teams.

Agent Mulder had reminded her of how many images of similar creatures existed in the world's mythologies: dragons, cockatrices, wyverns, Chinese water dragons—and the more she thought about it, the more sense it made that such rare beasts might have indeed existed.

With the destruction of the Xitaclan site and the significant amounts of new volcanic activity there, Mulder had been unable to offer any corroborating evidence. His alien artifacts remained unconfirmed, his derelict spacecraft destroyed. She felt that, while she would include his verbal eyewitness account, she could do nothing more than let it stand on its own.

She sipped her bitter coffee and scanned over her notes as she turned to her computer. She crossed out a few lines scribbled on the legal pad, tried to arrange her thoughts on paper, then rested her fingers on the keyboard.

She would have to smooth everything out in her final report. Scully could say only that the many anomalies at Xitaclan remained unexplained.

40

X Though FBI Headquarters never shut down entirely, the Sunday afternoon quiet surrounded Mulder with a warm peacefulness unlike the usual bustle of a normal business day.

Only one bank of fluorescents shone from the ceiling, the others were gray and dark. The atmosphere inside the FBI offices surrounded him like a tangible presence: the thousands of investigations, the case files, telephones that would normally be ringing, photocopy machines whirring and clanking into the night.

The phone beside his desk remained silent—down the hall, the other computers, the neighboring offices, the adjacent cubicles equally quiet.

It was not a rare occurrence for him to come in on the weekend; Scully had often joked about his lack of a social life.

Now he sat pensive, with the miniblinds drawn and a desk lamp switched on. Rubbing the bridge of his nose, he pushed aside his stack of books on Maya myths and archaeology.

He studied a sheaf of satellite photos he had obtained

through sensible use of two Washington Redskins tickets. He had invested in season passes, though his caseload rarely allowed him the time to go to the actual games. However, the tickets often proved to be a useful form of currency for getting unofficial favors done in the Bureau.

He sat down and looked at the finely detailed photos, a few of them showing the devastated crater remaining where a Mexican drug lord's private villa had once been. Curious, he turned to another photo, studying the close-in target of the hellish, blasted landscape around the ruins of Xitaclan.

The volcanic hotbed had already generated enormous excitement among geologists. That part of the Yucatán should have been geologically stable instead of giving birth to an erupting volcano, much like the mysterious appearance of Parícutin in 1948. The cone of the new volcano had already begun to take shape, and early geological reports suggested that the new eruption would continue for years.

Mulder wondered if there could be any connection between Parícutin and Xitaclan, but dismissed the thought.

He would have no chance to go back to the Yucatán. He had no reason to return, because the erupting lava and volcanic tremors would have annihilated all evidence, even down to the mundane archaeological ruins. Not a scrap of Xitaclan's ancient glory remained.

Mulder picked up the precious jade artifact, the slick-smooth stone of whitish green carved into the design of a feathered serpent.

This time, the image struck him with an eerie chill, because he had seen the real thing. He ran his fingernail along the notches in the carving, tracing the feathers, the fangs in the open mouth. So many centuries of mystery lay locked in that place, and in this artifact.

But since Xitaclan had been destroyed, no one would believe his explanations. As usual.

Mulder set the jade carving on his desk with a sigh. At least he could use it for a decent paperweight.